HIS SCANDALOUS LOVE

CUFFS & SPURS, BOOK ONE

ANYA SUMMERS

BLUSHING BOOKS

Published by Blushing Books®,
a subsidiary of
ABCD Graphics and Design
977 Seminole Trail #233
Charlottesville, VA 22901
The trademark Blushing Books®
is registered in the US Patent and Trademark Office.

Anya Summers
His Scandalous Love

EBook ISBN: 978-1-947132-13-9
Print ISBN: 978-1-947132-32-0

Cover Art by ABCD Graphics & Design

FREE BOOKS FOR AMAZON CUSTOMERS

RIGHT TO YOUR KINDLE

Do you love Blushing Books and our spicy stories by your favorite authors? Do you love Maren Smith, Addison Cain, BJ Wane, Anya Summers, Alyssa Bailey, Carolyn Faulkner, Jane Henry, Maisy Archer, Tabitha Black, Abbie Adams, Zoe Blake and dozens of others?

We give away one or two novels / novellas per month, and can send these monthly free stories directly to your Kindle device. They will also come automatically if you're using a Kindle app on your smart phone or tablet. You don't need to do anything, pay anything or remember anything. Every month, free stuff will just magically appear. (Depending on your settings, you may have to go to your "Library" and select *download*.) While the free books may contain short promotional material on our other new titles, you will not receive spam or any other unwanted promotions from us.

Here's how:

1. Email us at promotions@blushingbooks.com, and put FREE KINDLE STORY in the subject line of your email. The email address you mail FROM will not be kept or added to a

newsletter unless you also sign up for our newsletter with that address.

2. You will receive ONE email from us in return (typically within 24 hours) with detailed instructions on how to add our mailing address to your Kindle's list of approved senders.

Once we get an email from you, you'll be added to our free monthly story list. You'll receive two free stories per month. And remember, while we always have free material at www.blushingbooks.com, we do often put books in our Kindle promotion that are NOT offered free anywhere else.

CHAPTER 1

*T*here was hot, and then there was the fourth level of hell that was the middle of July in Wyoming.

Heat rose off the distant fields in iridescent waves, turning the customarily verdant green fields of grass into pale shades tinted with brown.

They needed rain.

Carter lifted his Stetson and swiped a forearm across his brow as he stared at the bright blue, cloudless sky. Sweat slicked his form and slid down his back. It was barely noon and the temperature had already shot into triple digits. He, Herb Henderson, his cantankerous foreman, and Kyle Renner, his young, college age ranch hand, were working as fast as the heat would allow to keep the horses cool. Each day since summer had roared in with sky high heat in June, it had been a grueling race to keep Carter's prized herd from expiring from heatstroke.

Due to the heat, Carter had postponed the breeding schedule for some of his mares to the following year. There was nothing for it. His ranch could sustain the loss in production of a new herd to cull and sell. What he couldn't do was replace his horses should the heat become too much. So the men worked to keep them hydrated. As it had been a hell of a dry summer, it had been a bit like trying to piss out a forest fire. A steady wind blew plumes of dust and dirt across his ranch, the Double J, just outside of Jackson Hole.

The Double J sprawled over a thousand acres in a basin of the Gros Ventre Valley. The meadows were surrounded by sharp spears of granite of the mountain known as the sleeping Indian. Carter had been born here. He'd grown up on this land, learned the value of things and become a man here. It was home.

Yet he could only pray they would see relief soon in the form of rain, otherwise the risk of forest fires increased. And that was a nightmare he didn't even want to contemplate, let alone face. Although the chance for it, what with the evening lightning and lack of precipitation they'd experienced this past week, dangled precariously as a more distinct possibility with each day that passed with no rain.

Luckily, they had a misting system in the stalls running round the clock, along with giant fans circulating the air, helping to keep the horses cool. His two prize stallions, an ebony thoroughbred, Odin, and a mahogany colored Arabian, King Tut, were being downright finicky in the scorching temperatures. King Tut wouldn't drink his water and Carter had to install a salt block in his stall. Odin preferred water with added electrolytes.

As it was, Carter currently had ninety-six horses on his ranch and under his care. Doctor Josh Barrett, the local vet, had already been by that morning to treat a few of Carter's pregnant mares. While they'd finished their breeding for the year early, due to the heatwave, Odin and King Tut had each covered six mares. So while it wasn't a full stock of pregnant mares, he still had to watch them closely, with the heat spike catapulting them from merely hot into the fiery pits of hell fourth of July weekend. The blasted weather showed no signs of letting up.

The Double J was Carter's life. He enjoyed it. Lived and breathed the ranch day in and day out. Loved training the offspring of his mares into the finest trail horses in the Northwest. And yet, he'd been walking around with a hole in his chest since the previous August.

He'd not found her.

As much as he'd promised himself that he would track Jenna down, it was like she had disappeared off the planet. He'd even toyed with the idea of hiring a private investigator to locate her. But there was a part of Carter that wondered, now that almost a year had passed—eleven months and one week to be exact—since he had first set foot on the tiny strip of an island in the Bahamas, whether he was being obstinate and downright idiotic. If Jenna wanted to be found by anyone from the island, she would have left a way to be reached. Jared, the owner of the Pleasure Island Resort, had assured Carter that he'd not been in contact with her, and that perhaps it was best if Carter let her go.

And wasn't that just the problem?

Jenna had rocked his world. The feisty submissive had wormed her way past his hard-fought defenses and had set up residence inside his soul. He dreamed about her. Woke up in the dead of night reaching for her. Carter used to joke about Doms who became whipped and would cave to their submissive's every desire.

It was karma, perhaps. Because now the fucking joke was on him.

He'd been living a half-life, cursing himself that he'd failed to take action after their week together on the island. That he had waited too long to contact her afterwards. He'd tried to be a gentleman. And, he admitted to himself, he'd let his ego get in the way. Because he would forever regret that he hadn't hauled her to the fucking plane with him and carted her back here to his ranch. He knew now that he should have gone all caveman, tied her up if he'd had to, and even gagged her if necessary to get her on the damn plane.

Because now she was lost to him, and Carter had no idea how to move past it. Past her.

"I'm back from my lunch break," Herb said, breaking Carter out of his maudlin and rather depressing thoughts. "You should go take yours. My Dottie has put together some brisket sandwiches and her famous potato salad."

"I will in a minute. Just need to check on Daisy and Morningstar," Carter replied. If he buried himself in his work, he tended to get a reprieve from thinking about Jenna. It was the only time he did. The nights were the worst.

"Carter, the horses aren't the only ones who need a break from the heat. Now, go on with you. Kyle and I can take care of those two mares without any assistance from you. What we can't do is run this place if you drop dead of heatstroke," Herb challenged. The craggy bastard might be in his mid-fifties, but he was still a powerfully built man. His old-school handlebar mustache was almost completely gray, and the weathered lines upon his face bespoke of his life working outdoors. He was a deep in the bone cowboy, part of an era of men who were passing into legend. Herb did things the way they'd been done for a hundred years or more, and rarely embraced any type of technology.

"You do realize I'm the boss."

"Boy, I've known you since before you had your first woman. Now get. Kyle and I have got it covered. When you come back we'll talk about hiring some more help," Herb chewed out with his hands on his hips.

Realizing that Herb wouldn't let it go without a fight, Carter tipped his hat and said, "I'll be back shortly. More help? Really?"

"Another hand or two wouldn't hurt. 'Sides, I hear Kyle might take off for the big city in the fall. Eat your lunch. Take your time and we'll talk when you get back. Besides, it looks like you've got company." Herb nodded toward the main house.

Carter swiveled his gaze and, sure enough, a black souped-up pickup truck was pulling into the drive and parking. He knew the vehicle well. With a nod at Herb, he strode out of the stables and up the path to the main house.

The ranch was located in the Gros Ventre Valley, surrounded by unforgettable views of the Teton mountains. The main house had been modified from its earliest beginnings. Carter's great grandfather, Jedediah Jones, had purchased this land back in 1901. The original cabin he'd built still existed and had been turned into a home for Carter's foreman, Herb, and his wife Dottie some years back. It had been his father who had built the main house, and crafted it into a bit of a showplace. Carter certainly didn't need the twenty some odd extra bedrooms when it was just him. Although, when perspective buyers came to the ranch, it demonstrated the work he did and added an elegance that people tended to like. The exterior of the house gave the appearance that it was a large wooden cabin, the logs a smooth, golden pecan color, and when the sunlight illuminated it, it tended to bring out golds and oranges that made it seem like it was on fire. But that was where any similarity to a real log cabin ended.

Large double pane windows graced the estate with premium views of the mountain range. Inside was modernly appointed with honey colored pinewood floors, soaring vaulted ceilings, and all the furniture and décor held a Western flare. He'd updated the kitchen in the last few years. Although Carter's favorite room—besides his personal dungeon, which hadn't seen any action lately—was the indoor pool and hot tub.

Leaning against his pickup, his arms crossed over his chest, waiting for Carter, stood Spencer Collins. Spencer was one of his best friends. They'd gone to high school together. Founded the BDSM Club Cuffs & Spurs together. Spencer ran their club night and day in Jackson Hole for the group. Cuffs & Spurs wouldn't be possible without Spencer guiding the helm. The rest of the members had ranches, tourist attractions, and other businesses to manage. But Spencer made certain everything ran smoothly for the members and that those in the area who were in the lifestyle had a place to attend.

Spencer gave him a sardonic grin as he approached. While Carter was covered in dirt and grime from working in the elements in the stables and paddocks, Spencer appeared fresh and clean in his spotless jeans and crisp lemon linen dress shirt.

"Look what the cat dragged in. What can I do you for, Spencer? Good to see you, man," Carter said, shaking his hand.

"Fuck, it's hot. Thank heavens I work in an air-conditioned space," Spencer muttered and returned the handshake.

"That just means you're a pansy," Carter teased. It was a long running joke that Spencer wasn't a real cowboy, and only wore the black Stetson to attract submissives, considering he was one of the few members whose life and job wasn't outdoors.

"Please, motherfucker, I did two tours in Iraq. I'm anything but soft and you know it." Spencer snorted. His large frame rippled with the full bearing of a Master. Those tours had honed his best friend, made him hard, and he bore scars, both internal and external.

Carter offered a wry grin. "Just yanking your chain. Why don't you come inside and cool off? I was just about to grab some lunch. You're welcome to join me."

"Dottie's cooking?" Spencer asked.

"Of course. Do you really think I have the time or the inclination to stand over a stove?"

"Lead the way," Spencer said with a nod toward the back door before he trailed Carter up the back steps to the porch.

Carter wiped his boots on the outside mat before he opened the back door and stepped inside the washroom. Cool air that would have made penguins feel at home blasted him. Carter sighed at the relief. Hot damn, but it was hotter than the blazes outside. The washroom—or mudroom—was the size of an extra-large walk in closet, and was a place he could store his boots and outdoor supplies when they were covered in too much filth to cart through the house. There was also a top of the line washer and dryer, which Dottie had rumbling away. The woman was always cleaning something. In addition, there was an industrial sink where he could wash the dirt and grime from his hands, and occasionally his face, if warranted.

"Oh, Mister Carter and Mister Spencer, come have a seat at the table. I'll fix you both up a plate," Dottie Henderson said, bustling about the kitchen and dining area beyond. The kitchen exuded warmth and was one of the parts of the house Carter had put his stamp on. The ceiling was crème colored, with exposed wooden beams in the same honey colored wood as the floors. The extensive cabinetry was a shade deeper in color than the floors and housed just about every gadget known to man—for the kitchen, at least. It was his gift and something of a bribe for Dottie to keep her here. The industrial size stainless steel range would make a five-star chef weep tears of joy. And the refrigerator was also industrial size, which made it easier to overstock, since at times in the winter, roads became impassable.

They had a storage room in the basement as well, with deep freezes and extra shelf space for dry goods.

But it was the killer scents wafting in the air that made his mouth water. Without Dottie, he'd likely starve or live off microwavable dinners. She kept him fed and his house clean. The woman was worth her weight in pure gold. And her cooking was some of the finest in the county. Her chili had won the blue ribbon at the county fair three years running.

"Thank you, Dottie," Carter said, washing his hands in the sink and putting his hat on the nearby hook inside the door.

Spencer did the same. Dottie was a stickler when it came to proper manners, but for her cooking, it was worth it. She was still an attractive woman, her dark hair streaked with silver strands and always pulled back away from her expressive face in a long braid. A little plump in the hips and thigh region, and a good foot and a half shorter than he, she'd been cooking and cleaning for the Jones family going on twenty years. And since Carter's mom had passed a few years back, she'd taken on the role of surrogate mother.

As much as he owned the place, it was Dottie and her husband who ran him most of the time. He preferred to keep her happy because while she rarely showed any type of temper, she had no compunction about beating him over the head with a wooden spoon if she thought he was out of line. He and Spencer each took a seat at the large oak table, which was a shade darker than the gleaming honey floors. Dottie brought two plates and set them down before them.

"Dottie, you've outdone yourself as always. Tell me what I have to do to get you to come work for me," Spencer said, glancing at the loaded plate and licking his lips in anticipation. On the porcelain white plate was a beef brisket sandwich on thick slices of Texas toast, a mound of potato salad, and baked cinnamon apples for good measure.

Carter felt his own stomach growl in eager delight.

Dottie flushed, "Now, Mister Spencer, you know I wouldn't leave Mister Carter for all the money in the world."

Carter gave him a bemused smile at the first bite of potato salad. Spencer knew he'd have to fight Carter practically to the death for Dottie, because no way would he allow the woman to leave. Not when she cooked like a fucking dream.

"That's too bad," Spencer said and took a bite of the beef brisket sandwich, then emitted a muffled groan.

Dottie returned to the table and set down two tall glasses filled with sweet iced tea, and then a pitcher so they could refill it. "I'll just leave you boys to your lunch. Those sheets won't clean themselves."

"Thank you, Dottie. It's excellent as always," Carter said around a mouthful of brisket sandwich.

"Love you, Dottie," Spencer said, also eating his meal with relish. If there was one thing Spencer loved, it was food. He might go through submissives like he changed his underwear, but he appreciated good food more than most. Carter believed it was the two tours in Iraq and eight years in the army that had done it. But that was his opinion.

"So, what's up? You don't normally leave Jackson Hole unless its poker night," Carter said, studying his friend.

Nothing but crumbs remained of Spencer's sandwich, and now he was plowing through the homemade potato salad. Still holding his fork, he swallowed and said, "Me and the boys are concerned. The knuckleheads elected that I come speak with you."

"About?" Carter questioned, his body tight and rigid in his seat. They'd discussed him. What the fuck for?

Spencer cocked his head, his black eyes unwavering as he said, "Dude, you haven't been to the club in almost a year. That's a record, especially for you. And I know for damn sure you don't have any of the subs coming out to the ranch. That bunch couldn't keep a secret to save lives, as lovely and enter-taining as they are."

"I've had a particularly busy year with the ranch. Just because I'm not attending the club, doesn't mean I'm celibate," Carter said, folding his arms across his chest—even though that was precisely what he'd become.

After a long draught of iced tea, Spencer replied, seeming to choose his words carefully. "Normally, I would buy that and not press you. But you forget, I know you. And you haven't been the same since your visit to Pleasure Island last August. I know there was a sub—"

"Careful," Carter uttered, his voice deadly serious. He did not want to rehash the island or talk about Jenna with anyone. Not when the mere thought of her made his heart ache.

"Fuck that. You've been moping for almost a year. You searched for her and couldn't find her. It's time you moved on. I'm saying this not out of spite but because I'm genuinely concerned," Spencer said.

Carter grimaced and traced the line of a bead of moisture on his glass before he replied, "Look, I know I haven't gone to the club lately. I will. I just—hell, Spencer, it's the same old subs there. I realize your concern and while I appreciate it—"

"Just come, tonight even. It will do you some good to get out of the house for a night. You're not a recluse but this past year you sure as shit have been acting like one."

Had he? Deep down he knew Spencer was right. Carter needed to move on and forget about the past. Jenna was lost to him, forever. As bitter a pill as it was to swallow, short of hiring a private investigator to track her down, there was nothing he could do about it. He'd been standing still, letting life move on around him while his heart bled into the ground at the loss. And Jenna obviously didn't want to be found—at least not by him—because if she did, she would be here.

"Fine. I'll come this evening. So you and the rest of the idiot brigade will get off my case," Carter agreed and shook his head. The thought of attending the club was about as appealing as watching paint dry, but he'd suffer through it.

"And the sub from the island?" Spencer urged, with a black slash of an eyebrow cocked.

"Give it a rest, will you? I'll think about it, but no more talk of her. I shouldn't have told you about her in the first place and wouldn't have if not for the tequila that night. But for now, I have horses that need to be taken care of in the stables," Carter said, shoving his chair back and standing up from the table, effectively ending the conversation in his mind. He grabbed his plate and glass and placed them in the sink for Dottie. If he so much as tried to put them in the dishwater, he caught hell from her so he'd stopped doing it ages ago. That woman was scary when she was angry, and would feed him something horrid like tripe if he didn't follow her orders. Carter realized the irony in a Dom like him taking orders from his housekeeper, but some things were better left alone.

He turned to find Spencer was behind him with his plate and cup. "Look, I'm not trying to piss you off, Carter. We've all been concerned for a while now. I'm not trying to lessen the impact of what you felt for the sub but it's over. It's been over for a while, and the only way you're going to heal is by moving on. Best way to do that is to fuck her out of your system."

"Save the Dom crap for a sub who needs it. May I remind you that I'm the founder of our little club?" Carter snapped, anger swirling in his chest.

"Yeah, well, start fucking acting like it instead of moping and growing more callouses," Spencer said, setting his stuff in the sink and heading toward the door.

"I told you I would come tonight," Carter growled to Spencer's retreating back.

"See that you do," Spencer said. "It's Friday, the place should be hopping. And if you don't, come Sunday, the boys and I will ream you out on poker night."

"Get out of here before I change my mind," Carter snapped, putting his hat back on his head and following Spencer out the back door.

"I'm going," Spencer said, giving him a friendly middle finger salute as he climbed in his Dodge ram.

Ass.

He shook his head as Spencer drove down the lane, kicking up dust.

Was his friend right? Had Carter become a recluse in an effort to avoid the truth? As much as Spencer was his brother from another mother, he hated when the bastard was right.

Because there was truth in his friend's words—he was right. Jenna was gone from Carter's life. He'd searched for her and hadn't been able to track her down. It was like she'd vanished. Even Jared was no help.

Had it all been a mirage? That was the question that woke him up at night. Had the emotion and the feelings he'd seen in her eyes, that he'd felt in her touch, been nothing but a fantasy? And why had she chosen to stay on the island? Why, after everything that had happened between them, had she walked away from him? And how had he been too blind to see it coming?

CHAPTER 2

*a*fter Spencer left the Double J, Carter threw himself back into work for the rest of the day. With ninety-six horses to care for, feed, bathe, medicate, and train, there were days when the labor felt endless and like he was never quite finished. That was life on the ranch. Always far too much work and not enough hands. Herb had suggested taking on more help. They had the profits to make it work so Carter had told him to bring on whomever he thought would assimilate well on the ranch. Herb knew people, and Carter trusted him to make the right choices. There were a few high school kids who came and shoveled the stalls but during the summer, most were working at the ski resorts and other tourist places in town.

By five o'clock his body ached, but Carter would honor his word. When he promised someone something, no matter what it was, he followed through with it. Whether he wanted to or not.

So instead of taking a dip in his indoor pool and relaxing that evening, Carter showered and dressed for attending the club. Since the heat dipped into reasonable temperatures at night, he wore a black tank top with a blue button-down shirt which he left open, rolling the sleeves up to his elbows.

He changed hats from his work hat to his city hat, and added a black pair of steel toed shit-kicker cowboy boots he'd had specially commissioned for his size sixteen feet.

Instead of eating more of Dottie's mouth-watering beef brisket, he gave her the night off and headed into town for dinner. He drove to one of his favorite places, the Teton Roadhouse and Brewery Company. They'd only been in business in downtown Jackson Hole for some half dozen years, but they made one of the best steaks he'd ever eaten and brewed an exceptionally fine craft beer. A winning combination, in his book, and one he hadn't had for quite a while.

Carter had been denying himself the simple pleasures in life since Jenna. That ended now, tonight. Spencer had been dead on correct. If positions were reversed, with Carter addressing another Master, who had been acting like a reclusive monk the way Carter had this past year, he'd be the first one to suggest that the Dom needed to screw another sub's brains out to help him move past what had become an obsession. Perhaps even a few submissives if the first one didn't take—until she was out of his system.

Somehow, over the course of this year, Jenna's ghost had fucking neutered Carter. Not that he didn't care for her. Hell, he loved her—or loved who he'd thought she was and had been with him—but she was gone. Mayhap if he was balls-deep in another sub, the thought of her wouldn't cut him off at the knees.

At the Teton Roadhouse and Brewery, the hostess, a young brunette barely out of high school, seated Carter at one of the tables near the pristine bank of windows facing the main drive. It was high tourist season. The streets were lined with families and couples, milling about in search of food, entertainment, shopping. Jackson Hole made the bulk of its revenue from tourism. Yet it seemed to get busier and a bit more crowded every year. The sight made Carter wonder if Jackson Stone would make it to the club that evening—most likely, on a Friday, he'd be out patrolling the congested traffic; both foot and car.

Carter people watched a bit while he waited for his dinner. It provided him with the opportunity to ease himself back into being more social without actually having to interact with folks just yet. Life on the Double J was sedate and secluded. Here in the heart of town it was far more active and chaotic.

The interior of the brewery had been crafted to appear like a western saloon. Everything out here had a similar décor. It meant lots of wooden floors, wooden tables. The wall bar had been erected with an eye toward the tourists. Designed and carved out of a dark mahogany, it looked like what one would have found a century past.

That was part of the charm of his hometown.

Although it was also interspersed with technology. On the walls among the western décor of buffalo and elk heads were flat screen televisions with all manner of professional sports being played on them. On the back of the menu were listed events; trivia nights and other social gatherings.

That was a little too social for his book. He liked people just fine, but most days he just didn't have it in him to drive into town.

Carter was halfway through his porterhouse steak, a twenty-one ounce marbled beauty of a steak cooked medium rare, when he spotted a ghost. The succulent bite of meat turned to charcoal in his mouth and nearly lodged itself in his throat. Either she really was there, or his brain had finally cracked with the forced social interaction. It couldn't be who he thought it was, but he'd recognize her silhouette anywhere.

Not willing to lose his ghost, he shoved his chair back and stood just as his waitress returned.

"Is there a problem with your meal, sir?" Becky Tanner asked. They'd gone to high school together. She was a mother of three, but still managed to waitress with the best of them.

"No, Becky. It's perfect as usual. I just have to leave, immediately. Here, this should cover the bill and tip," he said, handing her a hundred-dollar bill.

"What about your change?" Becky asked.

"It's all yours. If you'll excuse me," he said and strode around her shocked form. Without a backward glance, he hurried out the door and shot a look down the street. Carter caught sight of a trail of blonde tresses that shimmered with the multi-faceted hues of gold, and threaded his way through the crowd.

She strode around a corner near Teton General Store. Carter cursed beneath his breath when he lost sight of her for a moment. There was no way she was getting away from him again.

It was her—had to be.

Carter's long strides closed the distance between him and his prey. At this time of night on a Friday evening, town was packed with tourists and locals alike. His above average height gave him a distinct advantage as he trailed her movements through the throngs of people. His gaze remained trained on her as she threaded and wove through the crowd, her golden hair trailing behind her in the breeze. He remembered those tresses had felt like spun silk in his hands as they whispered against his chest when she rode him, and they were just vibrant as he remembered.

Yet, she wasn't moving as fast as he remembered. She'd usually zipped at lightning speeds from one location to the next over the island. It caused a fingerling of doubt to wriggle in his mind.

Was it really her?

Was she really here? If so, why would she be in his town? They lived worlds away, in more ways than one. Or was he perhaps seeing ghosts because he was finally attempting to move on and now found himself following an innocent woman?

That wouldn't end well if that was the case.

And Spencer and the boys would die laughing at the tale. Jackson would joke that he'd have to arrest him for harassing an innocent woman. If anyone found out, it would put a chink in Carter's reputation and standing in the community. While he might be a Dominant, as far as the rest of the world knew he was lily white and a good old boy. Business associates wanted to purchase trail horses from him, not hear about the latest bondage technique. Or that he preferred his women bound and restrained while he paddled their asses before he fucked them.

Which was something he had every intention of doing with Jenna once he got his hands on her again. For every sleepless night during which he'd replayed the events on the island. For every time he'd fisted his cock and developed callouses masturbating to her memory. And for the chance to feel her come undone beneath his hands once more.

Her steps segued away from the main hub of town into the more residential section. Not that Jackson Hole was an overly large city by any measure. It was really more of a blip; the nearest large city was Cheyenne a few hours south. On their trek, not once had she turned or looked over her shoulder in his direction. It was like she was in her own little world, hefting two reusable grocery bags from Lucy's Market.

He just hoped like hell it wasn't a case of mistaken identity.

She stopped at a duplex building. Really, the structure was nothing more than an oversized home that had been split into two residences. So, clearly, if it was Jenna, she was living here in Jackson Hole. Why? Not that he was one to complain if it was her. If it was, he'd be elated for the chance to get some answers. Like why she'd fallen off the face of the earth only to end up in his town. The exterior of the duplex was finished in a deep, dark, cherry-colored wood, much darker than his ranch house but with the log cabin rustic theme that a majority of the homes in the area tended to have. His intended target climbed the wooden set of stairs up to the second-floor dwelling.

Gotcha!

She was no sooner inside the front door than Carter took the wooden stairs two at a time. At the top of the stairs he drew in a deep, calming breath. To be this close after so much despair these past months. This was what he'd been waiting on for almost a year. A chance to see her again—hold her, paddle her fucking ass for ever leaving him, and bury his aching cock inside her welcoming heat.

Or he was mistaken and had just followed a strange woman —who could have passed for Jenna's twin—all the way home. If so, he would apologize profusely and leave at the soonest opportunity.

Lifting his hand, he curled his fingers around the brass knocker and banged it twice. If it was Jenna, what was she doing here? Why hadn't she sought him out? How long had she been in Jackson? A myriad number of questions ran through his mind as he waited for her to answer the front door.

The oaken door opened, the hinges creaking in protest at the movement. Sunlight from the setting sun bathed her visage in gold. And the pent-up breath he'd been holding expelled in a rush.

Jenna.

A smile spread over his face and a part of himself that had been missing these past long months slid back into place. His eyes roamed over her, drinking in the sight of her standing so close.

"Well, well, darlin', fancy seeing you here," Carter purred, stunned at finding Jenna in his own backyard. She was so fucking beautiful. Her face was devoid of artifice. Those corn-flower blue eyes of hers were framed by thick golden tipped lashes. Her bow shaped mouth, her top heavy upper lip still the plump delight he remembered. How often had he imagined those lips on his cock? Remembered how good her mouth had felt sucking him down.

Shock riddled her frame. She blinked at him like a doe caught in his truck's headlights, like she couldn't believe he was standing on her doorstep. She could have been a statue for all her movement.

Well, the shock was mutual. He also felt the lust roaring in his ears. He hadn't wanted another woman since her. None had engendered a response in him like Jenna did. It was crazy that he could desire her, crave to have her writhing beneath him as he buried himself in her seductive heat, but he did, like he wanted air to breathe. There was a part of Carter that wanted to hoist her over his shoulder, head to the nearest bed, tie her down, and not let her up until she confessed her transgressions and he'd finally fucked her out of his system.

The problem was, he'd tried that once on the island, and had lost more than just his head.

"Carter. What do you want?" Jenna asked defensively. Her hand gripped the door like she was ready to slam it in his face. He'd love to see her try to push him away now that he'd found her again. It would give him an excuse to put his hands on her. Carter could recall with startling clarity the way she'd stared at him when he'd left the villa. The tears that had suffused her bright blue gaze. The sky above his ranch at midday always reminded him of her eyes. Then again, he'd seen her everywhere and in everything he did. Except today, the warmth and welcome that used to flow from her were conspicuously absent, replaced by trepidation and a lingering hint of fear.

If anything, she was more beautiful, her delicate cheekbones more pronounced. Her bow shaped mouth pursed in annoyance at his interruption. Her hair looked longer. Her knockout body left him hungering to feel her wrapped around him, her pillowy breasts smooshed against his chest while he sank himself inside her.

Why the hell would she be afraid of him? She'd never cowered during their week together. Quite the opposite, in fact: she'd challenged him, gone toe to toe with him repeatedly, and left an imprint on his heart and soul.

"To know why you're here," he replied. Using his size and body to his advantage, he pressed forward—not waiting for an invite he surmised would never come—and entered her home. Jenna backed away as he pushed his way inside her apartment. He took in the quaint living room. The hardwood floors and furniture were clean, but everything had a sheen to it, a worn quality. The rocking chair in the corner looked as if at any minute it would give up and collapse. The couch's stuffing appeared misshapen, the seating bowing inward a bit, although the faded sea green fabric was clean. And it was cozy in a purely feminine way, with a few knickknacks and a small television near the fireplace. A forgotten coffee mug sat on a small wooden end table. There were splashes of color, bright blue and green decorative pillows on the couch, that gave the appearance that she wasn't just passing through.

Carter backed her up until she had nowhere left to retreat. He caged her against the wall. Christ, he felt like he was possessed. Jenna glared up at him. Her blue eyes blazed in fury. He'd missed her spark of fire. Leaning his head down, he breathed in her scent, jasmine and vanilla. It was a sucker punch to the gut and fueled a desire that was for her alone. One of his hands caught a strand of her hair, the feel of the silken thread nearly bringing him to his knees.

He lowered his head, yearning to feel her lips on his once more. Her delicate hands stopped him, pressing against his chest, pushing him away. Her hands upon him felt like brands and made his groin ache.

"Carter, please leave. Please—" Her eyes widened. Horror

crossed her expressive face, the gorgeous face that had haunted his dreams nightly. At the shrieking wail emitting from an unseen room, Carter rocked back on his heels. His world spun, and all the air vanished from his lungs.

It was the high-pitched wail of an infant.

Dazed didn't even begin to cover the roiling mass of disbelief infiltrating his system. Jenna raced from the living room and left him standing there, reeling. She hurried back beyond the tiny, eat-in kitchen, with the bags from the market still sitting on the counter—likely because of his untimely disruption. Shaking himself from his stupor, Carter trailed her, unwilling to let her out of his sight now that she was back in his life.

He blinked at the scene before him, wondering if he was hallucinating and had indeed gone off the deep end.

"There, there, my love. It's all right. I know you're hungry. Hush now. I've got you," Jenna murmured, her voice soft and infused with honeyed sweetness as she lifted a squalling bundle from a crib. Tiny fists waved angrily in the air from the swaddled blanket covered with tiny sailboats on them. Carter stood rooted to the spot.

Jenna was a mother. She had a baby. Who was she with? Did Carter know him? Jackson Hole wasn't that large a town, and he knew the majority of the residents. Anger clawed at his chest. It was irrational, to be sure, but he wanted to howl and shake his fists at the heavens at the unfairness of it. To finally find her again and see that she had moved on while he'd been stuck in a quagmire of their past...

"Jenna, you have a baby? When?" he asked, his heart aching in a way he didn't quite understand.

"You're still here? I thought I told you to leave." She nodded toward the door in a dismissive gesture, her eyes blazing with self-righteous indignation. "Please go, Carter."

"Not until I get some answers." He approached her with the

infant cradled in her arms and was brought up short. His world didn't merely spin but did an entire one eighty as he stared at the child.

"That's my baby," he said with awe clouding his voice. Carter would know that face anywhere. There was an image of him, nearly identical at that age, in the living room at his house. Of all the things he'd expected to find when he followed her, this wasn't it.

Jenna winced, and moisture rimmed her dark blonde lashes. "Carter, listen to me, please. He's hungry, he's—"

"Give him to me, Jenna. Let me see him," Carter ordered, unable to quell the rising tide of emotions battering him. She didn't fight him when he went to lift the child out of her arms. His son waved his fists and kicked his feet, his tiny face scrunched up in fury at being denied his meal. Carter laughed at the tiny wail. Euphoria infused him. Carter had never seen anything so beautiful in all his life.

His son. He had a son. He was perfect; loud, and red-faced, but the most beautiful thing Carter had ever seen.

I love you. I know this is the first time we've met, but I love you more than I've ever loved anything.

"His name?" he asked, his voice thick with emotion. He was a father. He had a son.

"It's Liam," Jenna said quietly.

"Liam. It's a good name. I'm your pa, Liam. That's it." Carter grinned as his son quieted and stared up at him with identical eyes to his own. It was a singularly unique experience; meeting his son, seeing himself—parts of himself—passed on. He and Liam stared at each other, Liam's little hand curled around one of his fingers, his grip firm and strong. They studied one another intently, and the peace lasted for about two minutes. Then Liam's face creased in fury and he howled again at being denied his meal.

"Carter, please, he's hungry. I was just about to feed him

before you arrived. Please, he needs me," Jenna pleaded, her hands on his arm attempting to gently remove Liam. He felt her touch to the marrow of his bones.

He looked at her then. Tears streaked her lovely face, her lower lip trembled. She seemed to fear he would take him, take Liam and leave. She'd given him a son. The woman he'd never expected to care for had borne his child.

With care, he handed Liam back to his mother. She instantly tried soothing the angry bundle as she sat in a corner chair that resembled a small, feminine lazy boy recliner in a paisley pink fabric.

"I know, sweet boy. I've got you. I know, you're so hungry. Carter, if you don't mind..." She nodded toward the door, dismissing him. But he wasn't missing a second more of his son's life.

Carter took a seat on the edge of her bed, as close to her and Liam as possible. When she opened her mouth, he stopped her, putting a hand up. "Jenna, I'm not leaving. I've already seen your charms. Feed our son."

He gestured for her to proceed. Liam's angry wail pierced the air, Jenna harrumphed and then ignored him entirely. She directed all her focus toward Liam. It was an achingly private and intimate moment, watching his son's tiny mouth latch on to Jenna's nipple and begin to suckle.

Liam's furious cries diminished. His miniature fist rested against her breast and his eyes were focused on Jenna, his mouth working as he nursed.

"There, that's better isn't it, my love? That's it," Jenna murmured, rocking him slightly, her gaze soft.

"You love him," Carter stated, a little amazed and awed by the expression on her face. Maybe he shouldn't be, but in the days and weeks since their interlude on the island, he'd questioned what he'd seen in her eyes. Doubted the emotions she'd tried to hide from him. Doubted his own memory, if truth be told.

"More than life itself," she admitted, her gaze never wavering from Liam. And then she blushed; her cheeks pinkened beneath his gaze and some of the flush even spread over her exposed breast.

"Why didn't you tell me, Jenna?" Carter asked, with more force and accusation in his voice than he intended. But she'd kept this from him. How could she do that? She'd hidden his son away from him. He wanted to pull her across his thighs and blister her hide. And he would, the moment the opportunity presented itself.

Her eyes slid shut, a grimace crossed her features and then she said, "I meant to, Carter, please believe me when I say that. My life got complicated really quickly. I never meant to keep him from you. I swear I didn't. I didn't even know I was pregnant until I left Pleasure Island and my life imploded."

She gazed at him then, regret swimming in her blue eyes. He hadn't forgotten how beautiful her eyes were, but he hadn't remembered the knockout punch to the gut a single look from her could give his composure. She continued, "But now you do know about Liam. And you can come see him and be a part of his life as much as you want. No pressure. If you don't want to be in his life, I'll understand, and I'm not asking or demanding that you do. But know this: if you decide to be in his life, then you are all in. I won't accept half measures where my son is concerned, or allow you to yo-yo in and out of his existence. If you need to take some time to think about it, I'll understand."

He hid his smile at her unexpected display of mama bear protective attitude. Carter's mind had been made up the moment he realized the child was his; Jenna just didn't know it. He said, "I'm all in. And I will be in his life on a daily basis from here on out. As soon as you have finished feeding him, I will help you pack your things and his, you're both coming home with me tonight. You'll live on my ranch from now on."

She shook her head in refusal. "Carter, I can't. I have responsibilities. I—"

"Is it another man, Jenna? What? Tell me." If it was another man, Carter would hide the body. He had a thousand or so acres of untamed wilderness. Plenty of places to hide one. Nothing was keeping him from his son—or his son's mother, for that matter.

"No, it's nothing like that. It's my sister. She's in the shower, getting ready for work tonight."

The gut clenching fear slackened, and he listened to the sounds in the apartment. He heard the water quietly running in an unseen bathroom. It was something he had missed entirely when he'd entered her place, but Jenna's presence and reappearance had consumed him, given him blinders to everything else. Carter could deal with a sister. Another man, no.

Jenna stated rather defiantly, a spark in her gaze, "I can't leave her here by herself. And I have a job that I'm starting in a few days. Without transportation into the city, it will just be easier for us to live here."

"Well, your sister can come live at the ranch too. As for your job, that's taking care of our son," Carter replied. If she wanted to fight him on this, she could try. But she would lose. His son would live with him.

"But, but…" she sputtered.

"You kept him from me, Jenna—whether intentionally or not, the result of your actions kept me in the dark about his existence. I won't miss more of my son's life because of your misplaced sense of pride, or whatever other reason you're trying to come up with to finagle a way out of coming with me. This is the most practical scenario for everyone. I can't get into town frequently with my duties on the ranch. Hell, this is the first time I've left the ranch in a month. You will have your own room at my house, and I will get a nursery put together for Liam. But I'm not leaving here without you and Liam. Fight me if you want to but you won't win on this. My son will live with me."

"So you would take my son from me? Just like that? Muscle in here, acting like a big bad Dom and—" Her voice rose an octave and she clamped her mouth shut.

"No. I won't take him away from you. How could you even think that of me? I never treated you poorly and that's the truth, so don't try to impose warped views of my character because you want to be a brat about the situation. But I will have my son under my roof. And it's going to be that way because I'm bigger and stronger."

"Don't pull that Dom bullshit with me, Carter. It won't work," she snapped.

He almost smiled at her response. God, he'd missed that spark she had in her. He knelt before her and put an arm on either side of the chair, completely trapping her. Mindful of the baby with his eyes shut, his mouth still moving and drinking from her tit, he said in a low voice, "You and Liam are coming with me, Jenna. If I have to handcuff you to my pickup truck, I will. And I will do it, because I will have my son in my house. I'm not doing this to hurt you or Liam. This truly is what is best for everyone. When he's done eating, pack your things. We're moving you both to my house tonight. Understood?"

She was rigid, but she nodded and then said, "On one condition."

"What's that?" he asked, feeling downright testy over her attitude. This little sub had forgotten the way to behave, and he would take premiere pleasure in reminding her who was boss.

"You don't touch me. I'm not your submissive or a convenient screw because I'm in the same house as you. Liam and I will live there, but we're roommates, nothing more," Jenna replied, studying him.

He stared at her, trying to decide how to answer. "I will agree that I won't touch you unless you beg me to, and then all bets are off."

"I won't beg you for anything," she said with a shake of her head.

"Then you've got nothing to lose or worry about. Are we agreed?" Carter asked, holding his breath, watching a myriad number of expressions as they flickered over her face while she decided. She was still so expressive, held nothing back. Everything she felt was in her eyes, and right now they were wary but resigned.

"Yes. We'll come with you," Jenna replied, her voice barely above a whisper.

Carter swallowed the momentary victory. She hadn't established any parameters for their agreement. For instance, just because she'd said she wouldn't beg him, that didn't mean he couldn't do everything in his power to change her mind by seducing her. Carter knew her body, knew how to drive her crazy and entice her into his bed. He wasn't certain why she had erected barriers between them. Perhaps it was the year between their parting, or maybe she hadn't felt anything more than a passing fancy for him. But he'd get to the bottom of it before long.

Carter felt a sense of purpose and forward momentum for the first time since he had left Pleasure Island.

She'd be under his roof and back in his bed by the month's end. And this time, he wasn't playing to own her merely for a week, but for keeps.

CHAPTER 3

*C*arter was here, in her apartment.

His inky, dark chestnut hair peeked out from beneath his Stetson, the tousled length longer than the last time she'd seen him. His shoulders appeared broader. But that was Carter; big and alpha to the core, and larger than life. Jenna was shocked at the unexpected desire thrumming in her veins at being near him again. She shouldn't be when it came to him. Carter's presence, the energy that made him who he was, infused her small bedroom and overwhelmed her. He'd done that from the first moment on the docks of Pleasure Island. And in the time since they had parted, it seemed like none of that had changed—when everything else had.

What had she just agreed to? Live with him? See him night and day?

Jenna couldn't stop the tremors that seized her at the satisfied glimmer in his eyes.

She did her best to hide her trepidation from Carter as Liam nursed. His intrusion into her room and back into her life left her dazed. She couldn't deny the apprehension she experienced at seeing him again. Before, when they'd been together on the island, he had dominated her world. It had been the best week she'd ever had, and had given her a renewed purpose in life when her own had become so bleak. Looking down at her son still rootling for more milk, she switched Liam from one breast to the other. Her little man was a hungry boy.

Probably because he took after his father. She didn't know how Carter had known Liam was his son—although, now that the two were side by side, she could see they had similar physical traits. Liam's eye color had already begun to shift toward hazel, just like Carter's. And he'd already had a mop of dark hair when he was born.

Carter knew about Liam and wanted him—wanted to be a father to him.

That was something, at least. Jenna had to look at this new development positively. Carter knew he was a father and appeared ready to pick up the gauntlet. Jenna could attempt to release the guilt and remorse at keeping Liam a secret, and move forward with her life. While having the news of Liam's existence sprung on Carter inadvertently wasn't ideal, or the way she'd wanted him to find out, the fact that he knew was good.

She had been working on building up her courage to drive out to his ranch with Liam for weeks now, but she'd chickened out each time, using her son and his tender age as an excuse not to, telling herself to wait just another week or two so he was older and then she'd make the trek. That driving for an hour with an infant was silly and she should wait. What if her sister's car broke down? What if Liam needed his diaper changed or got fussy?

She couldn't deny the relief flowing through her that it was no longer a secret. It certainly was one she'd never intended to keep.

The whys of her secret didn't matter now. Carter was justified in his angry accusations. It was guilt more than anything that made her agree to go with him. The man was stubborn as a mule and would get his way regardless. She didn't want to deny him access to Liam, either. And that was guilt. If Carter truly wanted to be a part of Liam's life and help her raise him, maybe it would be for the best if they lived at his ranch. At least for a little while so Carter could get to know him. As uncomfortable as she was with Carter in her room, his gaze was all for their son and didn't carry a hint of heat.

Unlike before, when Liam had suddenly made his presence known. Would he have kissed her if Liam hadn't intervened with his cries?

She'd been weak-kneed and flummoxed at being near him again. His scent, that woodsy spicy scent of his she loved so much had wafted over her. She'd waged an internal battle not to surrender to the overwhelming flash of desire flooding her system.

Jenna was hopeless when it came to Carter. He'd enjoyed her, cared for her, but it had been a week-long fantasy. Still, that didn't curtail the disappointment she felt that his gaze no longer held any heat. Becoming a father and learning about her inadvertent betrayal would do that. What had she expected? That he would see her again, learn about Liam and declare his love for her? While that might have been a secret fantasy she'd entertained over the long months of her pregnancy, she knew it wasn't the reality of their situation.

He was moving her to his ranch because of Liam.

With the condition she'd requested firmly in place, she didn't have to worry about any potential advances from him. Surely that would make life easier. She could ignore the constant sexual tension that seemed to always be present.

What they'd had on Pleasure Island had been a little slice of heaven in her life. And it had brought her the best thing in her life: her son. She didn't regret a moment she'd spent with Carter, even the unconventional way she'd ended up in his bed.

There was no remorse over her week with him. Just sorrow that so much had occurred in her life since then that she wasn't the same person she'd been on the island. Her dad had succumbed to his illness shortly before Christmas. Between her dad's funeral arrangements and then finding out she was pregnant while dealing with his estate, Jenna had barely kept her head above water.

When Liam finished nursing, she covered her breast and burped him. Her little man tended to get a little irate about needing to be burped when he would prefer to go right to sleep.

"That's it, my love," she murmured as she got a few out of him. He snuggled in her arms and it soothed her. Regardless of her concerns about living with Carter herself, she knew deep down it was the right thing to do for her son. Liam came first in everything.

They would have to set more parameters—like she absolutely did intend to work and support herself. So Carter could forget that one. But she would compromise with him. As long as he provided her the same courtesy, they would get along... somehow.

Rising from her chair with Liam secure against her chest, she side-stepped past Carter. He sat with his elbows on his knees on the edge of her bed. It was a queen-sized bed, more than large enough for her, but Carter was such a huge man that he made it appear almost doll-sized. Sliding her closet door open, Jenna withdrew her small tan suitcase to cart Liam's things: clothes, blankets, washcloths, and his bedding. The sheer volume of items babies needed was amazing. Then there were his binkies, her breast pump, his diapers, wipes, lotion, soap, special detergent, bottles, and so much more.

She'd use the larger suitcase for her things. This was a tentative move, temporary even, to see if it would work out. She'd pack enough to get them through the first few days. A few days with an infant and Carter might toss them both out on their butts. She wouldn't give this place up just yet, and then they'd see how things went.

"Hey, what's all the hubbub?" Meghan, her bright, funny kid sister asked, strolling into Jenna's room in her black and tan waitress getup. She'd been working as a waitress at one of the nearby resorts that Jenna could never seem to remember the name of, but it had 'mountain' something or other in it. Yeah, that whole pregnancy brain thing and mothers losing their minds a bit due to lack of sleep—it was a real thing. She could remember everything about her week with Carter. But for the life of her, Jenna didn't have the foggiest idea what she'd eaten for breakfast that morning.

Meghan skidded to a halt at the sight of Carter perched on the bed. Meghan was a younger, shorter version of Jenna and gave Carter a glare chock full of disdain.

"You're him," Meghan said, studying Carter like he was one of her science experiments.

"I'm Liam's father, yes," Carter said and stood, holding out one of his mammoth hands for Meghan to shake.

Meghan glared at him for a moment with an eyebrow raised, probably wondering how quickly she could draw blood if it was warranted. Jenna loved her sister, but she was not a wallflower by any means.

"Meghan," she finally muttered and accepted the proffered hand. Jenna was tempted to laugh at the idea of her younger, shorter sister going head to head with a man twice her size, but that was Meghan: she of the 'take no prisoners' variety.

"Why are you packing Liam's clothes? What did you do? Did you threaten my sister?" Meghan accused, her hands curled into fists.

"Meghan, it's nothing like that. Carter would like for Liam to live in his house. So we are moving in with him. The three of us," Jenna explained, trying to quash a potential confrontation before it began.

"One, I'm not going. Two, is he forcing you? Say the word and I'll call the cops." Meghan directed her gaze her sister's way. Jenna knew all she had to do was say the word and Meghan would cause problems. And make good on her threat to call the police. That was why she'd been able to leave her little sister in college while she'd worked on the island. Meghan had no problem taking care of herself—or others, for that matter.

"No. He's not forcing me," Jenna replied.

And then Carter said, "Call the police if you want. I'm sure my buddy Jackson would love to stop by and mediate."

Jenna fought the urge to smack the man upside the head. Didn't he realize his response was akin to dropping a match on lighter fluid when it came to her sister?

"Bring it, big guy. Even if you do have an in with the police, that doesn't mean you can toss your weight around like you own the place because you don't, I know the owner and you aren't him. So why are you moving Liam and my sister to your house?" Meghan asked, shooting Carter an even frostier glare, ratcheting up the tension in the miniscule bedroom.

Jenna wanted to thunk her head against the wall and then get more than an hour of undisturbed sleep. Yet these two knuckleheads were arguing—and over *her* life.

The man didn't back down. Not that Jenna expected him to, from past experience. He stood his ground and gave Meghan a rather direct and dismissive glance and a shrug of his massive shoulders. He said, "Because my son will live with me."

"Just like that?" Meghan prodded, snapping her fingers. Jenna knew she should intercede. When her sister blew her gasket—which, thankfully, wasn't often—rivers changed the course of their flow for days.

Carter blithely replied like he was swatting at a fly, "Yep. If

33

I'd known about him sooner, he would already be there."

"Meghan, can you stop interrogating him and help me please?" Jenna asked, a bit exasperated. Between holding Liam while she tried to pack and mediate a potential skirmish between these cotton-headed morons, she was liable to start knocking heads together. Starting with the sasquatch and man of the hour.

"Let me hold him while you get yourselves ready," Carter ordered and approached her. His long legs ate up the miniscule distance in no time and he towered over her.

Jenna hesitated as she craned her neck and looked at him. Sweet heavens, he was still the most handsome man she'd ever met. His dark stubble was shorter than it had been on the island, only a day or two's worth of growth. But his eyes were no less magnetic and drew her in until he was all she could see. Her body softened internally at his nearness. After so much time, her body couldn't still want him, could it? She glanced at his firm lips, remembering the ways in which he'd been able to render her brainless with merely a kiss.

Fear churned in her breast and she clutched her sleeping son to her chest. She couldn't go there with him again. The first time, watching him walk away, had almost destroyed her.

Her life was about her son and caring for him.

"Promise that you're not going to leave without me," she said and cursed that her voice trembled instead of sounding fierce as she intended.

That was her greatest fear. That he would take their son and shut her out. Jenna knew deep down it was an irrational fear but it was one that had woken her up at night. Carter was stronger, not only physically, but from the sheen on his boots she knew he came from money. Money equaled power. The power to legally take her son from her. And she would fight him—to the death if she had to—in order to keep Liam.

"Jenna, you know me. I would never do that to you. Hand

him to me and get your things. I'll wait," Carter directed, his exasperation evident. He held out his hands to take Liam out of her arms.

Jenna hesitated a moment longer before she caved. On the island, she'd trusted Carter without question. Her dad had always said she needed to have a little faith. She couldn't pack while holding Liam, at least not quickly. Grudgingly, she nodded and transferred her sleeping bundle into his father's arms.

The two made a picture, that was for certain. The huge, six-and-a-half-foot cowboy cradling a ten-pound infant against his wide chest. The sight of Carter holding their son stirred her. He looked almost ridiculous. And masculine. And alpha to the freaking core of his being. But it was the wonder on his face as he studied their son and walked out of the room that gave her courage.

She understood the sentiment well. The overpowering and not a little frightening depth of love for her child. All told, Carter was handling the news much better than she had expected.

Meghan started tossing Jenna's clothes into the larger suitcase.

"Are you sure about this?" Meghan whispered furiously, keeping her voice low while she removed Liam's clothes from the top drawer of the small dresser. The walls in this place were notoriously thin.

"No, not at all. But I do know it's what's best for Liam. He needs to know his father, Meghan. At least for now I think it's the right choice. Long term, we'll see," Jenna replied quietly so only her sister could hear her response. She didn't want to give Carter any ideas and make him think it wasn't permanent. They had more than their fair share of issues to work out, with living together and raising Liam. She didn't want to add to the pot.

Meghan nodded, her high blonde ponytail swinging, and replied with a whisper, "Pack what you need for now. I'm not going anywhere. If you go and it's all a mistake, you can come back here."

"You're not coming with me?" Jenna asked, her voice louder and filled with more panic than she intended. Meghan was supposed to be her buffer against Carter. Without her sister's presence, alone with Carter, she worried she would do something infinitely idiotic. Like fall for him again.

"No offense, but no. I have very little desire to live on a ranch in the middle of nowhere. As much as I love science and nature, here's fine for me. Just get me the address for the ranch and I will still come watch Liam for you while you do your classes," Meghan replied.

"Are you sure?" Jenna asked, hearing the whine in her own voice. It would be bad form to beg her sister to come stand guard and make sure she didn't sleep with the father of her child. Especially with the man in question in the other room and only paper-thin walls between them. Jenna couldn't give him the upper hand otherwise she'd drown. For Liam's sake, everything had to be kept above board.

"One hundred percent," Meghan replied with a shake of her head.

Carter walked back in and surveyed what she had packed so far. "I need to go get my truck. You have way too many things that we will need to take with us and I won't risk him with our arms full."

"Set him in his bassinet over there. We'll need to take it with us, too. I hope that's all right. And I have to get his diaper bag packed. We need the car seat base out of Meghan's car. You sure you know what you're getting into with all of this?" Jenna asked, glancing around the room at everything she still needed to pack.

"Jenna, I'm not backing out of this, now or ever. You may as well get used to it. We're in each other's lives from here on out. It'll take me fifteen minutes or so to get my truck. But I will be back and then we can go," Carter ordered, almost daring her to defy him. As much as she wanted to, Jenna just didn't have the energy. Liam had barely let her sleep last night and she was functioning on fumes.

"If you want, I can drive you to your truck. I have to get to work anyhow, and that way we can just transfer the car seat base into your truck," Meghan offered.

"I'd be much obliged," Carter said, tipping his hat toward Meghan. The man looked every inch the gentleman cowboy, and heaven help Jenna, but her knees trembled at the sound of his voice.

"Let me grab my purse and we can leave. Jenna, call me if you need anything," Meghan said, giving her a knowing stare. That was basically her sister saying, *call me if the shit hits the fan and I'll come raise hell and get you out.* Jenna replied with a slight nod.

Then she watched the two of them, her petite sister, and the man she had loved once, leave the apartment. With Liam asleep in his bassinet, Jenna walked into the kitchen with his diaper bag, grabbing extra binkies, and finally surrendered to the tremors threatening to wrack her frame.

She leaned against the kitchen counter for support. Her life had felt like one crisis after another for so long. It shouldn't be a surprise that it was all being upended yet again. What she wouldn't give for the teensiest amount of stability and not to continually have the firm ground she thought she stood upon ripped out from beneath her.

Would she find that on Carter's ranch? A place she could finally call home, a sense of security and peace of mind she'd never known? Especially now that it wasn't all about her anymore, but making certain Liam had a stable environment to grow up and thrive in. She'd sacrifice herself, her own wants and needs, if it gave Liam a proper home.

That was her purpose in life. Liam. Nothing else mattered.

Frustrated—mainly with the situation and herself, because a part of her had dreamed about reuniting with Carter, had craved him in the dead of night—she shoved away from the counter and finished packing. She knew Carter well enough; he'd want to leave the moment he returned.

And Jenna was so tired, all she really wanted was a comfortable bed and her son soundly sleeping nearby.

∼

CARTER FOLLOWED Jenna's sister Meghan out of the apartment. She looked very much like a younger and shorter version of Jenna. She was no less disarming and beautiful than Jenna, but she was also much more 'in your face' defiant. The woman would drive him crazy if he had to contend with her in his home. He already had Dottie ordering him about daily. Perhaps it was good that she'd opted out of living on his ranch.

Jenna would be enough of a handful. Carter folded his long length into one of the smallest cars he'd ever seen, let alone ridden in. It was one of those mini Coopers in a brilliant candy apple red that had been built for people much smaller than him.

"Sorry about the fit," Meghan murmured, a hint of laughter in her musical voice. She started the car and the engine made the entire vehicle buzz.

Chagrined over the ride and the company, he snorted. "No, you're not. Look, I realize you don't know me, but know that I don't mean your sister any harm. I just believe that my son should live with me, and that means your sister needs to come too. Head west on Broadway to Willow. I'm parked at one of the meters there."

Meghan gave a small nod, then pulled the car out onto the road before she responded, "All I will ask is that you be kind to her. She's been through more than you can possibly imagine. Jenna's the one who held our family together through thick and thin. And believe me when I say there's been a lot of thin. She's had the weight and burden of our family on her shoulders through crappy circumstances that anyone else would have buckled under. I understand your need to know your kid. And I have to say, I'm glad you feel that way. Jenna shouldn't be alone in raising him."

"But?" he asked, wondering what Meghan meant about the 'thin'. From the moment he'd met Jenna, he'd wanted to be her protector, wanted her to place her trust fully in him. And she'd tried, he knew that, but there had been parts of herself she had held back from him and kept private.

"Hurt her, and there is no place you will be able to hide where I won't find you and bury you," Meghan said with utter surety.

"You're threatening me?" He barked out a laugh. She was even smaller than Jenna, although her attitude was a bit more badass and a whole lot more defiant.

And then she swiveled her gaze toward him for a brief moment, whereupon he was able to see the one startling difference between her and her sister. Where Jenna's eyes were vibrantly blue, her sister's were a verdant forest green. She murmured, "That's not a threat. It's a promise."

Carter could appreciate how protective Meghan was being of her sister. He applauded her efforts to that end. But he wasn't going to hurt Jenna. Mayhap he'd push her buttons and try to get to the bottom of why she'd withheld Liam's existence from him. Discover why they were living in Jackson. That was one little nugget he could start on now. He asked, as Meghan turned onto Willow, "So why are you here in Wyoming? Jenna said you lived in Florida."

"I did. Graduated with my science degree this past May, and am now interning with The Alpine Science Institute that researches the Greater Yellowstone ecosystem. They don't offer a graduate degree but it's the work I really want to do. So they will train me and I can earn credit toward another college degree."

"Go about halfway down the street, my truck is the big navy blue Chevy. You like the mountains?" he enquired, making small talk not just with Jenna's sister but his son's aunt. By his reckoning, that made her family, even if it was of the extended variety.

"Yep. I know it's weird, being I had the Gulf of Mexico just outside my front door, but the mountains have always given me a peace that the ocean never did. And I happen to love the science and biology of mountains and want to study climate change so we as a society will have an idea of what to expect."

"Well, my ranch is located in the Gros Ventre Valley, with a clear stretch view of the Tetons and the Sleeping Indian. If you change your mind about living spaces, you are always welcome."

Meghan pulled her tiny car up behind his truck, parked what he had dubbed a baby carlet that wasn't suitable for living in the mountains, and said, "Thanks for that, big guy. I think I'll manage on my own just fine. Granted, I might want to come take a peek at your mountains."

"You're welcome anytime, Meghan," he said as he exited the vehicle and stretched his body from the cramped quarters. And he meant it. He liked Jenna's sister. She was a bit mouthy, but he could deal with that. It was her loyalty to her sister, and need to protect her—even from him—that stuck out for him.

Meghan helped him get the car seat base out of the back of her car and into his truck. It struck Carter, as he fastened the base into the back seat of his truck, how he'd left his ranch single and unattached, and would now be returning with his son and Jenna.

As she was getting back into her car, Meghan pointed at him and said, "Just remember, be good to her or else…"

Then she climbed into her Cooper and drove off like a red flash.

Carter climbed into the cab and drove his truck, a navy blue Chevy Silverado, through the streets of downtown Jackson. His emotions were in a tumult. His cell phone beeped again but he ignored the text messages from Spencer. The man was dogging his ass, asking where the fuck he was at and why he wasn't at the club. Carter set the ringer to silent. There was no way in hell he was heading to the club. He'd catch hell for it from Spencer and the rest of the crew, but he didn't give a damn.

Carter had just discovered he had a son. Tonight was about getting his son under his roof and marveling over his existence. The last thing he would do was get Jenna and Liam to his ranch and then head off for the night. That would sit real well with Jenna—so much so, he could just imagine the headache it would create in his life. The damn club could wait, as far as he was concerned. He wanted tonight. Just one night with his son before the rest of the world butted in.

Christ, he'd been a goner the moment he'd held him. He hadn't known he could love another with such startling depth and clarity. Liam existed, therefore Carter loved him.

And then there was his mother. Jenna's return into his life was just as cataclysmic as her first entry. She was still as beautiful as she'd been when they'd met. Her hips were a bit more rounded from childbirth, and her killer cleavage was even more so now that she was breastfeeding. He knew it shouldn't be erotic and shouldn't have aroused him, but seeing their son greedily latch his mouth around her nipple had made him hard as a fucking rock.

41

He pulled his truck up alongside her apartment and breathed a sigh of relief at the sight of her hefting her suitcases out to the landing at the top of the stairs. A part of him had worried that he would return only to find that she had vanished on him again without a trace, and this time with his son.

He'd trusted her without question on the island. The thought of Liam and the fact that Carter didn't even know exactly how old his son was put a rather large crimp in her trustworthiness. Only time would tell if he could trust her again.

Exiting his truck, he climbed the stairs. When Jenna went to lift one of the suitcases to carry it down, he stopped her. She looked like a strong wind would topple her over.

"I've got these. I don't want you lifting them when you could hurt yourself," Carter said, noticing her gait was a bit unsteady, as if she was in pain. He wondered what that was about.

It didn't take him all that long to secure her suitcases and the bassinet in the back of his truck. Once her stuff was stored and secured, that left Jenna and Liam. She exited the apartment toting her purse and a large diaper bag slung over one shoulder, with their son in the carrier part of the car seat in the other hand.

"Here, let me help you," he murmured, taking the stairs back up two at a time, reaching for the bags at her shoulder.

"If you could just lock the deadbolt with my keys, I'm fine with the rest," she said, handing them over. Then she navigated her way down the stairs while he locked up her place.

He was back down the stairs in a blink, opening the door and taking the diaper bag and purse while Jenna fastened the carrier onto the car seat base. Then she surprised Carter by climbing into the back seat and sitting next to Liam.

"Jenna, are you sure you don't want to ride up front?" he

asked as he climbed into the cab on the driver's side.

"If memory serves, you said your ranch is almost an hour outside of Jackson, right? That's a long time with an infant. He's sleeping and behaving now, but give it ten minutes and he could be fussing up a storm, with me needing to climb back here. It's just easier all around for me to sit back here to begin with. Trust me on this," she said with a yawn.

"You seem tired. Is everything all right?" Carter asked pulling away from the curb and heading toward the highway.

"Yep, just one of the joys of being a new mom. He's still not sleeping through the night, which the pediatrician tells me is perfectly normal, but it also means I haven't had a decent night's sleep since he was born. I tend to try and sleep whenever he does," Jenna explained and yawned again, although she tried to hide it.

"Then why don't you get some shut-eye while I drive. It will be about an hour until we make it to the Double J," Carter said, his chest tight that she was clearly suffering but also a bit piqued that she still didn't ask for help when she needed it.

She gave him a tremulous smile and replied, "If you don't mind."

"Not at all, Jenna. I'm not an ogre. You need your sleep to keep your strength up so you can take care of Liam. I'm here to help you but there are certain things you can do that I can't," he explained.

She blushed and said, "Thanks."

Then she leaned back in her seat and her eyes fluttered shut. One of her hands covered their son's little belly, like she wanted to ensure that Liam was safe even while she napped. It did something to him, seeing how protective she was, how much she clearly adored Liam. He felt it, deep in his chest.

Carter drove the rest of the way to his ranch in silence, glancing in his rearview mirror from time to time at the precious cargo in the back seat. And it wasn't just his son.

CHAPTER 4

"Jenna. We're here," Carter's voice infiltrated her dream.

A good dream—a memory, really, of when she and Carter had met on the island. The dunking into the ocean she'd given him that had set the wheels in motion and had brought her here, to this time and space. She cracked open an eye and gazed into Carter's face. He was leaning over the car seat, careful not to disturb Liam.

She'd missed his face. The rugged lines of his square jaw. The way his cowboy hat sat on his head. Her gaze dropped to his lips; his wide, sensual lips shrouded by a shadow beard. She remembered how they tasted, how they moved against her lips and over her body.

"Jenna," Carter whispered on a groan.

She glanced back into his eyes and heat, the intoxicating lure of him, barreled through her midsection. His mouth descended toward hers. She licked her suddenly dry lips. The potent chemistry she'd thought lost to the annals of time surged to the surface like a Spartan on his way to do battle.

Carter's lips were an inch from hers, his gaze transfixed on hers, when Liam sputtered a pitiful cry.

Jenna jerked back. Heat flushed her cheeks and embarrassment flooded her system. "Let me get him settled and I can help you get our things," she said.

"I already took care of it all. You and Liam were sleeping so peacefully, I didn't want to wake you until I had to," Carter said, helping her out of the truck.

She turned back and lifted Liam's irate little body from his car seat carrier.

"Could you get the carrier seat for me?" she asked, fixing a tight smile over her face. She couldn't believe she'd almost kissed him. She hadn't been in his presence again for more than a few hours. Heaven help her.

"Sure," Carter murmured.

While he removed the carrier from the truck, Jenna took her first look at his ranch. 'Wow' didn't even begin to cut it. Fields stretched and rolled in green waves. Pine trees and oaks danced in the warm evening breeze. The sun was setting behind a patch of dark slate-colored mountains, illuminating everything in its path a fiery orange and gold. The stables were huge. And as she listened, she heard the whicker of horses, the clomp of hooves against the earth, and could smell manure, loads of it.

There were other, smaller structures—a barn, a small row of cabins—that were aglow in the sun's golden, dying embers. Hopefully she'd get a closer look at them tomorrow. Jenna gently swayed with Liam, calming his cries until she could change his diaper while she swiveled her head and viewed the house they'd be living in with Carter.

It was the biggest log cabin she'd ever seen; two stories, with possibly even a third. It dwarfed the duplex she and Meghan had been residing in. She knew Carter had money, that he was well to do, but this? She'd never expected this. The main house, while it could have been a monstrosity due to its sheer size, actually looked like a warm beacon against the background of approaching darkness. The interior lights glowed in welcome, and the exterior just took her breath away.

Carter placed his palm against her lower back and ushered her toward the door. Jenna shivered and felt his innocuous touch clear down to her toes. How was she going to survive, living with him so near and not wanting him? She had no answer, only uncertainty about her future. With Liam complacent in her arms, she let Carter lead her up the steps of the back porch. She took it all in, her head spinning, wondering just how wealthy Carter must be to own such a place.

He opened the back door and held it for her. She entered, noticing the mudroom before Carter led them through to the kitchen and dining area. Jenna stopped when she spied a woman at the kitchen stove. She was older, perhaps in her early fifties. Her dark black hair was streaked with silver.

She turned and set a dish towel on the nearby counter before clapping her hands and approaching.

"Jenna, this is Dottie Henderson. She cooks, cleans, and takes care of everything inside the house," Carter said.

"Oh, it's a pleasure to meet you, Jenna. And you have a baby!" Dottie exclaimed, clasping her hands at her bosom.

"It's nice to meet you. And yes, this little guy is Liam. Sorry to invade you on such short notice," Jenna replied.

"Oh, it's no bother at all. In fact, it's the best news and most excitement we've had on the ranch in ages. And I just love that there's another woman out here. It can get a little lonely at times. He's just beautiful. It's been a long time since we had a baby on the ranch, too," Dottie said.

"So you live here, in the house?" Jenna asked.

"Oh no, with my husband, Herb, whom I'm sure you will meet in the morning. We have a small house on the grounds."

"Dottie's husband is my foreman," Carter explained and set the carrier next to the kitchen table.

Liam started to fuss and squirm. Then the smell hit Jenna. Yep, it was diaper changing time.

"Where did you put the diaper bag? And is there some place where I can change him?" she asked as Liam began to really make his discomfort known.

"Certainly. Oh, the poor dear. I don't like long car rides either. Let me show you where you can change the little master," Dottie said.

"Here," Carter said, holding the diaper bag out to Jenna. She took it and followed Dottie's matronly form down a short hall to a guest bathroom.

Dottie followed her in and helped her get the changing pad, wipes and a fresh diaper out.

"He's just precious, and looks so much like Mister Carter I would know him as his son anywhere," Dottie murmured.

"I'm sure you find it a bit odd that he didn't know about him right away," Jenna said as she cleaned up Liam.

"Not really. When you live long enough, you begin to understand that everything happens in due time, when it's supposed to. I'm sure you had your reasons. And when we get to know one another more, perhaps you will tell me—or you won't. But I will be here just the same, and help you adjust to life out here," Dottie responded, and Jenna was surprised at her kindness. She knew what the situation looked like and wasn't sure she would be so non-judgmental if she were in Dottie's shoes.

Jenna fastened a new diaper on Liam and replied, "Thank you, Dottie. I'd like that."

When Liam was all cleaned up, she followed Dottie out of the bathroom and back into the kitchen.

"Now, I have dinner all ready for you. Have you eaten yet?"

Dottie asked, moving about the kitchen like a whirlwind of energy.

"No. I was about to make some dinner and then Carter arrived," Jenna said. *On my doorstep without warning, completely upending my world once again.* She tended to forget a lot whenever Carter was near.

"Let me have him while Dottie gets you situated," Carter said, waltzing back into the kitchen. He held his hands out. Jenna wouldn't fight him, not on this. They were here. He wanted to make up for lost time and be with his son. She couldn't deny him that. The first week after Liam was born, she'd barely slept worrying something might happen to him and had just stared at him, amazed that he belonged to her. She relinquished Liam into Carter's care without a thought. He wanted this, he could help, and she had to admit, she was starving. Breastfeeding burned megawatt calories and Jenna was always hungry.

"Well, let me get the brisket heated and I can give you a tour," Dottie said, loading up a ceramic oven dish with the brisket and putting it in the oven to heat up. The woman had put so much more on the dish than Jenna could eat, but perhaps Carter would eat with her as well.

While they waited for the food, Dottie gave Jenna a tour of the kitchen. It was larger than the living room and kitchen in her apartment combined. It contained amber-hued wood cabinets and glossy granite countertops in a golden tan with veins of muted gray running through it. She'd never seen such a large refrigerator in her life—well, not outside a restaurant. And this one was double-doored stainless steel, and stockpiled with goodies.

Dottie showed her where everything was housed, from plates to bowls to pots and baking sheets, and told Jenna to make herself at home in the kitchen, and that if there were any dishes she wanted Dottie to add or any food allergies she needed to know about, to just inform her and she would make note of it for grocery day.

Jenna took it all in. She wasn't going to have to worry here about whether there would be enough food to make it to the end of a paycheck. Not that Jenna had ever starved but there had been plenty of times over the last few years where she'd had to make things stretch and ration her portion sizes to make it over the finish line until payday. In all her years, Jenna had never seen such a well-stocked kitchen or lived in a place with such bounty. It made her feel a bit like orphan Annie. Sure, she'd lived on Pleasure Island for a few months, with all its luxury amenities, but this was different.

As overwhelming and daunting as it may be for her, this meant her son would never go without, would never know lack. That had to count for something.

Liam began to fuss once more and her breasts actually ached with their fullness. He was hungry—again.

"I'm sorry, Dottie, this is all wonderful, but I need to feed Liam. He tends to eat quite a bit," Jenna explained.

"I'm sure that he does, and you don't need to apologize. Just make sure you are eating enough yourself. In fact, while you're feeding him I'll make sure there are a few premade snacks for you in the fridge, so you don't have to worry about a thing," Dottie commented, jotting a few notes on her list.

The woman was quite simply wonderful. Jenna hadn't known what to expect at Carter's home, but here certainly was a housekeeper and cook whose temperament reminded her of Glinda, the good witch.

"Thank you so much. I'll just be a minute," she said and walked over to Carter to rescue Liam.

"Is there someplace I can go to feed him?" Jenna asked, lifting him from Carter's arms.

"Here, why don't you use the living room back beyond here. It will be more comfortable for you," Carter said and escorted

49

her down yet another hallway into a living room of sorts. To Jenna it appeared much more like a great room with its soaring ceiling, massive fireplace, and plethora of leather couches that were made with large men in mind.

But over by a large bay window was a leather chair piled with sapphire blue pillows that faced the window. That was where he led her. The view from the seat was breathtaking. It looked out over the ranch and surrounding area. The sun had dipped behind the mountains, casting the land into twilight. She got to live here. Her son would grow up with this stunning scenery right outside the front door.

"Will this work for you?" Carter asked and shot her an unreadable glance.

"It's perfect. Thank you," she said and accepted the seat, where she discovered it wasn't just a chair but a glider; a bit like a rocker that she could use to put Liam to sleep.

"Good. I will leave you to it and see you both in the kitchen when he's done. After dinner, I'll show you where I've put you and Liam tonight," Carter said.

"Okay. That sounds great. Thank you, Carter, truly," Jenna said and held his gaze for a minute. He returned her stare, his expression reserved, like maybe he was wondering if he'd made a mistake. God, she prayed it was just her overactive mind, and that he wouldn't toss them both out.

CHAPTER 5

*C*arter strolled back down the hall into the kitchen. As much as he would love to watch Liam nurse again, the air between him and Jenna had become a little too overheated. They both needed a breather. Everything had occurred so swiftly this evening: his world had shifted from standing still to sonic boom strides forward. From what he surmised, Jenna's life had been unsteady and uncertain during the time they'd been apart. She'd looked so lost as Dottie had shown her around the kitchen. It had gutted him that her independent, feisty spirit that had always made her defy him, dare him, thrill him, even, had displayed trepidation.

All he'd wanted to do then was protect her. Even if he never touched her again, he would ensure she had no cause for uncertainty in her new home. He had meant what he'd said; they were in each other's lives now for good. Liam connected them. Carter would never allow her to be homeless or forced to struggle. He knew Jenna didn't come from money and that she worked incredibly hard. It was one of the qualities in her that had attracted him. But her response to his home made him wonder just how badly off she had been.

And oh, what the sight of her in that chair in the living room had done to him. That had been his mother's favorite place to relax in the evening. She had whiled away countless hours in that chair, reading, cross-stitching, and sewing. His mom would have loved to know her grandson would be nursed there.

He rubbed his chest. Liam had him wrapped around his tiny little fist and didn't even know it. Already he was making plans for the nursery. He'd make sure Liam had everything he needed.

Spencer had left him a final text message that read: *Sunday, you will be explaining yourself. Can't believe you ditched. Fucker.*

Instead of replying, Carter ignored the text message. One problem at a time. Spencer and the rest of the boys would get their panties out of a twist when they discovered why he'd avoided the club tonight. As it was, he didn't have the energy to text Spencer back to explain. He wouldn't even know where to begin.

Ah yeah, I'm not at the club because I found Jenna, living in Jackson Hole of all places, followed her home, and discovered I have a son. Mazel tov, it's a boy!

"Thanks for throwing this together last minute, Dottie. I owe you one," Carter said, entering the kitchen just as Dottie was setting the table with plates of brisket, mashed potatoes, and green beans.

"Oh, it's no bother at all. I must say, Liam is just a doll and the spitting image of you, Mister Carter," Dottie replied.

"Why don't you head on home? I'm sure Herb will be wanting his dinner and I can make sure Jenna gets what she needs."

Dottie gave him a smile. "If you're sure you will be okay or don't need anything."

"I'm positive we can manage for one night on our own. Git on with you. Tell Herb I said thanks for the loan and I will see you both in the morning," Carter ordered with a smile, nodding toward the backdoor.

"Congrats on your little one. I cannot wait to tell Herb we're grandparents," Dottie replied with a bounce in her step.

Dottie hastened out the back door. She'd been like a second mother to Carter and he knew beyond a shadow of a doubt that she would spoil Liam, dote on him as any grandmother would. And since both his and Jenna's mothers were no longer alive, his son was lucky to have Dottie. He watched her from the mudroom as she went home to make sure she didn't run across any predators out for an evening stroll. Kyle stayed in an apartment over the barn and tended to watch all the horses at night. But, when it got this dry out, the big game came out searching for water and, on their trail, the predators.

Herb had been right in his estimation earlier that they were short a few hands. Some of the college kids who had worked the ranch over the last few years had moved on, either to another town or to another ranch, or to one of the nearby cities for better work opportunities. Carter didn't blame them, but he also hadn't made sure their positions had been refilled— choosing instead to work himself like a pack mule.

But now that Liam was here, now that his son existed, Carter didn't want to miss a minute more of his life than absolutely necessary. When he saw Dottie alight the steps to her front porch, he shut the back door and headed back into the kitchen proper. Jenna trailed quietly back in with their son in her arms, uncertainty dotting her visage. The woman was wound tight, and while their new living situation was a change, to be sure, Carter didn't like the stress he was seeing.

All the protective urges she'd engendered in him on the island were cascading back into his being. He wanted to ease her mind, ease her burdens, and help her relax. He wanted a return of the sassy, mouthy woman who made him burn like a thousand suns and gave him cause to redden her behind.

He craved the chance to touch her. Not just to sate his lust, but to make sure she was real. A part of him, the part that had doubted he would ever see her again, doubted that this was all real, and figured he was hallucinating her return into his life. That it was too good to be true, having Jenna here, installed in his home with their son. Liam was utterly perfect, a son any man would be proud to call his own. And Carter couldn't get past the fact that he was real. That Jenna was here, and living in his home.

"Where's Dottie?" Jenna asked, her gaze a little frantic as she searched for his cook and housekeeper.

"I sent her home. It's later than I normally keep her here."

"Oh. Sorry, I didn't mean to make anyone late," Jenna said, putting Liam in the carrier with a binky.

"It's fine. She was thrilled to get to meet Liam. And during the day, if you need any help, she will be here for you," Carter explained, hoping the news would help her relax.

Jenna eyed the table.

"What would you like to drink?" Carter asked, wanting to put her at ease. She was like a spooked mare, ready to race off at the slightest provocation.

"A glass of milk, if you have one. Or just some water, or both. I tend to need to hydrate like crazy and am always thirsty now that I'm nursing Liam every few hours," she explained, a blush spreading over her cheeks.

"It doesn't seem that unusual that you need more fluids with feeding Liam. A lot of my mares are the same way after they foal. I will get you both to help you replenish. Why don't you have a seat at the table and I'll bring your drinks over," Carter gave the subtle command.

He poured two glasses for her, milk and water, then nabbed a bottle of Corona for himself. Tucking the beer under his arm, he carried her drinks over and joined her at the table. Their son slept soundly in his carrier, his little mouth slack around the binky.

After depositing her glasses near her plate, he slid into the seat beside her at the head of the table and opened his beer with a twist. He took a long draught, studying her, and wondered why she wasn't eating. Was she not hungry? Not feeling well? He had to admit, while his plan to get her here had seemed sound, now that the logistics were done with, he was a little lost in the woods himself.

"So what are your plans for us?" she asked.

"Us?" Christ, but he wanted there to be an 'us'. That's what he had been feeling from the moment he'd found her and Liam. He wanted to erase the months of separation between them and pick right back up where they had left off. He wanted her to belong to him in every way possible. He wanted to possess her heart, body, and soul.

"Liam and me. You got us here. Now what?" she asked, and it was then that he noticed how tightly clenched her hands were in her lap. The knuckles were white with her unease.

What was she so afraid of? What had happened to her in the time they'd been apart?

"Now we live, like normal people. I work my ranch. You take care of Liam during the day, and we just go from there. But you have help now. In the evenings I will be here to help you with him."

"And my job? I can't live off you, Carter. I won't," Jenna said defiantly, some of her old spunk returning.

"Let's not address that topic tonight, shall we? Can we just eat dinner and get the both of you settled in? Give me a chance to become acquainted with my son," Carter said, wanting to get to the bottom of her disquiet—but it wouldn't be tonight.

"Okay, I guess we don't have to solve everything right now," she murmured.

"Good, now eat. Trust me, Dottie's cooking is just the best you'll find in the state," he said.

She did as he asked and took a bite. At her blissful expression and tiny moan of delight, he grinned. Dottie's cooking was just this side of heaven. They ate in companionable silence for a few minutes. Hunger had taken over for Jenna. He was glad she was eating heartily. She needed it. For a woman who'd just given birth, she was decidedly too thin. What with the half steak he'd plowed through at Teton Brewery, he wasn't famished, and had only taken a half portion for himself.

"When was Liam born?" he asked, curious about his son.

"May first at Tampa General," Jenna replied, wiping her mouth with her napkin.

"And you moved here to Jackson Hole so I could be near him?" he questioned, wanting answers to some of the questions that plagued him.

"Yes and no. Meghan was accepted to intern at the Alpine Science Institute. She applied without telling me. Did it after I had discovered I was pregnant. We've only been here since mid-June. We had to wait until Liam was old enough to make the drive from Tampa, and I had some complications with his birth. It took us almost a week because of how often we had to stop with him."

Her answer mollified him a little, but still... "What complications? Are you all right? Why didn't you contact me when you discovered you were pregnant? Let me know that I was going to be a father? I really don't understand why you didn't. Jared had my number and I told him to give it to you if you asked for it. I looked for you, you know."

"Wait, you did?" Jenna said, sitting back in her chair, her shock evident. It seemed like it hadn't even occurred to her that he might have wanted to further their relationship.

Well, perhaps if he had told her as much... While he'd asked her to spend more time with him, he'd never let her know his feelings for her. He could be so dense and thick sometimes, never realizing that she'd needed the words, not just his actions. "Yes, I did. I wanted more with you after that week. Surely you knew that. I asked you to come with me that day, and figured you understood it went a hell of a lot deeper. Why didn't you contact me?"

Jenna's eyes welled with tears, turning them into liquid sapphires. "I wanted to, Carter. Please believe me. I left the island in September. My life just went to hell and back."

"How? Why did you leave the island? I thought you needed that job—although you never told me why."

"My dad was sick. I was the one taking care of all his medical bills and the costs for him staying in an assisted living facility. He had dementia and needed round the clock care. I had just found out I was pregnant with Liam when I got the call that his condition was deteriorating rapidly. So I left the island to be with him until he passed away."

Oh, baby. Carter wished she would have told him. He could have kicked himself for failing her. He'd wanted more and had let his ego get the better of him instead of putting her first. If he'd done his job properly as her Dom, he would have drawn this information out of her on the island. He asked, "When did he die?"

"Right before Christmas. And between the last of his medical bills and making sure Meghan finished college, I was working nonstop. I'm so sorry, I truly never meant to keep him from you. This last year has been one for the record books. We had to sell my parents' house to help cover the last of Dad's medical bills and liquidate his estate."

He threaded his hand around hers. The urge to protect her, be her bastion against life's storms gripped him. While there was a part of him which felt cheated, betrayed by her even, over missing the first two and a half months of Liam's life, he let it go. He finally understood the shadows in her eyes that were now mingled with grief. This was what her sister had meant in her car earlier. Jenna had been the one handling her dad's care, funeral, everything. Ensuring her sister was taken care of, footing the bill for it all, too, it seemed. Christ, when his mom had gotten ill, his dad had stopped working to be at her side, but he'd been able to afford it. And still the stress of the loss, watching the cancer eat away at his wife—the stress had sent his dad's health into such a severe decline, he'd followed her a year later.

Carter could only imagine not having that luxury, the weight of responsibility that she'd carried on her delicate shoulders. "Jenna, I'm sorry. Truly. Watching a parent die is hellish to begin with, but I didn't know the rest. I remember that you needed the job on the island but I hadn't understood how much. I do wish you would have called me, though. I would have helped you, surely you know that."

She shook her head, inhaling a deep breath before she replied, "It doesn't matter now. I can't change the past or the choices I made. It wasn't done to hurt you. Please believe me. Just know I'm ashamed that I didn't tell you sooner. I was working twelve and fourteen hour days. I kept telling myself that I would contact you the next day, then something would happen with my dad, or work would call me in early. I lived in this bubble where the outside world sped by while my days seemed to blend into each other. Before I even had a chance to catch my breath from it all, Liam was born. And I still hadn't let you know."

It took everything inside him not to pull her into his lap and comfort her. Any anger he felt melted away. There was no lie in her eyes, only sorrow and remorse. He asked, hating to press her further but needing his lingering questions answered, "And you've lived in Jackson Hole for a month? Why didn't you come to me?"

Her voice a ragged whisper, she replied, "Because I was

afraid. Carter, I didn't ask you if you wanted to be a father. I just went ahead and had him. I know I cheated you out of that choice. And, deep down, I was terrified that you wouldn't want him and would hate me for my decision. Liam's the most precious thing in my life. Before he came along, I didn't have a direction in my life other than working enough to pay bills. I love him more than I've ever loved anything or anyone before. And if you didn't want him, I wanted to delay that confrontation because he's the best thing about me. I hadn't done anything meaningful or worthwhile until I had him."

"Jenna, look at me," Carter softly commanded, then waited until her tear-filled gaze rose and met his. "While I wish I had known sooner, it's water under the bridge. We can't change it but we can move past it, you and I. You had your reasons and I don't fault you for them, nor will I punish you for them. I want him. Never think for a second that I don't. He will always have a place here with me, and so do you. You're not alone in this anymore. We will raise our son together."

Jenna replied, "Just like that, all is forgiven? You're not worried that we will get on your nerves, or that—"

"I'm sure I will get on yours from time to time. If I recall, you tended to want to strangle me on occasion on the island. In fact, I can remember a particularly wet occurrence when I first arrived," he said, and got a small watery laugh from her. "Are there concerns? Sure. But that's just life, Jenna, you can't stop living it out of fear. We'll figure it out. And the best part is, we have time. It doesn't all have to be decided tonight, thank goodness. If you're finished, why don't I show you where your bedroom is and while you unpack your things, I can hold Liam for a bit. Sound good?"

"Yes. Carter, I... truly I am more sorry than you will ever know that I didn't tell you sooner. I'm glad you want to be in his life." Jenna disentangled her hand and glanced at Liam still asleep in his seat.

Resisting the urge to heft her onto his lap and cuddle her, Carter collected their dishes and set them in the sink for Dottie the next day. There would come a time when he would push and make her confront her grief. And he would be there for her. Carter would prove to her that she wasn't alone anymore.

As he turned from the sink, he saw Jenna near the table, holding the handle of Liam's seat. Carter wasn't going to let her carry him up the stairs when she was clearly exhausted.

"Here, let me help," he said, gripping the handle and lifting it out of her hands. With Liam secure, he pressed his free hand against her lower back, escorting Jenna to her room. He'd put her in the room next to his, for a couple reasons. One was that he wanted her and Liam nearby. There was a room across the hall from his he had in mind for Liam's nursery. Second, his plan to seduce her would work better if the distance between them was negligible. The ever-present sensual current between them would be hard for either of them to resist with such close contact, and he was counting on that fact to give him an edge. Third, this room had its own bathroom, which he thought Jenna would appreciate. And fourth, the bed in here was large enough for him to fit on, and since he had every intention of seducing her, that made it convenient for him.

When he opened the door, he studied her expression. It was a beautiful room, with blue-gray walls and exposed, pecan-colored wooden beams in the high ceiling. There was a bank of arched windows with a seating area that would be nice for her to sit with Liam. The hardwood floors gleamed. The king-sized four poster bed had thick columns at its four corners that resembled Greek columns, and were partially made with a gray marble and golden leaf design.

"It's a lovely room," she murmured, but seemed almost hesitant to touch anything.

Liam yawned and started to fuss. When Jenna started

toward them, Carter said, "I've got him. Get your things put away, or as much as you can."

He lifted Liam from his seat and went over to the window. His son blinked up at him, his eyes so much like his, and studied him. At the window, Carter explained in a low voice what lay beyond. How, when Liam was old enough, he would teach him to ride horses, how to care for them, and muck their stalls. Liam responded to his voice, his fists waved in excitement, and he grinned as he peered up at Carter with interest.

As he and Liam enjoyed each other's company, Carter paid attention to Jenna peripherally. It was hard for him not to when her scent was all around him. Her very presence electrified him. Jenna unpacked, and while some of her tension had dissolved now that they had cleared the air, hints of strain lingered in her frame. They would work on that; Carter would help her relax and feel comfortable here.

After an hour with Liam, who'd begun to doze in his arms, Carter noticed Jenna's eyes were drooping with exhaustion.

"That's enough for tonight. Why don't you get some sleep," he said, nodding toward the bed.

"But Liam—"

"Is already asleep," he replied and laid him in the bassinette next to her bed. He watched her wearily climb in before he headed toward the door.

"Good night, Carter," Jenna said with a sleepy sigh.

"Sleep well, Jenna," he replied, flipping the light off as he exited. The room remained lit by a small nightlight Jenna had placed near Liam's bed.

Carter shut the door quietly and then headed to his room. He was totally, one hundred percent enamored with his son. He couldn't wait to watch him grow. Teach him how to ride, how to manage the ranch. He'd have to make a call to his attorney in the morning, to make sure Liam was made his sole beneficiary. If anything were to happen to Carter, he would make damn certain his son was protected. And that included his son's mother.

The most startling thing to happen to him today wasn't the fact that he'd discovered that he was a father. No, that little bit of news—while certainly unexpected and out of left field—felt right and made him deliriously happy. What was most surprising wasn't how swiftly his love for Liam had come, but the fact that he was still in love with Liam's mother. All the feelings he had for her had come rushing back to the surface.

The intensity and size of his feelings staggered him. They'd grown—or maybe they'd always been this deep and life-altering but he'd corralled them over this past year. Much like his herd. This changed everything. His seduction wasn't just a campaign to entice her back into his bed. He didn't want to expel her from his system—and heart. No, Carter planned to integrate Jenna into his life and keep her there. This time for good. She was his submissive, and had been from the moment she given him a wet welcome on the island.

CHAPTER 6

*J*enna quietly paced the floor in her room, attempting to soothe Liam. It was definitely the largest room she'd ever called her own, that was for certain, and gave her a ton of room to walk the floor with her little man. There was an elegant, canopied, four-poster king-sized bed, the walnut and marble structure covered with acres of soft blankets, fluffy pillows, and the smoothest sheets imaginable, all in a feminine periwinkle blue. All the furniture in the room, from the twin nightstands to the dresser and armoire, matched the bed. It was an actual bedroom set. That shouldn't have surprised her any more than the rest of the place.

The floors in the bedroom were wooden and gleamed in a blond honey walnut. There was a bank of windows along one wall, and a seating area with a pair of dark brown leather chairs complete with matching ottomans. Beside them was a rocking chair that didn't match the rest of the furniture. Something told Jenna Carter had salvaged it from another part of the house. She had her own bathroom which was larger than the kitchen at her shared apartment with Meghan. Inside there was a luxurious shower stall with a clear glass enclosure, and a bathtub that she could imagine taking a long hot bubble bath within. It was feminine in appearance, ivory marble with veins of light gray running through it on the counter and tub. The granite tile floor in ivory complemented the slate blue walls.

Jenna had unpacked her clothes and hung them up in the large walk-in closet, marveling at all the space. The room was bigger than her apartment on Pleasure Island. Her possessions didn't even take up an eighth of the closet. As she'd hung them up, even though they were clean, she'd felt a bit like a pauper. Just how well off was Carter, and why did it matter?

Because it worried her, even after they'd cleared the air at dinner. The owner of her dad's assisted living facility had sat her down in his office, his suit alone worth more than Jenna made in a month, and insisted the final bills she was protesting were legitimate. He'd threatened legal action if she didn't pay every cent.

She shoved the unhappy memory away. It was over. She had paid the man. Used what little surplus there was from the sale of her parents' home to help wipe the slate clean. And Carter was better than that jerk with his fancy suit and luxury car.

Jenna had used the top drawer of the swanky dresser for Liam's clothing and then in the second she stored the extra diapers, wipes, blankets. She'd reorganize if the living arrangement here became permanent, putting the mat from his diaper bag on top of the dresser to create a changing station.

Liam's cries escalated as she ambled with him, swaying back and forth as she walked to try and soothe him. His poor tummy could be so finicky and acidic at times. The pediatrician had suggested getting him on some medicine to help with his acid reflux. She'd refused, hoping it would ease on its own a bit. Yet her little man's tummy wasn't getting better. She'd contact the doctor on Monday and have him write the script for her.

Maybe she could go with Dottie when she did the shopping for the week.

"Hush, honey. Oh, I know your tummy doesn't feel good," she murmured, so sad at his discomfort. And then the front of her tank top and chest grew wet. Liam had spit up and it trailed down her front. Holding him away from her with one arm, she spot cleaned as best she could.

Liam screamed, his face scrunched in fury at having spit up. His cries escalated. He normally pooped after he spit up. And then the smell hit her. Yep, now he had a dirty diaper, which seemed to enrage her little man further.

This was their nightly routine. She woke up to him fussing, he would spit up a bit, poop. Then she would clean him up, feed him, and rock him back to sleep.

She was just fastening a clean diaper on him when Carter barged into her room looking wide-eyed and panicked, in nothing but a pair of dark gray boxer briefs, showing acres of chest muscles, his dark chestnut hair tousled with bed-head. She'd forgotten how good the man looked without his clothes on. Her gaze raked over his form, remembering how he had felt beneath her hands.

"Is something wrong? What do you need me to do?" Carter asked, looking at Liam's angry red face as he howled.

"Nothing. Sorry we woke you. He's okay, just a bit of gas and an upset tummy. Liam has a tender stomach, is all, which is perfectly normal for newborns, and this seems to be our nightly routine. Don't you, my love?" she said to Liam, scooping him up off the makeshift changing table.

"Can I help?" Carter asked. Carter was so damn earnest in his offer. He truly wanted to aid her and Liam. If he really wanted to be a part of it, then she would let him.

"Actually, yes. If you could hold him for a minute so I can change, that would be great. He spit up down my front and I'd love to put something else on."

"Certainly," Carter said, lifting Liam from her arms. Liam's fists were clenched and angrily waving in the air.

"Here, you'll need this." She gave him a clean burping cloth, then handed him a binky.

Carter didn't hesitate, giving Liam the pacifier and positioning him upright against his shoulder. Then he walked with him, his big hand cradling Liam against his chest, wearing nothing but a pair of boxer briefs. It was without a doubt one of the sexiest sights she'd ever witnessed. Her ovaries pretty much sighed.

To see a man so big and strong, so dominant, holding his infant son with such tenderness and concern for his welfare... if she'd not already had a child with him, she'd ask him here and now to knock her up.

Jenna grabbed a clean cotton nightie from her closet and headed into the bathroom. She stripped out of her soiled clothes and sponged off the dried vomit as best she could. As she did so, a bit of breast milk seeped from her boobs.

Why didn't they tell women everything that came with having a baby? She'd been puked up on, peed on, pooped on. Her breasts leaked. She'd torn, even with the episiotomy, and had needed stitches. She was still a bit sore from the birth, which she was told was perfectly normal. Her stomach had stretch marks on it, as did her boobs. Then there was the unending period that had lasted weeks.

She wouldn't take any of it back. Not one second of it, because that would mean taking Liam back and she'd never do that. Still, she felt like she had been constantly leaking for ten weeks. If women knew what they were getting into beforehand, their species would probably die out.

Jenna slid the white cotton babydoll nightgown on. Her milk-infused breasts were about three cup sizes larger, and spilled over the edges. It wasn't the look she was going for but at this time of night, with only a few hours of sleep under her belt, she was too exhausted to care.

Even if the thought of Carter in nothing but his underwear made her want to fan her face. The man had to simply breathe near her and she was aroused. Nearly naked, he devastated her composure and battered her desire for restraint.

Heaven help her, it was only the first night. How was she going to survive living with him?

Squelching her naughty thoughts, she headed back into the bedroom and was brought up short. Liam was cooing up at Carter, who looked down at him with a wide grin that stole the breath from her lungs. He'd gotten Liam to calm down when she'd not been able to yet. Relief flooded her. Perhaps this really was going to work out between them.

"You two seem to be getting along," she murmured.

Carter gave her a smile and said, "Yeah. He seems to respond to me, like he knows I'm his dad."

The pleasure in Carter's voice at that statement caused a fresh bout of guilt to swamp her. She'd been such a blundering ninny. Carter was correct. She'd known him—that he was honorable and a gentleman, even if he did like to flog a submissive from time to time. What Dominant didn't? It wasn't like she didn't enjoy being on the receiving end of his discipline. Dominant or not, he was the best man she'd ever met. That she had convinced herself that he wouldn't want Liam, wouldn't take up the reins of fatherhood with much the same temperament he did everything else, would always be the biggest mistake of her life.

She had much to atone for and made a solemn vow that she would do her best to work with him when it came to Liam.

"Here, let me take him and get him fed. A full belly will put him right back to sleep. Won't it, my love?" she murmured as they transferred Liam into her arms. Carter's fingers lightly and innocently grazed the exposed skin on one of her breasts.

That one simple innocuous touch rocketed through her body as she sat in the rocking chair.

Carter took a seat in the leather chair beside her as she fed Liam. A flash of lust crossed his face as he stared at her chest while Liam suckled, before he schooled his features and asked, "Tell me about his birth. How long were you in labor? Did he come quickly? How much did he weigh?"

"Well, let me tell you, your son was not an easy camper. I had the absolute worst morning sickness for the first trimester and a half. Rarely was I able to eat anything before noon without barfing it right back up. And then I had to stick to things like chicken soup and crackers."

Carter chuckled a bit. Then asked, "But it did clear up for you?"

"Yeah, it was about the end of the fourth month, I think. I became as hungry as a bear. I ate everything in sight. I would eat a full breakfast and was hungry again two to three hours later. The doctor said it was my body making up for lost time at the beginning of the pregnancy. I even added carnation instant breakfast shakes just to help supplement and appease the hunger. They aren't kidding when they tell you that you're eating for two. I made sure to keep it healthy, for the most part. Although I had the most wicked cravings for ice cream and peanut butter. Ate those by the bucket load."

"Good choices, nothing too weird about that. And what about the last trimester?"

"Yeah, I was glad about them, but you can imagine I gained some bulk with those two cravings. In the last two months or so, Liam liked to move—a lot. I carried high, which meant by the time I was eight months along, my belly went out like a shelf, right beneath my chest. And he tended to kick me—my ribs, lungs, stomach, all my internal organs—like he was playing soccer. I would lie in bed and his foot would poke out so I could see the entire shape. Meghan called it the alien foot."

"I would have liked to have seen that," Carter said quietly, almost to himself.

Of course he would have, because he was deep in the bone a good, decent man. She offered, "I have pictures; his ultrasounds, the different stages of my baby bump—including my imitations of a beached whale. You're welcome to look at them. I think I forgot that album in our hurry tonight and can ask Meghan to bring them when she visits this week. Although I will ask that the beached whale photos stay between us. And we can make copies of anything you would like."

Carter hid his grin. "I'd appreciate that and will keep your secret safe with me. And the labor, was it hard?"

"In a manner of speaking. I went into labor on the evening of April twenty-eighth, at my last checkup. But because I was only a centimeter dilated, my doctor told me to wait until my water broke or the pain became too intense for me to withstand to go to the hospital. She was going to have everything prepped and on standby for my arrival, but it was a waiting game. So, I spent that night walking the floor, trying to help speed the process along, anything to try and get my water to break. Meghan was there, making me laugh and helping me through the worst of it. The following morning, we headed to the hospital and I was admitted. I was still only at four centimeters and my water hadn't broken but the pain of the contractions was too much. I needed the drugs at that point and am not ashamed to say it. Along with the epidural, they gave me some Pitocin. It helps speed up contractions and helps the birthing process progress a bit faster."

"It sounds like quite the ordeal. But I'm familiar with the birthing process—just in horses. I always feel so bad for my mares, usually I bed down with them in their stall for the duration of it."

"I won't lie, it was the most painful thing I've ever experienced, physically, at least. But it was worth every bit of it, tearing and all, when he arrived at five of seven the following morning."

"Tearing? What tore?" Carter asked, his gaze running over her and Liam with concern.

She winced at her admission. That had been one little factoid she'd planned to omit, but her lack of sleep had her blurting out more than she intended. She shifted Liam from one breast to the other. "Well, your son has a rather large noggin, so even with the episiotomy I still tore a bit. He was eight pounds, two ounces, and twenty-two inches long at birth. I think they said his head was like thirteen centimeters in circumference. Women dilate ten at the most."

"Christ, Jenna. I'd noticed you weren't moving as fast as normal, but I had no idea."

"Well the stitches are out but my mobility is still on the sore and tender side of things. It's all perfectly normal, I can assure you," she murmured, moving Liam from her breast but not before noticing Carter's heated gaze on her boobs.

She covered herself and started to position Liam on her shoulder to burp him when Carter said, "I'd like to do that, if you don't mind."

"No, not at all," she said, handing him over, and then proceeded to show him how to burp Liam. At the first tiny belch, Carter's face said it all. He was entranced by his son. She prayed it wasn't the newness of it.

And then Liam needed a nappy change. Carter wanted to do that as well. The diaper change took a wee bit more instruction on Jenna's part but he was eager to learn how to properly care for their son. She couldn't fault him in that arena one bit.

She made a trip to the bathroom and returned to find Carter rocking their son to sleep. Dammit, how was she going to keep herself away from him when he did something so innocuously sexy? Liam appeared just as taken with Carter. It warmed her heart, seeing the two of them together.

"Jenna, you're about ready to drop. Why don't you get into bed and I'll get him to sleep?"

"Are you sure?" she asked, trying to hide her yawn.

"Yes. We need to get more than one nightlight in here for you. I'll take care of it."

"Thanks for all the help," she murmured and climbed into bed. It should feel weird that he was in her room, that Liam wasn't beside her in bed, but it didn't. She watched them as her eyes started to close.

"He likes you, Carter," she said.

"You think?" he asked with a half grin.

"Umhmm. You seem to be able to get him to settle down," she murmured sleepily.

Carter traced a finger over Liam's cheek, still a bit awestruck over him. She settled into bed, with the small wedge pillow from his bassinette beside her that helped with Liam's acid reflux.

Then Carter stood with their sleeping son and moved quietly over to her bed. He handed her the tiny slumbering bundle, then startled her when he climbed in.

"What are you doing?" she whispered furiously over their son's little body between them.

"Relax. Besides, it's not like we haven't slept in the same bed before. I want to sleep next to my son tonight. I have to be up in a bit anyhow, so it won't be for long," Carter said. And it was then that she noticed how tired he was. After how gracious and nice he'd been to her, and how loving to Liam, she didn't have it in her to tell him to find his own bed. Nothing was going to happen between them anyway. He was right, they had slept in the same bed, enough to make the miracle now lying between them.

"Okay, you can stay. Wait, it's three in the morning?" Jenna questioned with a large yawn.

"And living on a ranch, my day begins before dawn. Just go to sleep, Jenna. It will be all right," Carter commanded.

With Liam nestled at her side, she allowed her eyes to close. But not before she caught the look of wonder on Carter's face, his hand over Liam's belly. She fell asleep with her son safely cocooned between her and Carter.

CHAPTER 7

*A*t his office desk in the stables, Carter chugged his third cup of coffee while he studied the schedule to see what each horse needed on the rotation. There wasn't a break in the heat yet, nor any rain on the horizon, which meant they had to order more salt blocks and electrolytes for the finicky animals. Herb and Kyle had been up at dawn, beginning the daily rounds. Derrick Wimbly would be by later that afternoon to check on his pregnant mares.

If they didn't get any rainwater soon, Carter would have to check their water reserve levels. He might have to divert some of the tributary crossing his land for more. They'd have to run it through the filtration system but in this heat, his herd needed hydration.

He rubbed a hand across his face when he found himself reading the same section of the schedule for the third time that morning. Between being dog-ass tired from lack of sleep, and inner turmoil over Jenna, he was having difficulty focusing on the task at hand. Although, he did have a newfound respect for Jenna and the sleep deprivation their son was putting her through. And he'd only done it one night.

Last night, he'd loved hearing about Jenna's pregnancy with Liam. Learning that she'd fought to bring their child into the world. The way Liam gazed up at him, like there was some inner biological component that made him recognize he was his father.

Christ, he'd never thought he could love anything so much, but Liam had proven him wrong. Moving on from the schedule, he made a few calls, starting with his lawyer, Kent O'Brien.

"Are you sure you want to do this without a paternity test, Carter?"

"He's my son. He looks just like me at that age, so much so that it's uncanny," Carter replied.

"Well, I must tell you as your attorney, it is ill-advised and against my advice that you change your will in this manner without a paternity test. As your friend of more than twenty years, I think you're being a fucking moron. But if you're happy and there's no talking you out of it, I will get the paperwork drawn up over the next few days and then drive out to have you sign it," Kent replied.

"Thank you for your concern. I'd also like to include something for Liam's mother, Jenna," Carter added.

"Fuck me. Has she put a spell on your dick or something?" Kent barked through the phone.

"Now that's no way for a counselor to talk," Carter chided with a deep chuckle.

Kent snapped, "Bite me, Carter. So has she put your dick in a clamp? Say the word and I will get the rest of the boys over there with voodoo priestesses or some shit to help you get rid of her curse."

"No. I'm completely of sound mind and body. She's the mother of my child and I want her cared for, the end. While I appreciate your concern, this isn't up for debate," Carter responded. His decision would ensure that Jenna was cared for. Regardless of where their relationship went or didn't go, she had given him a son. To Carter, that counted, and he would see that financially, at least, she didn't have to worry anymore.

Call it Dom pride, the cowboy code, he didn't really give a damn. But from what little he'd surmised, Jenna had been the one to take care of everyone and everything. She'd not had anyone watching her back and ensuring her safety. He wasn't going to leave her with nothing should something happen to him.

He didn't care if she ended up hating him one day, he'd rather she be okay and pissed as hell at him than continuing to struggle when she didn't need to.

"Jesus, I was worried you would say that. You got it, I will include the stipend for one Jenna Mallory—after I have a drink or two, or ten. If only my clients would actually take my sound legal advice instead of ignoring it. Would make my life and my blood pressure so much better," Kent said without rancor.

"Thanks, Kent. Don't worry, you know I hear you, but in this I already know I'm Liam's father."

"Suit yourself," Kent said and disconnected the call.

At the knock on his door, Carter glanced up and found Herb standing in his doorway.

"Herb, I was just getting ready to come help you and Kyle, what's up?" Carter asked, rising from his desk.

Herb wiped a red bandana across his forehead, swiping at sweat, and said, "Tallulah and Starlight are going to need the vet. The heat seems to be getting to them something fierce."

Carter's gut clenched. Two of his prize mares. He asked, "They aren't taking the electrolytes well?"

"Nope, and avoiding the salt licks. I already called the vet. Josh Barrett is on the way. I know Derrick's scheduled for the pregnant mares later, but Derrick can't get out here this morning."

"Thanks for handling that. And I don't remember if I told you to do this or not, but hire as many hands as you think we

75

need to fill slots. You're right that we need extra and I'm sorry I didn't see it sooner."

Herb shrugged his shoulders. "It happens. A man gets busy trying to outrace something, he doesn't lift his head up to view the rest of the world."

Carter wiped a hand over his face. And there he'd been thinking no one on the ranch had noticed his malaise. Apparently, Spencer and the gang weren't the only ones this past year who had. He replied, a bit miffed, "Well, you have my permission to tell me to get my head out of my ass. Especially now with Liam here, I can't guarantee I won't be sleep deprived—or what sleep will be like for me in the foreseeable future, so I might need you more, or we'll need more help than just four additional hands."

"A newborn will do that to you. We've got your back. And you and the missus will adjust," Herb said with a shrug.

That was part of his—or should he say *their*—problem. Carter wanted to seduce Jenna back into his bed but after the insights he'd gained when she'd let slip about the injury she'd sustained bringing Liam into the world, he was at a loss. He didn't want to harm her or cause further injury. When he finally got a chance, he'd conduct some research. As it was, his plate for today was overfull. Shoving his phone in his back pocket, he strode around his desk.

"Let's get a look at Tallulah and Starlight. See what we might be able to do for them until the vet gets here," he said, following Herb out of his office.

He didn't correct Herb about the 'missus' part. Especially not when he'd had that same thought since he'd woken up across from her, their son nestled between them: that he wanted more permanence with Jenna. Starting with getting her back into his bed. He would have to check and see how soon a woman could have sex after childbirth. He wouldn't rush her, but the seduction to get her there began now.

∼

CARTER MADE the short walk from the barn to the main house just as the sun dipped beneath the western mountain range. Dottie strode down the path with a smile on her face.

"Evening, Dottie." He tipped his hat her way and got a smile from her.

"Mister Carter, have a good night," she said with a small grin and passed him by, meeting Herb at the stable doors before heading off to their house.

He climbed up the back porch steps and opened the back door. Liam's voice was oh-ing at something. And pleasure unlike anything he'd known settled in Carter's soul. The homey sound of his son's voice hit him right in the chest. Carter had been an avowed bachelor, living in this huge house alone going on five years now since his father had passed. He hadn't realized how solitary and lonely he'd become. He washed his hands and wiped his boots, hung his hat up and then entered the kitchen.

Inside, he discovered Jenna at the kitchen sink with Liam, giving their son a bath. Liam waved his hands and feet in excitement, his eyes trained on Jenna. But it was the smile on Liam's face that rocked Carter.

"There, my love, cleaning every nook and cranny," Jenna said in a sing-song voice that drew a high-pitched giggle from Liam.

"That's it. So, what should we read tonight? I know last night with moving here to your daddy's house we missed our reading time, but what about your ducky story tonight?"

Liam cooed, his tiny little fists pumped in the air. Carter took that as a yes to the book.

"Yes, I know you love that one."

It charmed him, watching her with Liam. It was clear she

adored him. He stomped his boots on the doormat, not wanting to startle her.

She shot him a grin over her shoulder. "Oh, hi. We were just having bath time. It's one of Liam's favorite things. I hope you don't mind that I'm using the kitchen sink. It's just better with his baby tub since he's so small."

"Jenna, it's fine. This is your home now. Whatever you and Liam need." He approached.

Liam's eyes, so like Carter's own, stared up at him. His mouth formed a tiny circle and he cooed and held his fists out.

Carter bent and kissed the tiny hand. Then he said, "Let me go wash up from today and I can help you with whatever you need."

"That would be nice," Jenna replied with a hesitant grin.

Carter left her and showered quickly, opting for a tank top and pair of Under Armor black pants. His hair was still wet as he walked barefoot back into the kitchen. Jenna had Liam in his carrier with one of his toys dangling above him, keeping him occupied while she set the table for dinner.

"You didn't have to do that. I could have helped you with this," Carter commented, his stomach growling at the heady aroma of the lasagna and garlic bread.

"I know, but you've been working out in the heat all day. And all I did was reheat dinner. Dottie's the creator of the feast," Jenna replied. She'd even put a beer by his plate.

"Good to know." He took his seat. Liam was in his, watching them. "I've been thinking. I'm sure there are items Liam needs. I'll give you a credit card and you can order whatever that may be."

Jenna winced around a bite of food and said, "Carter, we're already living here. It's enough—"

"Jenna, when I told you I want to be involved in his life, that includes taking care of his needs; clothing, toys, diapers, you name it. Now, I'm not skilled in the art of buying things for a baby, especially a newborn, and I'm sure there is stuff he needs. I didn't see much in the way of clothing or other items for him."

She stiffened, her eyes flashed, and she replied, "It took us a lot to get here to Jackson Hole. We had to liquidate all of Dad's things—"

He put his hand over the one of hers closest to him that was gripping her fork—mainly to keep her from stabbing him with it—and said, "That's not a judgement of you, darlin'. I know things have been tough for you but I'm here now to help with him. That encompasses everything. Either you do it, with an eye for what he needs, or I will make the best guess and buy things for him," Carter said with a shrug. He didn't want to injure her pride, but he wouldn't negotiate on this when it came to their kid.

"Okay. I will. Thank you." She nodded.

"What did you and Liam do today?" he asked, not really used to having anyone with him at dinner.

"Well, we finished unpacking. We FaceTimed with Meghan. He really loves his aunt, couldn't stop laughing. She does these funny faces with him that he really gets a kick out of. He ate a lot, pooped a lot, we took a nap, and that's about it."

"Sounds fascinating," he commented.

"Don't lie. You and I both know that it's not rocket science, but this time with him when he needs me this much won't last forever."

"No, it won't. Tomorrow I'll give you more of a tour of the place, show you where everything is in the house."

"That would be great. On Monday, we're going to ride into town with Dottie to see his pediatrician. Because of his tender belly, she suggested putting him on some medicine to help with his acid reflux, and I think that's something we should do," Jenna explained.

"Has it been that bad?" Carter asked, concern surging in his chest.

She shrugged a single shoulder, acting like it was no big deal. "Well, I didn't want to at first, hoping his issue would correct itself. Babies can have stuff like this crop up and it not be serious. We tried the non-medicine route with his pillow and the way he sleeps, but it hasn't corrected itself. I just want to give him a little relief, especially at night."

"What time is the appointment? I will take you," Carter said, already thinking about what he would move around on Monday. It would be tough, but doable.

"You don't have to take off for this, really. We can manage, and Dottie already said she would take us."

"What time? And I'm taking you two. Don't worry about the ranch, that's my job," Carter directed.

"Carter, I don't think—"

He flexed his hands. Jenna always pushed the limits of his patience. He growled, "Just because I can't spank the hell out of you right now, doesn't mean I won't figure out another way to discipline you. Stop baiting me and acting like you have to figure it all out on your own. You don't. You have me. We will go to his doctor's appointment together."

"Fine. You're still a badass Dom, I get it." She rolled her eyes and he smothered his grin. The moment he knew she was no longer hurting from childbirth, he would redden her behind. He should start keeping a tally.

Then Jenna stood and took her empty plate over to the sink. When she put the rinsed off dish into the dishwasher, he held his tongue.

"If there's anything you need to do for yourself, I can watch him for a bit," he offered, noting she still had dark circles beneath her eyes. Whatever he needed to do to ease the work-load on her shoulders, he would do.

"I would dearly love a shower, if you don't mind. Here's his binky and his favorite toy, and he's not ready to eat for a bit. If you need diapers, they're—"

"Go, Jenna, it will be fine. Liam and I can hold down the fort, right, son?" he said with a wiggle of his brows as he scooped Liam out of his carrier. Liam raised his fists and kicked his tiny legs in response. They'd go sit on the back porch and have some father and son time.

"All right, I will be quick," Jenna replied and left with a last glance over her shoulder that seemed to sizzle the air between them.

"Take your time." The attraction between them was as potent as ever. There were other ways Carter could love her without vaginal penetration. Carter remembered how wild she become when he'd given her oral. Which meant he just needed to adjust his approach to her seduction. With a final glance at the now empty hall, he shifted his focus to his boy. He and Liam headed out the back door, where he sat in a rocker and Liam giggled at the fireflies.

CHAPTER 8

*J*enna had been dying to try out the shower in her bathroom. She shook her head. Inside of twenty-four hours it had become her bathroom. Hopeless was what she was. The stall was large enough that she could put pillows along the basin and curl up for a nap if she wanted to.

She didn't hesitate to strip out of her soiled clothes and take advantage of the small reprieve Carter was giving her. Before Liam, she'd been the queen of fastidiousness and now, on her top alone she had breast milk stains, a spot of spit up—and it was in her hair, too, she believed—and part of her shirt still smelled like pee.

When she'd been changing Liam earlier, she'd turned to dispose of his diaper in the genie only to turn back to a clear stream of urine splashing him in the chest and face. Which of course had startled and enraged her little man. It was not the first time or likely the last that he had peed on himself—and her in the process. Nothing in the world said 'I love you' quite like wiping another's bum.

Jenna sighed, standing under the hot spray. She had kinks

in her muscles the size of Alaska. And she loved this shower. It wasn't right to love inanimate objects but she hadn't realized how much she needed this small slice of silence and self-care. Guilt washed over her. She adored her son but it was constant round the clock attention. Who knew that getting the opportunity to shave her legs and underarms would feel like heaven? Or washing the grime from her hair? The cleanliness of it now would feel so good.

Granted, she could use a bikini wax in the worst way, but her doctor had suggested she give her body a minimum of twelve weeks of healing before she did that. She already had her appointment booked at the nearby spa. Although she had no idea how she was going to get there, considering she didn't actually have a car.

That would change. She was only twenty-one credit hours from her degree in accounting. Then she could get a decent paying job that wasn't waitressing, become a bookkeeper and accountant for a company, maybe even start her own company after she gained some real world experience. It would mean she could finally pull her weight with a decent income. Be a mom her son could be proud of because she could support him.

It was a topic she needed to address with Carter. Jenna rebelled at the idea of living off him. It wasn't that she didn't appreciate his desire to see that Liam's needs were met as well as hers, but they were co-parents. She needed to feel useful. Even if her income barely dented the surface for a while, it mattered to her, deeply, that she play an integral role in financially supporting Liam.

Most women would likely call her an idiot for not jumping for joy at the size of Carter's bank account and how generous he was being. But to her mind, she would be taking advantage of him when she was perfectly capable of providing for their son. Perhaps not as lavishly as he could, but that was part of the whole co-parent gig. He'd pick up the slack, and it relieved her to know that Liam would have what he needed from here on out.

But she wasn't letting go of her need to work and support herself. Just because her body zinged to life whenever Carter was near, they weren't a couple. And she wouldn't live off him, although she would give them a few more days to get settled before she approached Carter about the matter. And yes, she realized her impersonation of an ostrich was spot-on and award worthy.

Jenna washed her hair twice, because it needed it, and she wanted to make sure all the vomit, spit up and drool were gone. Granted, she'd have more by this time tomorrow but maybe here, with Carter's assistance, she could at least work to keep it from building to icky proportions. She exited the shower and dressed in a tank top and pajama bottoms. She dried her hair, loving the feeling of it being clean.

When she emerged from the bathroom, she drew up short and stopped. Carter was standing in her room, changing Liam's diaper. Liam howled, pumping his fists in anger at being denied his nightly meal, and her breasts ached. Her little man definitely did not like missing a meal.

"Hey my love. Are you a little hungry?" she murmured.

"Sorry to barge in but he didn't care for having a wet diaper," Carter explained.

"No, he doesn't, just wait until you get a muddy one. Then he's really a handful. It's no bother. Thanks for watching him so I could shower," she replied, ignoring the ever present spark of electricity that flowed between them. His woodsy scent made her toes curl and she had the distinct urge to lean in to him.

Carter moved to toss the dirty diaper in the genie and she picked Liam up off the dresser—aka the changing table— grabbed one of his burping cloths and headed over to the bed.

Liam would be down for the count after his feeding. And so would she. She stifled a yawn.

"If you'd like to read to him while I nurse him, you could. His duck book is right on the nightstand there." She indicated, setting Liam down, then clambering up into bed. His reflux pillow was already present. She propped her back against the headboard with a host of pillows, making sure she was situated before she picked Liam back up.

"I'd like that," Carter said and walked over to them.

He settled his big body beside her, heat emanating off him as he lifted the book off the nightstand. He leaned in close, his gaze on Liam suckling on her breast. A flash of lust crossed his face and then it vanished. But it was enough to stir her, made her body pulse in yearning. Would she ever not want him? Because they'd been here for a day, and already she'd fantasized about him, nearly kissed him, and her body craved him even after all this time.

Liam watched Carter, his attention rapt with interest now that his belly was being satisfied. Then Carter began to read. "One little duckling swam through the pond. On his swim that morning, the little duckling spied one green frog leaping on a log..."

Carter's voice dipped and deepened as he read. Liam's face brightened at the story. He really did love this one. And he seemed to adore hearing Carter's voice tell it. It was just the strangest thing, seeing how connected Liam was to Carter already. It was as if he knew Carter was his father, that their DNA connected them.

Carter finished the story and murmured, "You know the story doesn't make any sense whatsoever."

No, it didn't. She glanced at him with a smile and said, "I know that, but Liam loves it, as you can see. So for now, it's the duck story."

Carter's gaze clashed with hers. Electricity vibrated through her. The current was a livewire, a potent passion that was almost tangible in its ferocity. Who was she really kidding? She had never stopped craving him, her desire for him violent and visceral. His face was so near, she could count his inky eyelashes if she had a mind for it. With the way they were positioned against the headboard, if she leaned in an inch or so, her lips would touch his.

She licked her bottom lip. Heat ignited in her veins. The air between them grew hotter. They were drawn together almost as if an invisible magnet pulled them. Carter's lips met hers halfway.

At the first whispered brush of his lips against hers, she moaned into him. When he sensed she wouldn't push him away, his mouth closed over hers and he kissed her roughly. His tongue swept against her lower lip and sought entry. This kiss was everything. Hard and potent. This was a reclaiming as their lips melded.

She surrendered to the heady intoxication of his kiss. No man, no Dom, had ever been able to render her brainless this way. At the dark rumble he emitted from his chest, she forgot everything and gave herself over to his kiss. His lips moved against hers like they were relearning their shape and size.

She'd forgotten how good he tasted. His smoky dark flavor, the way his tongue would slide along hers in a caress, how he tilted her head back and dominated her. Turning her world inside out until all she could see was him, with merely a kiss.

Her son at her breast was the only thing that kept her anchored. Liam, bless him, squirmed in her arms, ready to be moved to her second breast.

Carter, ever attuned to her and everything around him, finally released her lips and raised his head. She blinked open her eyes, fighting the desire pulsing in her body, and inhaled a shaky breath. In his eyes was a light and a heat that blazed with lust and need. Jenna felt a resounding ache in her core.

One of his hands cupped her chin, his thumb whispering against her bottom lip. The simple, gentle caress was like a lightning rod of pleasure exploding in her veins. It devastated her. Jenna clutched their son to keep her hands off him.

"I'll let you finish feeding him and get some sleep. If you need me, don't hesitate to come get me. I'm right next door," Carter said, slipping from her bed.

She watched him stride to the door, sure-footed and strong. Despite his size, he truly could be so infinitely tender, it made her want to curl into his strength and stay there. It was part of what had drawn her to him on the island. That, and the epic chemistry between them.

"Good night," he said. His hungry gaze slid over her, infused with desire and something else, something deeper and much scarier than combustible heat. Her exhausted brain was not ready to process the feelings his glance evoked just yet.

"Night, Carter," she said, her voice husky and infused with need.

"Night," he replied, hesitating, like he regretted leaving her bed—and her. Jenna tempered the urge to call him back to her side, to beg him to stay with her.

He nodded then—with an expression so reminiscent of the last look he'd given her on the island, her heart squeezed—and exited her room. She stared at the spot where he had stood. The similarity was not lost on her. Only this time, he would be there when she woke.

And because now she understood she had never stopped loving him.

CHAPTER 9

*T*he following morning, Jenna descended the stairs holding Liam, her growling stomach leading the way. She waltzed into the kitchen expecting Dottie. Instead of the matronly woman, Carter was at the stove, frying bacon. The mouthwatering scent permeated her senses and her stomach rumbled in eager anticipation.

She was always hungry these days. Feeding her little man, she burned calories in a way she never had before.

"Morning," she said, placing Liam in his carrier. He was happy in his seat. And it gave her a chance to actually eat and do other things when she needed to.

"Morning," Carter said and shot her a glance. His gaze held banked embers. "Sleep well?"

Jenna cursed that her nipples hardened and her pussy throbbed in response. The man had only to breathe and it aroused her. And the way he looked her up and down, staring at her chest with such longing—she had to dig her nails into her palms to keep herself from closing the distance between them and launching herself into his arms. She cleared her throat and replied, "A bit. It will be nice once Liam starts sleeping through the night. But last night was better than the previous one. Babies don't like change, so I'm sure the move precipitated the other night."

"How long before he starts sleeping through?"

She shrugged. "Well, his pediatrician indicated that infants begin to sleep in longer stretches when they are anywhere between three to six months old. It just depends on the child. So hopefully soon. I don't remember what it was like to sleep all the way through the night anymore," she admitted with a shake of her head and insta-guilt.

"If you'd like, I'd be happy to help you out. We could trade nights. Does he take a bottle at all?" Carter offered.

"Carter, you have the ranch to worry about. We're fine, really," she said.

"I'd prefer to help you out. Mayhap not every night, but my foreman can cover any of my slack on the ranch so it's a non-issue. I won't take no as an answer on this. I'm here and I want to be involved, even with the sleepless nights."

"Knock yourself out. I won't stop you. He prefers getting fed directly from the source but I have been attempting to incorporate bottled breast milk." She gave him a bit of an eye roll and a shake of her head. When it came to Doms, there were times when arguing with one was akin to trying to pull your bottom lip up over your face. Painful, unattainable, and not remotely realistic.

"Well, if you show me how to prepare a bottle, I can step in. How many eggs would you like?" he asked, opening the carton on the counter.

"Three. Can I help?" she said. Carter had a point on the bottle. She wanted to breast feed until he was six months of age, then begin to wean him off the boob and begin incorporating baby food. But she wanted to make her own so it wasn't preprocessed with all the added junk. Perhaps living here with Carter, even with having to battle the undercurrent of ever present desire for him, would end up being for the better. She could make sure Liam had the best there was to offer. Living here was a small price to pay if that was the payoff, even with her uncertainty about her footing on the ranch.

"I've got it. In fact, it's almost done. There's coffee. Can you have coffee while nursing?"

"Yes, but I have to pump and dump the next batch of milk. I tend to like to save that feature for the off-chance that I have a glass of wine," she murmured. Not that she had done that just yet, but living here with Carter, she wanted to make sure that option was kept open.

Carter gave her a bemused half grin. "Understandable."

Instead of waiting for him to offer, she left Liam in his carrier and fixed herself a glass of milk. She'd have loved some juice, but it tended to make her milk acidic and affect her little man's digestion. So again, it would be a situation where she'd have to pump and dump.

She topped off Carter's coffee for him in the mug sitting on the island. The way the man could drink the stuff black with nothing in it made her shudder in revulsion. As much as she loved coffee, she had to add a little cream or milk to it to soften the blow to her belly.

She also sliced up some apples and took them over to the table.

Carter joined her with their plates.

"What are you up to today?" she asked after her first bite. She didn't really know anything about his ranch.

"Well, I thought you and Liam might like a tour of the grounds. If you're up for it, of course."

"No. That sounds great. I still haven't seen most of the inside of the house." Mainly because she'd felt odd nosing around the place without Carter there. As much as she enjoyed the bedroom she and Liam were in, a part of her worried it was all too good to be true and that the rug would be snatched out from underneath her.

"Well, we can rectify that today," Carter said.

They ate breakfast in companionable silence, with only Liam making noises. He was just beginning to test his vocal cord skills, and would crack himself up when he made a loud piercing scream.

"He do this often?" Carter said, shaking his head and wincing at the shrill, piercing sound.

"Lately, yes. It's his way of learning to use his voice. Isn't that right, baby? The first time he did it, it scared the blazes out of me. I worried that something was wrong. But then he gave me a grin like the one he has on his face now."

"That's it, son, show them how it's done," Carter said, placing his dishes in the sink. Then he waltzed back over to the table and picked Liam up out of the carrier.

"Whenever you're ready, but we should do the tour this morning before the heat gets too intense. I just realized that we don't have a stroller for him, do we?"

"No. It was on my list of things to get once I was working. I do have a harness carrier for him in my room," she said, a bit ashamed. The fallout from her dad's illness had left her and her sister with very little in the bank. What small amount they did have was what remained from a forgotten life insurance policy that had helped pay off the remainder of her dad's bills and allowed her to take off work after Liam's birth. But her reserves were finite and she stretched every dollar.

"That wasn't censure, Jenna, just an observation. And I've got it. We need a stroller, so I will make sure of it. Add it to the order you're going to place this week. And if you have the type of diapers and wipes we need for him, make sure Dottie knows before tomorrow. She'll add that to the weekly shopping she does on Mondays."

"She'd already asked me and noted that, but thanks," Jenna

replied, planning to give Dottie some cash for the diapers without telling Carter. She'd let him help but that didn't mean she wasn't going to pay for stuff like her son's diapers.

"I'll stay with him, if you want to go get yourself ready. You'll want a hat, and boots, if you have them."

"Okay. I'll be right back." She hurried back to her room and slipped on a pair of tennis shoes. The only boots she owned were of the club gear variety. Although she did have a ball cap she could use, and plunked it on her head.

Jenna packed the smaller diaper bag, which was really just one of her old hobo style purses. It was already prepacked with a few diapers and small package of wipes, wet ones, antibacterial hand sanitizer and a binky. She added the portable changing mat and folded it up. She also grabbed a change of clothes for Liam, including a hat, and a blanket for just in case. While it might be hot outside, his tender skin had to be covered.

She picked up the harness, then headed back down to the kitchen, where she found Carter and Liam having a moment. Carter was murmuring something to their son by the door to the mudroom, their faces close together. And Liam was giggling up at him, his tiny hand against Carter's jaw. He really was going to be a great father. She hadn't expected this level of interaction and care from him, but she should have. It wasn't in Carter to do half measures and not invest himself fully.

"What are you two up to?" she asked.

"Just giving him some instruction on how to be a man," Carter said.

"I see. Why don't you let me change him quickly and we can leave," Jenna said.

Carter gave her a once over, his gaze stopping at her hat and shoes. "No boots?"

"Not unless thigh-high club couture with a four-inch heel

would be appropriate," she said and batted her lashes in an exaggerated fashion.

"No. Not for where we're going today. Although I wouldn't be averse to seeing them at another time," he added suggestively.

At the mention of her club gear and his obvious flirting, she blushed. One kiss and she was ready to cave to his potent magnetism. Idiot who was asking for heartache, party of one, she lambasted herself. Just because she loved him still didn't mean she could—or should—hop back into bed with him. No matter that her body was totally on board with that plan at the mere thought. Traversing that emotional minefield was folly.

And yet, her entire body electrified at the mere thought of standing before him in club gear. The thought of feeling his firm hand against her bottom as he disciplined her caused her core to liquefy into a mass of need.

Tamping down her lustful thoughts as heat spread into her cheeks, she held out her arms for Liam. Carter stared at her; the smile on his face slipped and his gaze darkened with hunger. For her. Carter wanted her. Her breath expelled in a rush and she broke the connection. When Carter transferred their son into her arms, she didn't look up at him and kept her attention on Liam.

Jenna strode to the nearby bathroom to change Liam. He cooed at her the whole time. He loved mornings. They were his favorite time of day. Until he was born, they hadn't been hers, that was for certain. But now, getting to see him alert and exploring the world at large, happy and laughing up at her, was the best part of her day.

Once Liam was properly attired, they rejoined Carter in the kitchen. He'd already had his boots on earlier, and had added an inky black Stetson while they were in the bathroom. Today he had on a pair of Levi's and navy-blue tank top. The guy had always worn jeans better than any man she'd ever seen. The tank top left his shoulders and arms bare, probably to contend with the forthcoming heat and not to make her week-kneed, but the effect was the same. And he'd taken it upon himself to strap the harness on with the seat for Liam in front.

She'd always loved Carter's arms and shoulders; so wide, he narrowly missed brushing against the doorframe. His arms thick with ropey muscles that attested to his strength. Those muscles rippled and flexed when he moved. And seeing the black harness against his chest made her think of another time, being bound before him and loving every minute of it.

"Ready?" he asked, lifting Liam from her arms and depositing him in the harness. Their son kicked his legs in excitement. Liam loved walks and being outdoors—something he didn't inherit from her, likely a trait he received from Carter.

"Yep. Lead the way," she murmured.

With the diaper bag slung over one shoulder, and Liam secured in the harness, Carter pressed his hand against her lower back as he escorted her out the back door and down the porch steps. She felt his big palm like a red-hot brand and shivered at his touch. It was simple and tame. It was possessive. Carter's hand on her declared to all and sundry that he considered her his.

What's more, she wanted to belong to him. It would be so easy. Jenna wouldn't have to worry anymore. A part of her craved it something fierce. Although another part of her fought hard against it, like it was her last stand.

She ignored the need igniting her veins, shoving it down under lock and key to focus on the tour of the ranch.

On the back porch were a pair of large cedar wooden rocking chairs with a small table between them. She'd missed those when they'd arrived the other night. They had a perfect, unobscured view of the nearby mountain range. Jenna could see herself sitting out on the front porch with Liam, a cup of tea on the table as she rocked with him or read to him, enjoying the majestic, breathtaking sight.

Everything about Jackson Hole was magnificent. The scenery and the man at her side.

"Now, this ranch has been in my family since my great grandfather settled here in 1901. Jedidiah Jones was a homesteader and original owner of the deed," Carter said as they walked down a wide dirt path toward the barn.

"That long?" Jenna couldn't imagine something being in her family for more than a century. The Mallorys tended to discard items at will.

"Yeah. It's been passed down to the oldest son going on three generations. And now Liam here will be the fourth," Carter added.

"What are you saying?" She glanced at him.

"Jenna, he's my son. This will one day be his," Carter said rather nonchalantly. As if the decision was a simple fact and done deal.

She peered at him. "That's too much, and you know it. I didn't come here for you to—"

"It's not your call. He's my son and heir, there's nothing to discuss. Get your panties out of the twist they are in. Did you honestly think I wouldn't make sure he's my heir?" Carter asked, his visage stern and formidable.

"But it's so much," Jenna said. The damn stubborn sasquatch. The man could irk her in ways no one else seemed capable of doing. Almost like he did it on purpose to get a rise out of her.

"And it will also be a ton of work and a source of frustration for him, along with stability. He will learn at my side just like my dad taught me," Carter said, opening the stable door for her.

The building up close was massive, larger than she'd originally thought. It was roughly an eighth of a mile from the main house. It had obviously been constructed with a similar wood to match the main house in physical appearance, except the undertones of the wood carried more of a red sheen. Carter held the door open for her to step through. Liam's gaze was riveted on the building.

She'd noticed the smell of horse manure increasing as they approached the facility. Being an avowed city girl her whole life, farm smells were not something she was familiar with. Jenna wasn't certain what she had expected to see in the stables, likely something out of a Hollywood film. But she hadn't expected the modern interior, the clean stalls, the technology they passed.

"It's impressive. Just how many horses do you own?" she asked, not even attempting to keep the awe from her voice.

"At present count, I have ninety-six in my herd. Although I have twenty mares who are pregnant."

"So many? And do you keep them all?" she asked.

"It's a fair sized herd. And the number of pregnancies is lower than normal. We had to stop the breeding early this year due to the excessive heat. I typically have double that. We rotate the mares we impregnate on alternating years. And then, when the mare is too old for breeding, we either keep her or sell her. I tend to cull a few new horses from the new stock into the herd and the rest are trained to be trail horses and then sold."

"I hadn't realized it was so involved. Silly of me, I suppose," she said, enthralled by the sights and sounds. And she wasn't the only one. Liam seemed just as enchanted by what they were seeing. His little face was rapt with attention as he stared from the harness. His little legs kicked in excitement.

"Someone seems to like it here," Carter said with pride in his voice at Liam's reaction.

"Yeah, he does."

Carter took them through the stables and introduced Jenna

to Herb and Kyle. His two prize stallions were the most gorgeous horses she'd ever seen. Carter explained his breeding system. That the foals from the previous year were already being trained but it would be in the fall that Carter began working with each horse individually, training them to accept a rider, taking them out on the trail with other horses, making them follow commands.

He showed her the misting system and his office, and then they left the stables and headed out the opposite end to view the paddocks and fields beyond. The horses were let out in groups to get exercise, to eat grass in the pasture, to socialize with other horses.

Then they walked past Herb and Dottie's home, which was the original homestead log cabin. It had been thoroughly updated, of course, and had been moved from its original site, which was where the current main house stood. The history of the Double J, the timelessness of it, the continuity of it passing from one generation to the next called to Jenna on some level —one that she didn't recognize. She'd been a tumbleweed, never settling, always constant movement, and no attachments to places or things—or people, for that matter—because it had hurt far too much when those things were taken from her life. Yet this land, this ranch, this man shifted her center of gravity and filled her with an emotion she'd long ago thought life had all but stomped out.

Hope.

It bubbled inside her chest. That her son was a part of the continuity of this ranch. He would never have to worry or wonder what his place in the world might be. He might be so secure here that he would one day chafe at it.

It had been a long time since she'd had any hope. The feeling was alien, it made her feel unsteady.

But she was falling for the land, just like she had for its owner. The horses were stunning as they lingered in the shade and munched on grass. She wondered what it would feel like to ride one. Have the wind in her face as they raced over the terrain. She could picture it.

"They're beautiful, Carter. I'd love to learn how to ride, if there's time," she stated, surveying the paddocks.

"There's time. When you're no longer hurting, we can start. Come on, there's more to see." His arm slid around her waist and he towed her away from the fences.

She got a glimpse of the extra cabins that would apparently be occupied soon with new help. The barns, filled with hay and extra supplies. Carter explained what they were. Tack, leads, blankets, harnesses, grain... so much that her head began to spin. There was so much involved with running this place and yet he still wanted to make time for Liam, for her, even, to make sure she felt comfortable.

That was when she knew that while the love she had for him seemed as constant, deep, and steady as the land upon which they stood, she still had so much further to fall with him. On the island, he'd been on vacation, with no stress other than the next time he got to fuck her. Here, he had the weight of responsibility for everything: the horses, his employees, the buildings, the land itself, and nothing made him falter. He was as steady and solid as the very mountains surrounding the ranch.

When Liam began to fuss, Carter led her over to a nearby oak. Jenna wasn't nature girl extraordinaire but this would do. She sat near the tree in the soft grass. Carter handed Liam to her, then removed the harness and set the diaper bag beside her. She got the blanket and laid it out with one hand, thinking he might want to nap a bit while they were in the shade. The fresh air would be good for them both.

"Here, let me help. You've got your hands full," Carter said, spreading the tiny blanket over the grass.

Carter surprised her then as he joined her, his back against the tree, then shifted her so that she was cocooned between his legs, her back resting against his chest.

"Carter," she exclaimed, starting to move away. Hard to do with a nursing infant.

"Just relax and feed Liam. This will be more comfortable for you anyhow," he murmured against her hair.

Liam was content, unaware of the tension his father had caused. But as she stayed within the circle of Carter's embrace, her body began to relax, until she finally sighed and surrendered to the comfort he offered. He was right, he did make a better backrest than the tree. The man made her want things and due to the way he acted, a part of her believed she could attain them. In the shade, staring at the unspoiled mountains, peace settled over her. She could envision staying here, building a life here, allowing herself to become embedded in the routine.

And it terrified her.

Jenna had a hard time counting on things, be it people or places. Yet Carter made her yearn to do just that, with him and the people here.

"The ranch is wonderful. Truly. I'm sure Liam will love growing up here."

"And what about you? Can you see yourself happy here?" Carter asked.

"The jury is still out. Ask me again sometime," she said, burping Liam.

"Then I will have to convince you. I haven't even shown you the pool," Carter added, his lips so near the tender skin of her neck that his warm breath slid over her.

She shifted her head and said, "You have a pool!"

That slight movement put her mouth a mere centimeter from his. Their breath mingled. Jenna felt like a woman possessed when she slid her tongue over his bottom lip. His guttural groan trembled through her. His hand cupped her cheek and his mouth closed roughly over hers, kissing her until her toes curled in her sneakers.

There was nothing tame about the way he kissed her. It was a claiming, as much as the way his hand on her back had put his possessive stamp on her for others to see. His tongue plundered inside her mouth, imitating sex, showing her that he wanted her and all she had to do was surrender.

Carter lifted his mouth and ordered, "Place Liam on his blanket."

She glanced down at their son, asleep, his mouth hanging open with a dribble of milk at the corner. On autopilot, she did as Carter asked, making sure he was comfortable and giving him a binky.

As she straightened, Carter's hands were at her shoulders, tugging her back against him. Then he was reclaiming her mouth, holding her lips captive as he gripped her nape with one of his big hands. The kiss was carnal, igniting her blood with torrents of need. His lips were rough, the kiss hard and nearly brutal.

When his hand snaked beneath her shirt and bra, a thumb scraped against her nipple and she moaned into his mouth. It had been so long since she'd been touched. The calloused pad of his thumb circled her areola. Desire arced from her tit to her pussy. Mewls erupted but Carter's mouth was there, drinking down her cries. He deepened his kiss and heaven help her but she followed. Her fingers dug into his thighs. The noticeable bulge of his erection was pressed against her rear.

Carter's hand descended from her cleavage. His fingers trailed over her belly to the button of her jeans. The man made quick work of her zipper, then he slid his hand beneath her panties to her pussy.

At the first touch of his two digits against her clit, she moaned. He stroked her nub, flicking his fingers back and forth. Pleasure rushed her body, her cries swallowed by his mouth as he kissed her.

Jenna's hands gripped his thighs. Carter didn't relent. He caressed her, teasing her bud, making it swell beneath the hood. Wetness coated her panties and she canted her hips, greedy for the pleasure, craving more friction. He swept his tongue against hers and nipped her bottom lip as he caressed her to a fevered pitch.

She came. Hard. Wailing into Carter's mouth.

Her climax was a mix of pleasure and pain. She rocked against his fingers. Her body turned fluid as her pussy clenched and spasmed in acute ecstasy. Only when her trembles ceased did Carter finally release her mouth.

"Carter," she whispered, gazing at him, shaken to her foundation. The connection between them was palpable. The way he could play her body like no other left her rattled to her core. There'd not been permanence in her existence but she wondered if perhaps he could give her that.

His hazel gaze burned with dark lust. He withdrew his fingers from her panties and lifted them to his mouth. They were damp with her dew. His eyes never left hers as he sucked his fingers into his mouth and tasted her.

"Looks like we have a visitor," Carter murmured, nodding toward the driveway. Jenna turned her head and spied the shiny red car. Meghan's silhouette stood next to her Mini Cooper.

Jenna scrambled off his lap, fixing her jeans. She wondered if her sister had caught anything between them from this distance. Not that it mattered, it was done. She doubted Meghan had witnessed her orgasm. If she had, well, she'd deal with it.

Carter stood, brushing off his jeans before he put the baby harness back on. Then he reached for Liam, who had quietly slept on his blanket, satiated with a full belly and obviously enjoying the outdoor air, although the temperature had risen since they'd first ventured forth on their tour.

Jenna packed his blanket back in the diaper bag and hoisted the strap onto her shoulder. "Is he good?" she asked, nodding at Liam.

"Yep, sound asleep," Carter said.

Jenna avoided direct eye contact and headed toward the house. Carter was on her heels every step of the way, his footfalls confident and steady while she was more confused than ever before. Shouldn't she be fighting her attraction to him?

CHAPTER 10

"*W*ell, I see you two haven't murdered each other," Meghan said, looking at them over the rim of her sunglasses with a lopsided grin. Meghan always looked fashionable and today was no exception. Even for a casual visit on a hot Sunday in the country she was wearing a cute mint green sundress that ended mid-thigh, and high heeled sandals that showed off her toned legs.

Carter said over Jenna's shoulder, "Meghan, good to see you. Why don't you come in? We were just getting ready to have lunch and then take a tour of the rest of the house."

"Yes, please come in and visit," Jenna said, praying that she would. She needed the distraction to get her mind off the man of the hour.

"You know me, I can always eat. Especially if I don't have to cook. Jenna, I brought some of your stuff that you'd forgotten to pack that I thought you might need," Meghan replied.

"Let's get you ladies inside where it's cool, then I can bring all those items in for you," Carter offered. His niceness, his deep in the bone goodness made Jenna want to scream and stomp her feet. The man wasn't making this easy on her one bit. In fact, he was making it damn near impossible for her to come up with reasons not to stay away from him.

Carter was too good for her and she didn't deserve him. Not after she'd withheld Liam from him.

"That would be great, big guy, thanks," Meghan said, following Carter as he trod up the stairs to the back door.

Jenna inhaled a deep, steadying breath, then straggled in behind them. Cool air enveloped her and she sighed. The heat was getting to be a bit excessive. She didn't think Wyoming got this hot. Dottie, bless the woman and her incredible cooking skills, was in the kitchen, fixing sub sandwiches and salad. Carter handed Liam to her before Meghan gave him her keys. Carter stepped outside, only to return a short while later, hefting a few bags.

"I'll just set these in your room for you," Carter indicated.

After lunch, Carter took the three of them on a tour of the house. There was indeed a pool—an indoor one—and a hot tub. Jenna was living in a house that had a pool. How was this her life now?

On the first floor of the house there was the kitchen, an informal dining area, a formal dining room, the great room, a parlor, of all things, a sunroom, an office, and the indoor spa with swimming pool. On the second floor there were ten bedrooms. Carter's was the master suite, and Jenna's was the second largest on the floor. As she had guessed, there was a third floor that was smaller than the rest but held an additional five bedrooms.

In the basement, Carter showed them the storeroom with the two deep freezes and shelves lined with dry goods. There was a game room that had a fully stocked bar, pool table, poker table, foosball table, a large screen television with a few gaming consoles, and couches. A theater room held a huge, wall-sized television screen and leather couches. There were an additional five bedrooms down here, and another room that was off limits. He didn't even let them take a peek inside. Jenna wondered what he was hiding. Knowing him, she had an idea, but she didn't want to speculate with Meghan around.

Then Liam needed a diaper change. Carter escorted the little group to her room.

"If you guys are okay, I've got to head to the stables for a bit," he explained.

"Go. We'll be fine here. Thanks for today," Jenna said and squeezed his hand. The light in his eyes at her touch sent a cascade of shivers through her frame. Then he tipped his head, his eyes never leaving hers, transmitting a wealth of meaning. She released his hand and retreated a few steps. At his knowing grin, she shivered again. He knew just how much he affected her. Her palm buzzed from the simple touch.

Then he left, shutting the door behind him. She finally breathed a sigh of relief. They couldn't be in each other's company and not have this potent electricity clouding the air.

"What was that all about?" Meghan asked while Liam dozed in his bassinette.

She tried to ignore her sister's question and headed into the gargantuan closet with the bags she'd brought. Her sister tailed her inside.

"Come on. You honestly aren't trying to avoid talking to me about your relationship with Carter," Meghan quipped, opening one of the bags.

"I don't know what you're talking about. We are roommates and happen to have a child together," Jenna replied, wishing like hell she couldn't feel the heat spreading over her cheeks.

"Oh no, don't you go deflecting on me. I have eyes, you know. So that wasn't the two of you smooching under the tree? And then just out there with you batting your lashes at him before he left? The 'Thanks for today, Carter,' with your breathy, sex kitten 'come hither and ravish me' voice? Spill. I want details. Are you two a thing now?" Meghan asked, holding one of Jenna's shirts hostage while she stood with her hands on her hips, her face so like Jenna's own, insistent on a reply.

"Meghan, it's not like that with us."

"Oh, so you weren't kissing him a little while ago. And it was at one time, because, hello, there's Liam." Meghan replied, gesturing toward the bedroom and Jenna's sleeping son with an exasperated expression on her face.

Meghan wasn't going to let her wriggle out of this. Jenna sighed. "Yes, I know. We've kissed. A couple of times. They were nothing. And it's not going to happen again."

There was no way she was going to mention the teensy little fact that he'd given her an orgasm under that tree too. She'd never hear the end of it.

"Why not?" Meghan asked, glancing at her dumbfounded.

"Well... because it would be bad for Liam. I mean, what if we didn't work out? What if all it is between us is sex, and then it putters out and we still have to live together?" Really stupendous, world-altering sex, but that wasn't the point. The point was Liam needed stability and security. To put his happiness and well-being on the line for her own desires would be foolhardy and selfish of her.

"Jenna, don't take this the wrong way, but you need to get over your hang-ups. I know life has not been easy for you, and I'm partly to blame for that. But you're not living, not really. You let yourself be insulated by the tragedies you've experienced and haven't really been living."

"I had a baby, Meghan," she defended herself with a furious whisper. Yet her sister's comments hit close to home.

"I know, and I adore my nephew. But you need something for you, too. I see the way you look at Carter. You still have feelings for him, deep feelings. Maybe it's time you stop running from them and start acting on them."

Was that what she was doing? Running from him? Maybe.

Probably. "What if he doesn't want me? I mean, a lot of time has passed since we were together. And it wasn't a traditional relationship even then."

Meghan snorted and asked, "Was I the only one on that tour? That man was all but waving his dick in your direction. I've never seen a man want to impress a woman more. If it were me, and a man I had feelings for went all out, saying things like: the pool is yours to use whenever you want, Jenna; whatever you need, Jenna... Does Liam need this? Let me take care of that. Wake up and smell the blatant seduction. Carter wants you in the worst way."

Her cheeks burned. Her heart trembled. Could it be true? Was she playing ostrich again where they were concerned? She thought about that afternoon. How good it had felt to be held by him. The way he'd seen to her pleasure. He was acting like he was her Dom.

She swayed a bit on her feet and plopped down on the padded bench in the closet. "Oh, god. I'm an idiot."

"You said it. I didn't. And take it easy on yourself, what with Liam keeping you up at night, I'm sure your brain is foggy."

"What do I do? Seduce him? Have him take me to his club?" Jenna said, flummoxed that it had taken Meghan holding up a mirror for her to see the truth.

"What club?" Meghan asked.

Not thinking, Jenna said, "He's the founder of a BDSM club in Jackson. It's how we met. That resort in the Bahamas caters to people in the lifestyle and I—"

Her sister gasped. "You mean like bondage and kinky sex stuff?"

Oh, crap. She winced, studying her sister's reaction and said, "Yeah, I know, I've never said anything about it before. Are you upset? Do we need to talk about it?"

"About the birds and the bees, no. The bondage stuff? Hell

yeah. Why didn't you tell me you were into kink? Is it like handcuffs and whips, or is there more?"

Jenna tried to backpedal on the conversation. "Well, maybe I shouldn't be telling you this stuff. Being a submissive is a choice. It's not one that is for everyone."

"Relax, I don't think I'm submissive in the slightest. I don't think I have the temperament for it. Granted, I'm not opposed to bedroom kink. So were you in handcuffs when Liam was conceived?"

"Possibly that," Jenna said, "or perhaps some Velcro restraints. Could have been the hot tub too. Not sure."

Meghan chortled, her visage awash with mirth. Jenna snickered in reply. And before she knew it, they were laughing so hard, she had tears streaming down her face. Meghan did likewise.

"What's it like being a submissive? Do you wear a collar and leather panties all the time?"

Jenna wanted to clear up some of her sister's perception, especially since she'd admitted she was not submissive material. It wasn't that Jenna was ashamed of being submissive but she was protective of Meghan and wanted her to have a clearer picture. She said, "It's not like that. A woman—or man, for that matter—does it because they like to please their partner. It's not being weak or abdicating responsibility. It's more the ultimate measure of trust one could place in a partner to accept whatever may happen without question, and it's a freedom unlike anything I've ever known. Submission is a choice and for me, personally, as I've always had to be in charge of everything else, I like knowing my needs will be taken care of without question."

"Huh. I might have to try it sometime." Meghan shrugged, but there was an interested gleam in her eyes.

"It's not for everyone. You don't think less of me because of it?"

Meghan shook her head and grinned. "No. I'm relieved, actually. I didn't think you had it in you, being as tightly wound as you are. So does Carter dress up in, like, leather pants and stuff?"

"Not him, no. He's definitely a Levi's man, but he sure as hell knows how to wear them." Jenna sighed. And that was part of the problem too. He looked the same—hell, he looked better than he had on the island. Whereas she had stretch marks, her stomach was no longer flat, and her butt was bigger, as were her boobs. Granted, he'd always enjoyed her cleavage, but she still felt frumpy and unattractive. On all the mommy blogs she followed, she was told it was a normal occurrence. And with that Liam woke up, most likely hungry.

"I can dig the Levi's. That's kind of a given in this area when it comes to available bed partners," Meghan replied, following her out of the closet.

Jenna picked Liam up from his tiny bed and sat with him in the sitting area to nurse. "Do you like it here?" She asked her sister the same question Carter had hours before.

"Nope," Meghan replied, and Jenna's heart sank. Then her sister said, "I freaking love it here. I know we're Florida girls at heart, you more so than I, but this place feels like home. I like my job, the people are nice here, and I'm looking forward to my internship starting at the institute next month. Truly, I think this place is great. I might not love it in the dead of winter, but we'll cross that bridge. And Dad would be thrilled to know that his girls were enjoying life for a change."

Some of the guilt Jenna had been carrying evaporated. She had been worried that Meghan had undertaken this move, applied for and taken the internship purely for Jenna's sake so she could help her with Liam and everything.

"Yeah, you're right. What do you think he would have thought of Carter?" Jenna asked, switching Liam from one boob to the other.

"Dad? Knowing him, he would have considered Carter the son he never had. So, are you going to stop sitting on the fence and do something, like jump the man's bones?"

"I'm thinking about it," Jenna said pensively. It was a huge step. Regardless that her heart already belonged to Carter—it had since the island—it wasn't just the two of them to consider anymore. Her decisions, and his, would impact their son's life, whether they admitted it or not, and she was being careful.

Meghan rolled her eyes and replied, "You're overthinking things, as usual."

Most likely. But it was what Jenna did. She'd probably overthink attending an overthinkers anonymous self-help group.

"Can you stay for dinner? I'm sure Dottie is probably whipping up something fabulous. And she always cooks more than enough." Jenna had enjoyed having Meghan here this afternoon and wanted to keep her as a buffer while she made her decision.

"Can't tonight. Maybe Tuesday after your online class, and I can finish watching the little dude for you."

Crestfallen, Jenna replied, "Okay, just don't be a stranger."

"I won't. What the hell is that?" Meghan asked as a rumble of loud motors pulled up to the house. The noise permeated the stillness. They raced over to the nearby window. Six trucks of various shapes and sizes had pulled into the driveway. In the fading light, men climbed down from their truck cabs.

"Crap. I think they blocked me in," Meghan said with a groan.

"I think you're right. Give me just a minute and we can head down," Jenna said, since she had finished feeding Liam and was just as curious as her sister about the men's arrival. Carter hadn't said that they were going to have visitors this evening. "Let me change his pants and burp him."

"All right. Can you burp him on the way down? I don't want

whoever is blocking me in to get too comfortable," Meghan said.

"What's your hurry?"

"Hot date. Really cute mountain climber staying at the resort this week. And yes, I will be careful," Meghan replied.

"Okay, fine. Just promise me you will stay for dinner on Tuesday," Jenna added.

"Deal," Meghan said as they left her room and headed down the main stairwell. They gravitated toward the sound of multiple masculine voices speaking in the kitchen.

"What the hell, dude? You haven't been to Cuffs in ages."

"Look, there are things—" Jenna recognized Carter's voice in the mix.

"Cut the bullshit. You bailed Friday, and have been ignoring my texts ever since."

"What we need to know is why?" said another.

Jenna and Meghan entered the kitchen, which was laden with an overabundance of testosterone. At their entrance, seven pairs of male eyes glanced at them and stared. Jenna wasn't certain who was more surprised by their entry, the group of devilishly attractive cowboys, or Carter. Did he really think she would sit back and not investigate the cowboy invasion?

"All right, which one of you cowboys is blocking me in?" Meghan queried, setting her hands on her hips that were cocked at what could only be termed a jaunty angle. Her sister never had a problem interjecting herself into the fray. There were times when Jenna had no idea how they had both been spawned by the same parents, considering their differences. Jenna noticed the way the men's gazes roved over Meghan. And the way they snapped to attention at her question.

Then it hit her: these weren't just cowboys. Every man in here was a Dom. And her kid sister had just tossed down a gauntlet challenge. Oy! Tonight might be her night for that glass of wine.

"If you're the owner of the little red hatchback that's really more of a go-cart than an actual vehicle, I am," one of the cowboys said, taking an intimidating step forward. He was tall, not a giant like Carter, but still a good six feet or more. His jeans were molded to his thickly hewn legs. His black tee was stretched taut across acres of rock hard muscle, displaying the lines and indents of each one. Tribal tattoos scored each of his triceps and they disappeared beneath his shirt sleeves. But it was the man's face that was the true dichotomy. If it weren't for the faint, thin, white jagged scar that ran from his left temple down to his jaw, he would have been pretty—like, Hollywood actor pretty. But that scar and the few days' growth of black stubble made him look like he was not a man to be trifled with.

Meghan didn't seem to care, and wasn't intimidated in the slightest by him. "That *go-cart* can go from zero to sixty in six seconds, has a twin turbo engine, and was tricked out by professional street racers with a three hundred-fifty horse-power engine. Not to mention, it's much more ecologically friendly than the gas guzzlers I watched pull into the drive."

"Save us all... a tree hugger," the man responded.

Meghan rolled her eyes. "You have something against wanting to save the planet?"

Carter thankfully decided to intervene, since it looked like her sister was about to go nuclear, and Jenna was fairly certain it wouldn't end well with the Doms. Meghan, bless her heart, had no idea what testing a Dom could lead to. Carter stepped between Meghan and her adversary, safeguarding everyone from any bloodshed, then said, "Guys, this is Jenna," he gestured to her, "and her sister, Meghan. She's working at The Alpine Science Institute."

"Jenna, Meghan, these knuckleheads are Spencer, Cole, Mason, Garrett, Alexander and Jackson." Jenna put their names with their faces. Meghan's verbal sparring partner was Spencer. Beside him was Cole, who made her think of mountain men and log cabins with his long brown hair that went past his shoulders. His beard, while trimmed and neat, was full. At least he tipped his hat their way. Next to Cole was Mason, and they had similar facial features, although Mason's face was shaved baby smooth. His hair was lighter, more of a golden walnut.

"And the kid?" the man Carter had called Garrett said. He wore a plaid white and black button down dress shirt, even in this oppressive heat. Both his dark brown hair and beard had hints of red but it was his eyes, the sharp bright green that reminded her of images of fields in Ireland, that really stood out.

Liam took that moment to make his presence felt and squirmed in her arms, almost like he knew all the attention in the room had been directed his way at Garrett's question. Carter strode over to her then and plucked Liam from her arms. The minute he spied his father, he cooed at him and grinned.

"And this is Liam, my son," Carter said, turning Liam in his arms for the group to see him.

This was one of those pin drop moments. The six cowboys looked at Carter as if he'd grown a set of antlers. One of the men—Jenna thought Carter had said his name was Alexander—he of the ginger hair and amber eyes, his mouth had dropped open.

Jenna didn't know how to proceed here. These were obviously Carter's friends. He'd been so generous, she didn't want to step on any toes.

"Wow, who knew an infant could turn cowboys mute? Spencer, how about we mosey outside so I can get out of here?" Meghan quipped, her voice dripping disdain.

"What's the rush? Hot date?" Spencer jibed. And it was clear to Jenna, although Meghan seemed not to pick up on the social cue, that she had derided the Dom in the wrong way and he was going to be a mule about it.

"Actually, now that you mention it, yes. And I'd really like to not be late." She gestured toward the door. Then she shot a glance at Jenna. "See you Tuesday."

She stopped by Carter and gave Liam a quick buss on the check. "See you Tuesday, little dude." Liam grinned and laughed at Meghan. She was one of his favorite people. "Carter, good to see you." Then her sister headed toward the back door.

"Are you always this bossy?" Spencer asked as he walked with Meghan.

"Are you always a stick in the mud?" Meghan asked with exasperation.

"I'm surprised someone hasn't gagged you before now," Spencer grumbled as he opened the door.

Meghan sailed through it, stopping under the frame and patting Spencer on the chest. "Many have tried, big guy, and all have failed." Then she went out.

Spencer shot Carter a look that made Jenna groan internally. Those two would end up coming to blows. She could see it, clear as day. She just hoped it wasn't tonight and that they wouldn't kill one another.

Jenna decided to cut the silence, ease the tension a little, and said, "So, are they all here for dinner?"

"It's our monthly poker night. Sorry, I forgot to tell you. We'll just end up ordering a bunch of pizzas. And we've got plenty of chips and beer. Don't worry about us," Carter informed her.

"I could make dinner, so you don't have to order in. I'd just need you to keep Liam occupied for a bit. He's fed and has a clean diaper—for now, anyway," Jenna offered. This was something constructive she could do, as a thank you to Carter for all he had done for them. While she didn't have the mad skills that Dottie did in the kitchen, she could hold her own.

"You don't have to go to the trouble," Carter said with a shake of his head.

"It's no bother. Really, let me do this for you, Sir," Jenna said softly, aware of their audience, and she lowered her gaze out of respect. And as an apology for her sister's behavior.

"All right, appreciate it. We'll be down in the game room. Just come get us when it's ready," Carter said. He put Liam in his carrier seat, pocketed a binky, and then led the crew—minus Spencer, who was still outside moving his truck—to the game room in the basement.

Jenna trudged into the kitchen and began pulling items out of the fridge. Everyone loved tacos so that was what she decided on. They were all big men, so she opted for a triple batch. They would also make great leftovers—if there were any. Her taco recipe had been her Puerto Rican grandmother's, and people tended to help themselves to extras.

Spencer slammed back inside just as Jenna had tossed ground beef into a pan to brown—a clear indication that he and her sister had likely had more words in the driveway.

"It's Spencer, right? Sorry about my sister, she can be a little forthright and she's not in the lifestyle, so please don't take what she said personally," Jenna murmured, stirring the sizzling meat in the pan.

Spencer stopped at the kitchen island, his black eyes assessing her, and then said, "You're the sub from Pleasure Island, aren't you?"

"Yes," Jenna replied. There was no point in denying it, but it rocked her world that he knew about her. It meant Carter had talked about her with his friends. That bit of news shifted her perception and some of the hesitation she felt melted away. They'd both bumbled things, hadn't they?

"You planning on staying?" Spencer said, his gaze judging

115

her like she was under a microscope. And, well, could she blame him? She'd be suspicious too.

"In Jackson, yes." The rest had to be worked out between her and Carter first before she could give him more of an answer.

"That's good enough for now. Nice to meet you finally, Jenna. Congratulations on the boy," Spencer said, tipping his hat, and walked out of the kitchen, seeming to know precisely where he was headed.

Jenna wished she had an idea herself. Clarity of direction had not presented itself. Had she received a few nudges today? Certainly. But her course was still littered with fog and debris.

Did she want Carter still?

God, yes. With every fiber of her being. Carter had been nothing but gracious and hospitable. And he had not hidden how much he wanted her. So what was holding her back? What exactly was she waiting for? She wished she knew the answer to that.

She loved him. That had to count for something, right?

CHAPTER 11

*C*arter felt the weight of his friends' stares as they entered the game room. He'd had a custom poker table crafted years ago. Most of these guys he'd known since high school, a few from primary school even. Poker had always been something they did to pass the time. They would sit around a table, play cards, talk the rodeo circuit—or any sport, really—drink a few beers and discuss the club if needed. It was at one of their poker nights a decade past that he'd proposed starting Cuffs & Spurs.

At the table, he put Liam's carrier by his seat and lifted him out. The guys were studying Carter a little like he had an alien in his hands. Well, some of them, anyway. Liam appeared entranced by his friends. Which made sense, considering the first ten weeks he'd mainly been with Jenna and her sister.

"Dude, seriously? When, how did this happen?" Alexander asked, not feigning his surprise.

Jackson and Mason carried over a bottle of Jameson and glasses for everyone. Jackson said, "I see your Dom training is lacking somewhat if you don't have any idea how babies are conceived, Alex."

"Hardy har har, dipshit. You know what I meant," Alexander replied gesturing to Liam.

"I say congratulations are in order," Cole said with a tip of his hat.

"Exactly," Mason said, pouring a dram of Irish whiskey for each one of them, then handing a glass to every member of their crew. Spencer waltzed in then with a self-righteous air and fury burning in his gaze. It made Carter wonder what barbs Meghan had tossed his way. Mason handed him a glass of whiskey.

Garrett said, "Congrats, dude. As the first of us to have progeny, we're thrilled for you."

"Yeah, no matter how he came to be," Jackson added with a smile for Liam that made his son grin.

"Are you sure he's yours?" Spencer asked. He obviously had a burr up his butt the size of Texas. Everyone turned to Spencer with 'dude, really?' expressions and he held his hands up defensively in front of himself like he was being held up at gunpoint.

"Yes. He's mine. He's my spitting image at this age," Carter snarled. He didn't care if Meghan had laughed at the size of his dick, Spencer's attitude was pissing him off.

"And you don't find it a bit suspicious that she showed up on your doorstep with him?" Alexander asked and Spencer nodded in agreement.

"What? I just think it's a bit odd," Alexander said when everyone glared at him.

"She didn't show up on my doorstep. Not how you think. I'm the one who moved them here to the house. They've been living in town for the past month. Jenna's sister is at the Alpine Science Institute doing graduate work," Carter explained.

"And they moved up here, just like that, no explanations," Spencer asked, apparently still unconvinced that Carter wasn't harboring a viper.

"Look, cut the shit, Spencer. I appreciate your concern. All I will say is that she has been through a lot this past year and doesn't deserve your disdain. I'm a big boy and I want my son in my home, period. It's not up for discussion. And I would ask that you be nice to her and her sister," Carter added.

"Jenna's not a problem. Can't make any promises about the sister," Spencer said with a shake of his head.

"Now that we've shared our feelings, can we do this?" Mason said, indicating the shot glasses.

"Why the hell not?" Carter said, Liam cradled in one arm, drink in the other.

"To Carter, on the birth of his son, Liam," Cole said, holding his shot glass in the air.

"Cheers," they all shouted and tossed back the whiskey.

Carter enjoyed the burn. But the chorus of cheers startled Liam and he started to cry.

"Great. Now see what you blockheads have done. Get the cards and the beers ready while I settle him down," Carter ordered, exasperated with the lot of them. It was his fault that he hadn't prepared them. He'd fumbled the pass on this announcement. But now Liam was breaking his heart with his cries and he tried to soothe him.

His friends winced.

"Maybe that wasn't the best idea," Mason said with a grimace.

"Would have been better if we hadn't been so loud," Jackson said, his face concerned as he looked at Liam.

Carter tried rocking Liam. Giving him his binky. Tried talking him down. But nothing was helping. He lifted him up and didn't smell anything in the diaper. Poor guy was unhappy and not calming down one bit.

Jackson and Mason tended to be the bar masters and were putting beers around the table, mainly because Mason loved playing bartender. And Jackson, as the cop of their ragtag group, liked to count how many beers each man drank and would confiscate keys when necessary. There had been more than one poker night where they all had crashed in one of the extra rooms.

"Here, give him to me," Cole sidled up beside Carter and held out his hands.

"Are you sure?" Carter eyeballed Cole with a raised brow.

"I'm good with babies," Cole said simply with a one shoulder shrug.

Since he was out of ideas for soothing the little guy, Carter handed Liam off to Cole. Cole was what some might call a free spirit and a recluse. Other than occasionally attending the club and coming to poker night, he tended to keep his own company. While he and his brother, Mason, owned the Black Elkhorn Lodge and Resort, Cole ran their outdoor guided horse tours, camping, fishing, and hunting tours, where he didn't have to interact with many people. When he wasn't taking a tour out, the man was usually off by himself at his cabin.

With care and a critical eye on his friend, Carter watched as Cole waltzed around the room, speaking to Liam in a low voice. Carter had no idea what he was saying. Within two minutes, Liam was giggling at whatever Cole was whispering to him. Carter had never witnessed anything like it. Jenna was good at calming the baby but then she seemed to anticipate Liam's needs. But Cole, calming Liam? So quickly?

Astonished, Carter slid into his chair at the table with a shake of his head. The group all began taking their seats as Cole finally strode over and sat in the chair beside him. Liam was grinning from ear to ear up at his friend.

"You have to tell me exactly what you just did," Carter ordered.

"Babies can pick up on moods. They're highly sensitive creatures. He probably perceived the initial tension in the room and then, when everyone shouted, it scared him. So just talk gently, like you would with a spooked mare, and they tend to calm down," Cole said with a shrug and a smile for Liam.

"Huh. Good to know," Carter replied, taking Liam back.

"Yeah, like the fact that perhaps we should set up a nursery at the club and put Cole in charge of it." Mason chortled.

Alexander snickered.

"I'd like to see you try that one," Cole uttered with a warning glance at his brother.

Garrett dealt the first hand of five card stud. Liam was relaxed and happy as a clam once more, paying rapt attention to everyone in the room, interested in the plethora of male murmurs. Glancing at the five cards, Carter grimaced at the piss poor hand. Bad hand with absolutely nothing.

"So are you and Jenna together again?" Spencer asked as he put down two cards and was dealt another two.

The question threw Carter. It shouldn't have. Spencer had a tendency not to let things go and that, mixed with a desire for the truth, made the subject bound to come up. He'd been hoping to avoid the question—for tonight, at least. Carter knew what he wanted with Jenna. But he wasn't necessarily prepared to discuss it with his buddies, not until he was more certain of her feelings toward him and he had discerned which way the wind blew.

"Leave it, Spencer. Tonight is not the time to talk about this." Carter gave him a biting look. He loved the dude, considered him a brother from another mother, but that didn't mean he wouldn't beat his ass if he got out of hand.

"But she's the one. The reason you've not been to the club this past year. If you've not claimed her and re-established contact, I'd like to know why," Spencer pushed.

"Spencer, leave the guy alone. He just found out he has a kid with her. Stop being an ass," Garrett said, exasperated, as he dealt Mason three new cards.

"Let's just play the game and leave that stuff for later," Alexander interceded, attempting to play peacemaker, tapping a poker chip against the table—one of his tells that he had a decent hand.

"No. I want to know. She's beautiful. I can see why any man, any Dom, would want her, but are you sure you trust her?" Spencer asked.

"Christ, you're like a fucking dog with a bone. I don't know, Spencer. How's that for an answer? Liam has changed the dynamic of everything. And while I'm totally in love with this little guy, when it comes to Jenna, I just don't know. I'd appreciate it if you would give me some goddamn space on the matter," Carter said with disgust lacing his voice.

Spencer sat back in his chair and said, "Fine. Peace offering. I'll get the subs to throw a baby shower at the club."

Jenna would like that. It would be good for her to get to know more people here. Carter nodded and said, "That would be nice. I know things have been hard for her and I'd like her to have the opportunity to fit into the community."

"A Dom thinks that way, he's thinking long term," Cole muttered.

"Consider it done. I will have the girls put something together for Saturday afternoon. We can make it a co-ed one, those are all the rage now, and everyone at this table is expected to attend with gifts in hand. But I'm not inviting the sister," Spencer stated.

"You have to invite Meghan. She's Liam's aunt whether you like her or not," Carter said.

"I tell you what that little brat needs is a firm hand and a red ass," Spencer replied.

"Be nice, Spencer," Carter growled. Meghan had grown on him today with her intelligence and obvious love for both her sister and Liam. That meant that, even if he had to protect her from Spencer, regardless of the mouth she had on her, he would.

"She's certainly a pretty one. Not sure she's a sub, though," Mason said, and Carter could see the wheels of interest turning.

"That one has teeth, brother, and is not one you'd want to tangle with," Cole said.

"Fine, she'll get an invite. But if she dares to speak to me again the way she did out in your driveway, I cannot promise enough restraint not to paddle her ass," Spencer chewed out, folding his cards.

"Ah, sorry to interrupt the manly ritual down here, but dinner's ready if y'all want to take a break and come eat in the dining room," Jenna said from within the doorframe. Carter wondered how long she'd been standing there. He hadn't heard her approach. None of them had, and they hadn't shown restraint in their conversation.

She approached him, but because of Liam. Their gazes clashed and then she lowered her gaze to Liam. "Hey there, my love, you having a good time bonding with all the boys?"

Liam grinned and cooed up at her.

"Oh yeah, it's been that much fun? Well, why don't you come with me so you can tell me all about it and we can change your pants, then join your new friends for dinner."

She lifted Liam out of Carter's arms and strode out of the game room without a backward glance.

"If it were me, I'd do whatever it took to keep a woman like that at my side and in my bed," Cole said quietly with a hand on his shoulder. Carter responded with a nod and rose from his seat. Cole was right. Absolutely one hundred percent. And he was working on it.

They grabbed their beer bottles and filed out of the room.

What he hadn't told them was that he was still in love with her. And as for getting her back into his bed, he was working on it. Hell this afternoon beneath the tree, he'd nearly come in his pants like an untried youth as he stroked her to climax. Just reliving the memory made his dick twitch in anticipation. Except, he didn't want her as merely a convenience because they lived together. Carter wanted to ensure that once he got her in his bed, she stayed there, permanently. He wanted to make sure she was physically recovered from giving birth to Liam. It wouldn't hurt him to press and be a bit more aggressive in his pursuit, though, not after her response to him today.

Tomorrow, the real seduction began.

But could he trust her after all this time? Could he trust that she wouldn't abscond and leave him floundering? And this time, she'd take his son.

CHAPTER 12

*L*ast night, Carter and his band of friends had given Jenna a ton of fodder to chew over. She'd overheard them discussing her and Meghan, although she'd never admit it to Carter. There were some mysteries that were better left unsolved.

Hearing Carter admit he loved Liam calmed her, settled some of the fear that had been rattling its cage in her chest. He really wanted Liam. And he had proved it in spades this morning when he'd driven them into town for Liam's doctor appointment. He'd asked questions of the pediatrician regarding the reflux medication. Paid for everything, from the doctor's visit to Liam's prescription. When she'd tried to pay at the pharmacy they'd nearly come to blows until Jenna had relented and caved.

While Carter was all in with Liam, he was unsure about her. She didn't blame him for that when she was just as uncertain about him. Jenna felt like she was walking through a minefield where a single incorrect step could make everything blow up in their faces. And Liam would end up harmed in the fallout.

After lunch, she sat in the sunroom with Liam contentedly

sleeping in his carrier. She ordered some things for Liam online to be delivered later that week. Then she worked on classwork that was due the following day. She was just shy of twenty-one credit hours before she received her bachelor's degree in accounting.

She knew most people thought it was a boring field, but she had always been good with numbers. Her ultimate dream would be to have her own bookkeeping business. It wasn't exotic work by any means, but people always needed accountants for taxes, estate planning, and other things. Now, after Liam's arrival, she wanted her dream more than anything. She wanted to be able to set a good example for her son, to prove that with hard work and dedication he could make something of himself. Even with the knowledge that one day this ranch would be his, she wanted to instill a work ethic in her kid. Part of that would come from providing him a solid foundation from which to springboard, one that didn't shift under his feet from one moment to the next.

And, this was purely selfish, but she wanted her son to be proud of her. Corny, she realized. But she never wanted Liam to think poorly of her or less of her. She knew that there would be times that he would roll his eyes at her or fight for his independence as a teen. That was a given when you had a child. But she didn't want him to have to parent her or be an adult before he was ready.

Jenna had become the other adult in the house after her mom's suicide. Her dad had shifted the responsibility of raising Meghan and so many other chores onto her shoulders while he'd wallowed in grief. By the time she was thirteen, she was the one who had run the household, not her father. She tried not to think less of him because she loved him so much. But he'd given her more responsibilities, forced her to grow up before she was ready, and then allowed her to take care of him.

Jenna never wanted Liam to have to be the adult in their

relationship. She'd fight to keep his childhood intact for as long as possible.

When she was twenty, Jenna had to leave college at the end of her sophomore year to help take care of their dad when he received his diagnosis. She had worked to support him. Had spent years running, from the moment her feet hit the floor each day to the moment she collapsed into bed in the evening. Yet, she'd still carved out time to take one or two online courses a semester toward her degree.

She'd done it in secret. Hadn't even told Meghan until she'd caught her studying while she was pregnant. Meghan had been super supportive and given her the stink eye for keeping it a secret. But Jenna had learned to keep the things she cared about most close to her chest. Not out of spite, or because she wanted to deceive the people she was closest to. But because when people knew about something that mattered to her, it became real. Once it was real, it could be taken away. So she protected what she cared about most by not mentioning it. That was another one of the reasons why she'd had such a hard time approaching Carter regarding Liam.

Carter strode into the sunroom then. The man simply took her breath away, much like the mountains around his ranch did. His nearness ignited a slow burn in her midsection.

Carter dropped onto the end of the leather chaise, his gaze on her open text book.

"Are you studying for something?" he asked.

"Yeah, actually. I'm a few classes shy of finishing my accounting degree," she admitted.

The dark slashes of his brows rose and he said, "Really? You never told me that. You want to be an accountant?"

She shrugged, attempting to deflect and make it seem unimportant. "More or less. I'd like to have my own business that would allow me to work from home while Liam's young and then work while he's at school when he's older."

Carter cocked his head to the side, studying her. "You're serious. Why did you never mention it on the island? I thought—"

"That I was just a bit of submissive fluff who liked to mouth off?" she replied. And wasn't that part of what her problem had always been? Not being taken seriously, even by those she loved and who loved her back.

His gaze hardened and he bit out, "Don't put words in my mouth. You just never mentioned it. I'm proud of you for working toward a goal like that. It's rather noble of you, I think. You certainly are more than capable and intelligent enough to handle it."

She flushed at the compliment and glanced down at her nails that were sorely in need of a good manicure. "Was there something I could help you with, Carter?"

"Yes, Cuffs & Spurs, my club, is throwing us a baby shower on Saturday. Spencer needs your sister's number."

She snorted. "Do you really think that's a good idea? Giving my sister and that man a way to contact the other?"

Carter chuckled darkly. "She'll keep him on his toes, that's for certain. And personally, I find it funny as hell watching Spencer deal with Meghan."

"Yeah, but you've never seen my sister when she goes nuclear. Rivers have change the course of their flow for days. I realize Spencer's a Dom and likely a capable individual, but even I pity him in this scenario."

Carter shrugged. "He'll be all right. And if not, well, the entertainment value alone will be worth it."

She jotted Meghan's number down on an empty sheet of notebook paper. Handing it to him, she said, "It's Spencer's funeral. Just don't blame me when they come to blows."

"No worries," he murmured. His fingers grazed hers as he took the piece of paper with Meghan's number scrawled on it. Electricity from the innocuous touch zinged throughout her body. Her nipples hardened. Her core fluttered. And she cursed internally when he noticed her arousal.

They were walking a tightrope ready to snap, only there was no net to catch them when they inevitably fell.

"Was there something you needed?" she asked, her voice husky with her arousal. The sensual tension crackled and pulsed. It would be so easy to cave to the desire she felt for him. Sex had never been an issue with him. Their desire had always blazed hotter than the sun. But she worried about trusting him with her heart. Before she did something stupid, like jump the man's bones, she scooted back as far as the chaise would allow, creating a safe distance.

Carter cleared his throat, but his deep bedroom voice carried a hint of lust as he spoke. "Yes, actually. I have to head back into town for a meeting at the club. Was there anything you needed?"

It wasn't lost on her that his gaze dropped to her lips. Nor that her pulse spiked. She sputtered, "No. I'm good. Thanks for asking. Here's the credit card you gave me this morning."

"You ordered stuff for Liam?" he asked.

"Don't sound so surprised. I did as you asked, and his things should be here at the end of the week."

"Will wonders never cease? Good. We'll get you both outfitted in no time. Don't wait for me to eat dinner but I should be back in time to read to Liam before he goes to sleep."

"Okay, have fun."

Carter leaned forward then, eliminating the small distance she'd erected. And, as if it was the most natural thing in the world, he kissed her. Just a brief, gentle brush of his lips against hers. More startling and pronounced because it was unexpected and short. The kiss removed whatever imaginary boundaries she thought she could maintain, and rocked her foundation with its simplicity.

When he withdrew, his hazel eyes blazed with banked heat, like an iron forge smoldering.

Their gazes locked on each other, kinetic energy swirling between them. How could she have thought for even a second that she didn't want him, that she could keep it casual and friendly between them without muddying the waters with lust?

The waters were already murky and infused with enough sexual energy to power the state of Alaska. And she wanted him, in an all-consuming way. Her gaze trained on his mouth, she started to lean forward for more, but before her lips could touch his, Liam emitted a tiny cry.

Jerking back, she climbed off the chaise and lifted Liam from his carrier, swaying a bit to soothe her little man. Carter stood, his big body dwarfing hers.

"See you later tonight then," Carter murmured. He reached for her. To do what, she wasn't certain, but he then seemed to think better of it and course corrected so that he caressed Liam's cheek instead. With a last heated glance at her, he swiveled on the heels of his boots and strode from the room.

Jenna was teetering on a ledge with Carter. She craved him. Loved him. A single push, and she'd jump. Toss caution to the wind and hope that, when she did finally land, she wouldn't be too broken.

CHAPTER 13

*L*ater that evening, Jenna and Liam were in her room. She'd just settled into the rocker, Liam excitedly straining in her arms because he knew he was about to get fed, when a knock rapped on the door.

"Come in," she replied, covering her exposed breast. Liam petulantly waved his fists. The door swung inward as she stood and approached to discover who was there. Carter was on the other side of the doorframe. He hoisted a piece of wooden furniture and hefted it into her room.

"What's this? Do you need help?" Jenna asked, advancing toward him, cradling Liam against her chest.

"It's a proper changing table for Liam. That way you don't have to use the top of the dresser anymore," Carter explained, positioning it up against the wall near the dresser and diaper genie.

It was very sweet of him and rather practical. She had to admire that.

"Thank you. I'm sure it will be wonderful," she said as Carter adjusted the table.

"It's no big deal. There's also one in the bathroom downstairs near the kitchen, one in the sunroom, and there will be a fourth for his room," Carter said, hands on his hips.

"You bought four changing tables tonight?" she asked, staring at him like he'd lost his mind.

"Well, yeah. It's needed, right? I also picked up more of those genie things and put one in each room with the tables." He shrugged, like it was no big deal. Didn't he realize how huge it was?

"Carter, I—"

He held up a hand, his gaze stern and immovable. "Don't tell me it was too much. This will help you out and make life a little bit easier. That way, when you're studying in the sunroom and Liam needs a diaper change, you don't have to run all the way back up here. Dottie will help keep them stocked."

Make life easier for her. She blinked back the onset of moisture filling her gaze. It shouldn't make her cry that someone wanted her taken care of, but it had been so long. Her voice thick with emotion, she said, "Thank you, Carter. Truly."

Liam fussed in her arms at being denied his nightly meal.

"If you give me five minutes to take a shower, I will be back in to read to him. I just want to wash all the dust off before I hold him," Carter said.

"Sure. He's ready to nurse but that takes a bit, so you have time."

"Be back in a few," Carter replied and left her room.

She gathered a few of Liam's books and placed them on the nightstand for Carter to read, then laid Liam upon the mattress. She climbed into bed and settled against the headboard. Liam wailed his frustration over not being fed.

"I know, my love," she murmured.

Lifting Liam into her arms, she positioned a pillow beneath him and fit her nipple into his tiny, bow shaped mouth. He rootled for a minute before he latched on and began to drink. Waves of protectiveness and love swamped her. She knew that it was partially a hormonal, biological component that made breastfeeding an activity mothers liked, but it was also so much more than that. She loved this precious time with him and the bond that grew deeper each time. It was unlike anything else in her life.

Even the connection she had with Carter.

Carter returned in sweats and a tank top, his inky hair damp. Sexy as sin. He always had been. Nothing had changed that fact. If anything, he'd grown more handsome. Perhaps it was because Jenna loved him so much. And then there was the teensy fact that she knew the scintillating body hidden beneath his clothing.

He skirted the foot of the bed and joined her. She liked him this way; relaxed, barefoot, the scent of his woodsy soap still clinging to him. Even with the constant livewire sexual tension between them.

"What should we read tonight, son?" Carter said, giving Liam a smile and wriggling his dark eyebrows.

Liam grinned up at him, a small stream of milk drizzling down his cheek before he re-latched and sucked, his stare intent on Carter. Jenna couldn't deny the bond that was forming between man and boy.

"The counting book? That's what I was thinking too," Carter said, lifting the first book she'd put on the nightstand.

The easy rhythm of Carter's voice filled the room. She felt the timbre and vibrations in her chest. His shoulder pressed against hers. It took everything inside Jenna not to give in to her yearning. She wanted to lay her head on his shoulder. Give him all her cares and worries. And just stay here with him.

When Liam had finished breastfeeding, Carter said, "Here, why don't you let me take over and you can have a shower if you'd like."

She wasn't going to turn him down. Handing Liam over, she headed into the bathroom. Her sister's words tumbled in her head as she showered. The only thing holding her back from enjoying Carter was she herself. Was she ready for sex again? Was she ready to re-forge that connection with him?

Yes. She wanted him. Needed him like she needed sunshine and oxygen. The first time would likely be painful, yet she'd get past it. Where it would all lead, she had no clear cut answer. And while she could keep attempting to ignore it all, there was a pressure cooker building inside her where she felt like if he didn't touch her, didn't put his big hands on her, if she didn't feel the weight of him over her, she would explode.

Her decision made, she hurried through her shower. By now, Liam should be asleep. In the evenings, on a full belly, he tended to conk out and sleep for a few hours. It was enough time to seduce Carter.

When she emerged from the bathroom in only her robe, Carter was putting a sleeping Liam in his bassinette. At the sight of her in nothing but her robe, he straightened and approached. His hazel eyes scored her with hunger.

She met him halfway until they stood a foot apart. The air shimmered with expectation.

"Jenna?" Carter asked the question, his gaze roaming over her form.

She gripped one of his big hands and lifted it to her cheek. She rubbed her cheek against his palm and beseeched him, "Touch me, Carter. I want—"

He closed the distance, his mouth claiming hers, cutting off her words. And her body went up in flames. Finally! Finally, his hands were on her again. His mouth, his wonderful, seductive, sinful mouth, moved over hers. His tongue swept inside, thrusting deep, drinking her moans.

She plastered herself against his front. Her arms circled his neck. She leaned up on her tiptoes. But Carter took over control, palmed the globes of her ass through the robe, and hoisted her into his arms. He carried her to the bed and laid her down on the mattress, his mouth never leaving hers as his body followed her down.

He tugged the front tie of her robe and spread it open. Her fingers clutched at his tank. She yearned to feel all of him. Every acre of firm hard muscle. He finally lifted his mouth from hers, his breathing heavy. His eyes raged with lust as he helped her remove his shirt.

She moaned deep in her throat at his nude chest.

Flames battered her core. Passion speared her veins. Drawn to him, of their own accord, her hands touched his chest. At the tingle created by his chest hair against her palms, she mewled. Then she caressed his pecs, circling the flat disks of his nipples, loving the grumble of pleasure he emitted. She traced down over his lats, the lines and ridges of his stomach, before she trailed her fingertips along the waistband of his sweats. The firm ridge of his cock pressed against her hip.

He placed kisses over her jawline. Down the sensitive hollow of her neck. Over the slope of her breasts. Her boobs were so much more sensitive now that she was breastfeeding. When he flicked his tongue against a nipple, pleasure coursed through her. He sucked the bud into his mouth. He licked and nipped at her flesh, and then he was drinking from her tit. There wasn't much left over. But she'd never considered Carter would want to taste her this way.

"Now I know why our son loves suckling your tits so much. Christ, I never thought it would be a turn on," Carter growled and moved his mouth to its twin, giving it identical treatment that left her gasping and writhing beneath him.

He traveled further south. Kneeling, he spread her thighs wide, then ran a finger through her folds. She hissed at the pleasure.

"Fuck, you're drenched. I promise I will be gentle. Let me know if anything causes so much as a twang, understood?"

"Yes."

"Yes, what?" he growled, giving her a dark heated glance.

"Yes, Sir," she murmured.

"Your safeword still red?"

"Yes, Sir." She nodded and gulped in a breath.

"Good. Your hands are to stay here," he directed, placing them on either side of her body on the bed.

"Don't move them for any reason, understood? Relax and let me love you. This is about reintroducing your body to the delights of the flesh," Carter ordered, his gaze intense and suffused with hunger.

The inherent command, the domination in his touch, caused shivers to erupt in her. She'd missed this, missed him being like this. Then he spread her thighs wider and wedged his broad shoulders between them. She dug her fingers into the mattress to keep them in place. Her breath clogged in her throat as his mouth descended. At the first swipe of his talented tongue through her intimate folds, her breath expelled in a rush.

Pleasure curled inside her core. Carter circled her nub of desire, teasing her with the promise of ecstasy. His tongue slid under her hood, lapped over her labia, before finally flicking over her clitoris. Pleasure rocketed inside her. He'd always enjoyed giving her oral. And goodness, but he was as hungry for her as she'd been for him.

He ate her pussy with relish. Like it was the best thing he'd ever tasted, and he wanted to dine on it for the rest of the night. He savored her, sucking her engorged bud into his mouth. She clawed at the mattress, needing surcease, her climax just out of reach.

He held her hips firm in his grasp and plunged his tongue inside her quivering folds. She tried to rock her hips into his thrusts but he wasn't allowing it. Her pleasure was at his command. It drove her wild.

"Sir." She gasped, her back arching at the waves of pleasure riddling her frame.

"Stop trying to control everything, Jenna. Surrender. Let go for me," he ordered, his tongue driving her out of her mind with need.

Was she trying to hang on to control? And if so, why?

She wasn't alone in this anymore. Hadn't he proved that? Carter had never done anything to warrant her mistrust. Somehow she'd forgotten what it truly meant to be submissive. She'd held on so tightly for so long. But she was denying them both —even when they'd been on the island she'd denied him. He, more than anyone, any Dom she'd ever known, deserved her complete submission. The ledge she'd been holding on to for so long her fingers ached crumbled and she inhaled a deep breath and just let go, trusting that Carter would be there to catch her as she fell. Her body went fluid beneath his touch and relief swamped her.

Carter lifted his head, his chin coated with her dew, his face hovering over her mound, and gave her a seductive grin, pride infusing his gaze. He winked and lowered his mouth back down to her pussy. His gaze trained on hers, he ramped up his speed, thrusting inside her channel with wild abandon at her surrender. Jenna couldn't stop her moans.

"Quiet, or you'll wake Liam. If I have to gag you, I will," he warned and nipped at her labia.

She bit her lower lip, attempting to contain her mewls.

Carter's teeth nipped at her nub and she came apart. Pleasure ricocheted through her body. Her pussy quaked. She strained at the waves as they bombarded her system.

Carter didn't stop his ministrations. When the vibrations from one orgasm ended, he drove her up another cliff with startling ease. Before Jenna knew what was happening, another climax hit her. He continued to eat her, sending her over the edge of delirium. With the next one, he added his fingers. His tongue flicked over her clitoris as he penetrated her with a single digit.

She hissed at the unexpected slice of pain.

"Carter, Sir," she whined.

"Relax, darlin'. I'm just trying to stretch you before I fuck you. I will go slowly but I know this time might be painful and I'll do what I can to lessen it."

She nodded. He thrust his finger, setting up an even rhythm. Jenna could feel her body relaxing around it, accepting the intrusion. And then he added a second finger, starting the whole process over again.

The pain wasn't horrible, more of a dull ache. And it eased with time and the way his tongue never stopped lapping at her clit. By the time he inserted a fourth finger, Jenna was sure this having sex again thing was going to be fine. Yes, there was pain, but there was pleasure also.

And she'd always enjoyed a little pain with her pleasure anyhow. With his tongue and fingers, Carter drove her body up another pleasurable peak of ecstasy.

Then he knelt before her. His cock jutted from his lean hips. He gripped his shaft as he spread her thighs further. Propped up on one thick, strong arm, he drew his cock through her wet folds. At his hiss, she glanced at his face.

Heat scored his features. Lust hardened his gaze.

"I will go as slow as I can. Use your fucking safeword if you need it," he commanded, his teeth gritted.

Then, with more control than she knew he had, he penetrated her channel. Inch by inch, he pressed his cock forward. Pain stole the breath from her lungs and her eyes watered.

"Carter," she whispered at the agony.

"Deep breaths. You're doing beautifully," he said, then moved his hand and rubbed his thumb over her swollen clit.

Pleasure spliced through the discomfort and he slid deeper inside. Carter thrust gently, progressing deeper each time until he was fully embedded inside, his balls pressed against her bum. She moaned, and not in pleasure. Tears spiked her eyes and coated her lashes.

Carter's big hands cupped her face.

"Look at me, Jenna," he commanded softly.

She opened her eyes and stared into his.

"Talk to me. Tell me what you're feeling, darlin'," he said.

"It hurts, Sir. I don't know…" She blinked back her tears.

"Easy, darlin', just trust me," Carter instructed.

She nodded through her tears. He didn't move his hips or withdraw his cock but stayed embedded in her pussy. His thumbs caught her tears. Then he fitted his mouth over hers and kissed her, deeply. The kiss marked her. Took her out of her mind so she relaxed. She returned it with everything inside her, pouring her need for him, her love for him, into it and even giving him her pain. Defying his command, she wrapped her arms around his wide shoulders. She needed to touch him. Jenna adored the sensation of his massive body atop hers, the weight of him pressing her into the mattress. It made her feel inherently feminine and submissive.

Carter continued to kiss her, his tongue dueling heatedly with hers. And still he remained motionless but for his lips upon hers. Slowly, the pain in her vaginal walls started to ease. The man had always known how to kiss her brainless. But now he grew even more in her esteem as his kiss drove away her pain.

Jenna clung to Carter as he delved inside her depths. His hands cradled her face. His mouth dominated her. Took her under. She wasn't sure how long he kissed her. Time suspended itself. With every thrust of his tongue, he drew her deeper into his sensual web. Pain gave way to liquid tugs of pleasure in her womb.

Her body softened beneath him, accepted his weight, accepted his cock. Her pussy clenched and fluttered around his girth. And still he kissed her. His kisses filled all the holes in her heart and soul.

Jenna's fingers dug into his back, clutching at him as her passion rose to startling heights. She needed movement, even just a hint of friction. She whimpered into his mouth. Her hands trailed down to his butt and gripped his ass, trying to show him without words what she needed.

When Carter finally lifted his mouth, his eyes were dark as pitch in his lust. With his gaze locked on hers he rocked his hips in a gentle seesaw motion. Her mouth opened on a gasp. Carter drew her hands from his body, held her wrists and placed them on either side of her head. His fingers threaded through hers and she gripped him, holding on as he ground his hips, his cock gliding in and out with ease.

Jenna canted her pelvis, meeting his thrusts. She'd never expected such gentleness, such aching tenderness from him. They'd always been combustible between the sheets. Yet this was different. She felt every measured thrust, each cant of his hips as he glided inside. Her body ached, the pain of penetration morphing with every thrust, adding to the eroticism of his lovemaking. And through it all, his gaze remained trained on her, watching every nuance of her reactions, ensuring that she wasn't in discomfort. Her body ratchetted up a sharp precipice of desire. Her fingers clutched his, her nails digging in to his hands.

"Carter," she moaned as her body tightened in on itself. Like a tidal wave crashing ashore, her body broke into a million pieces as her climax riddled her frame. Her pussy clenched with a fine line of pleasure-pain so intense she saw stars behind her closed lids.

He buried his face in the hollow of her neck as he thrust, need overriding everything. Carter's cock stiffened and swelled. His body jerked. He thrust, his body strained, and hot jets of liquid filled her pussy, setting off another round of sparks.

His groans filled her ears.

Tears pricked her eyes. Carter had made her first time post Liam beautiful. She wanted to burrow into his arms and never leave. And that terrified her. Love for him cascaded in her being. It was so huge, it brought tears to her eyes. Jenna wanted to tell him how she felt. That she didn't just want him. That she needed him—that, for the first time in her existence, she didn't feel alone. That she felt like she could lean on him and trust that he would be there.

And that everything she'd felt for Carter, everything she'd told herself she had buried in the sand, had just been lying in wait beneath the surface.

When Carter finally moved, he shifted and rolled onto his back. But he took her with him so she was cuddled by his side with her head resting on his chest. Carter looked at her then. His stare was tender, possessive, and instead of saying the words that were on the tip of her tongue, she played ostrich, burrowing against his chest.

And he let her.

Maybe he didn't want to break the spell of such world-altering sex. Well, she didn't either. Jenna closed her eyes and let herself fall into a dreamless sleep.

It felt like minutes, but was most likely hours later when Carter nudged her shoulder and murmured, "Jenna, Liam's hungry and needs you."

She opened her eyes to her upset little guy. "You mean he needs my boobs."

Carter chuckled and handed Liam over, then settled himself back beside her, spooning against her back. She fit Liam lengthwise and let him take root at her breast. She sighed, feeling the rush of hormones as Liam greedily slurped. Carter traced a finger over his son's cheek.

"I don't think I will ever tire of watching this. The way he looks at you while he feeds," Carter murmured.

"He's a charmer, much like his daddy," she quipped and shot him a sleepy grin over her shoulder.

Carter gave her a quick kiss on the tip of her nose and chuckled. "That he is."

Jenna nursed Liam until his belly was full. Then the three of them fell back asleep.

CHAPTER 14

*C*arter woke as the first rays of sunlight shone through the curtains. Careful not to wake them, he stared at the woman who continued to surprise him and his son. Christ, he'd never known such fierce protectiveness as he felt when it came to Liam. If his son needed him to corral the moon, he would figure out a way to draw the heavenly globe down to earth for him. When it came to Liam, he was a complete goner, and had no qualms about it.

Liam slept peacefully, secure with Jenna's arms around him. His little mouth was open and surrounding one of her nipples. They'd all fallen back asleep once he'd fed, and had stayed that way.

He hadn't expected to make love with her last night. Carter hadn't wanted to push her or her body until she was ready. He could honestly say that with all the submissives, all the women he'd slept with over the course of his thirty-five years, he'd never made love to a woman until last night.

Jenna wasn't ready for full on bondage and dominance. Hell, he had been more worried about whether she would buck

143

him off. Whether the pain would be too severe. And he had restrained his dominant nature to give her what she needed.

He still owed her a spanking. Yet he didn't want to cause her more pain, so he had his dominant beast collared. And last night, when he was buried deep inside her, he had shown her with his body that he loved her. He was too uncertain of her affections for the words to come easily. He'd never said them to someone else. Perhaps that was why, once they'd been together on the island, he wasn't able to attend the club. He'd already lost his heart to her. And for him, once he loved, it was forever; no take backs or refunds.

When he'd slid inside, her silken heat clamped around him, Carter felt like he had finally made it home. She was his home. His heart and soul had simply said: *mine*.

She was caving to him, and not just physically either. He noticed it in her eyes when she glanced his way or he caught her watching him.

Regretfully, he slipped from bed quietly and started his day.

∾

OVER THE NEXT FEW DAYS, they settled into a rhythm. Every night after his day out on the ranch, Carter would spend time with Liam while Jenna showered or did some school work. Her sister visited the ranch twice that week during the day to watch the baby. Carter could see the bond between the sisters. But they developed a pattern and rhythm, with Jenna sliding into his life rather seamlessly. At lunch the other day, he'd found her folding laundry with Dottie while Liam slept. When he asked her about it, she stuck out her chin and said that as this was where she was living, she would contribute. She wouldn't have Dottie do her wash when she was perfectly capable.

The woman drove him mad with her defiance. She challenged him, more of her spark returning the more comfortable she felt here.

It was the nights that were by far and away his favorite though. He enjoyed the homey routine, joining Jenna and Liam in her room. They took turns reading to Liam while he nursed. Once Liam was asleep, he and Jenna would have sex.

So far it had all been vanilla in their bedroom activities. Jenna was still sore and her body adjusting slowly to having sex once again. Carter didn't want to push her but there was an essential part missing, for both of them. He could feel it.

And they hadn't talked about their relationship. During the day, they could well be friendly roommates and nothing more for all the warmth they displayed. The closeness, the incendiary fires, only transpired in the dead of night.

He wasn't certain why. But he vowed to find the underlying cause of it. At the knock on the door to his office, he yelled, "Come in."

The door opened. As if his thoughts of her had conjured her up, Jenna hesitantly walked in, toting a picnic basket.

He leaned back in his chair when she shut the door behind her.

"Jenna? What can I do for you?" he asked, his body instantly alert.

"Well, you didn't come to the house for lunch today and I wanted to make sure you don't starve."

He steepled his hands in front of him, studying her. He noticed her hands trembled when she set the basket on his desk. "You didn't have to do that, but I appreciate it."

She hesitated, like she was about to say something and was having a raging internal debate.

"Spit it out, Jenna. You didn't just come to my office to deliver lunch. What gives?" he asked.

"Never mind. I didn't mean to disturb you," she said,

backing toward the door. Like hell was he letting her leave. He stood and prowled around his desk, his long strides eliminating the distance between them. Her hand gripped the knob when he came up behind her. Placing his palm on the doorframe, he kept her from opening it and escaping him. Jenna turned and glared up at him.

"What the hell, Carter? What's with the caveman act?" she asked. Yet as she scowled at him, he noted her pulse fluttering in her neck. Her pupils were dilated. Lowering his gaze, he saw her nipples were hard, beaded points under her top.

Fuck. She wanted the caveman act. Maybe he'd approached their nights together all wrong. He'd been so worried he might cause her pain that he hadn't dominated her, not the way he should have. Carter could make sure she wasn't harmed while affirming who was in charge. That changed. Now. She had come to him.

"I want you bent over my desk, bare assed," he ordered.

She inhaled a breath and licked her lips. Desire infused her gaze. "What?"

He gripped her chin. "You heard me. Don't make me punish you, Jenna. I don't know that your body can handle being spanked just yet, which means I will have to get very creative with your punishments for the time being. Do as I asked. I want you bent over my desk with your pretty ass in the air so I can fuck you. And that's what, *Sir*?"

He flipped the lock on his office door and drew down the interior shade. The last thing he wanted to do was give his foreman a heart attack.

Carter took a step back, just enough to allow Jenna movement to follow his commands. He held his breath. Would she comply? Had he read the situation correctly? If she didn't obey, he contemplated what her punishment could be without injuring her. Jenna surprised him. Sliding past him, her knockout body brushed against his and his eyes damn near crossed at the torture. Then she sashayed her way to his desk. He clenched his fists at her striptease. He fucking loved her body, even with the changes that becoming a mother had wrought.

He bit back a groan as she laid the top half of her body across his desk. Passion crashed over him.

He was so fucking hard. Carter bet he could cut rock with his dick. A haze of sexual need descended over him as he stalked to his desk. Yes, this was it. What they both needed.

"Very nice," he murmured, moving the picnic basket aside and then he pushed his office chair back so he could kneel between her thighs. He positioned her hands over the edge of the desk, wishing he had a pair of cuffs with him. That was something he would remedy tonight.

"Keep your hands here. Don't move them for any reason. Understood?" he demanded.

"Yes, Sir," she whimpered breathily.

Her pussy glistened with dew. She was as aroused as he. Good. It was about damn time. He slid to his knees. Parting her ass cheeks, without preamble or warning, he swiped his tongue through her crease. At her gasp, he grinned. Oh yeah, she needed his dominance every bit as much as he needed to dole it out. He tongued her clit, swishing around the bud as he parted the globes of her very fine ass. Even after having Liam, her ass was still fucking incredible. He nipped the nub, biting down until she cried out in pleasure.

This was what they'd been missing. They hadn't fucked yet. He hadn't dominated her. He ate her pussy. Laved her labia folds with his tongue. Held her steady when she attempted to buck her hips. Sucking the swollen bud into his mouth, he hummed while his tongue flicked back and forth. Then he slipped his tongue inside her channel, thrusting inside her sweet cunt. Her juices coated his chin. He circled her clit with

147

his thumb as he thrust his tongue, listening to the beautiful sounds of her arousal.

He stopped feasting on her cunt for a moment, gave her a love tap across her butt and said, "Quiet, or I will have to gag you. I don't want Kyle or Herb to hear you."

"Yes, Sir," she replied on a ragged moan.

Then he attacked her pussy with vigor. He wanted to have her flood his mouth with her dew, have her drench his chin with her essence. He held her steady as he plundered. Her pussy quivered, attempting to draw his tongue deeper as he thrust. Carter could feel her body reaching toward climax... then he pinched her engorged clit between his thumb and forefinger.

She shrieked as she came, defying his orders. Her pussy clutched at his tongue and her body quaked with the force of her climax. Carter stood and withdrew a clean bandana from his desk drawer, along with a tube of lubricant. He wasn't just going to fuck her pussy but her ass as well.

But he was gagging her.

He leaned against her, pressing her into his desk. "You disobeyed me, darlin'. And for that, you will be punished. Open your mouth."

She did as he commanded without qualm. It thrilled him. Even with her disobedience, she was the perfect fucking submissive. He fit the red bandana over her mouth and fastened it so that she was effectively gagged.

"You're not to come until I give you permission. Understood?" he growled in her ear.

She nodded her head.

Then he unzipped his jeans and freed his dick. Gripping his shaft in one hand, he parted her butt cheeks with the other. He fit his crown at her pussy entrance. Then he rocked his hips and thrust, embedding his length inside her clasping sheath.

At her muffled moan, he stilled, attuned to her body. She

wasn't bucking him off. In fact, the look on her face was one of sublime pleasure. The feeling was mutual. He gripped her hips as he began to move, shuttling his cock in and out of her glorious heat in long, smooth strokes. Fuck, he loved the way her pussy squeezed him.

He didn't hold back as he thrust, setting a wickedly fast pace, pounding his length inside her sweet cunt. From the beautiful sound of Jenna's moans behind the gag, she was enjoying every minute. While he thrust, he added a dollop of lube to her pretty rosette.

At her deep groan, he smiled. Oh yeah, they both needed this fucking. Pumping his cock in her pussy, he pressed two fingers into her ass, stretching her tight back channel. At the double penetration, Jenna's moans behind the gag increased. He worked her ass, stretching the taut muscles, adding a third and then a fourth digit, thrusting inside until his fingers were gliding smoothly without hindrance.

Jenna gripped the lip of his desk, issuing garbled moans in a never-ending stream. He jack hammered a few more strokes before he withdrew from her pussy. From behind the gag, Jenna protested.

"Don't you worry, darlin', I plan on fucking your pretty rosette and making you come so hard, you'll barely be able to walk," he growled as he coated his length with more lube. Jenna whimpered and wriggled her ass. He gave her a firm swat to still her movements and then pressed the crest against the tight ring of muscle of her back channel. He furrowed his length inside her until he was balls deep, then held still to regain his composure.

Christ, she felt like electrified silk clamping his dick.

Carter knew he wouldn't last long in her ass. Not when she was his every fantasy and constricted around his cock like a heated vise grip. He unleashed his inner beast, letting all the restraint he'd shown this past week fall by the wayside.

Pistoning his hips, he pounded his length inside her ass. A passionate fury drove him. His balls slapped against her pussy. Her muffled cries drove him wild.

He leaned forward slightly, changing the angle of his penetration. One of his hands slid around her throat. He ground his cock in her ass. Slammed his length so hard he nearly saw stars. It was the ecstasy on Jenna's face that drove him onward. She was the only one, the only submissive who had ever matched him for pure passion. She fit him like a fucking glove. And he knew he was a fucking goner where she was concerned.

If he had to move heaven and hell to keep her here with him, he would do it.

He snaked his free hand under her hips and strummed his fingers over her clit. His mouth beside her ear, he growled, "Come for me."

He hammered his cock in her ass, feeling his dick lengthen and swell. At his command she turned her face toward him, his hand gripped her throat and he felt the thrumming beat of her heart. He pinched her clit as he thrust, and her back channel spasmed and quaked around his cock. She wailed into the gag, her body trembling and quivering beneath him.

He relinquished his control. It had already been slipping, anyway. Lightning arced along his spine and sent shockwaves of ecstasy up his shaft. Now it was his turn to moan as his seed poured in rivulets into her clasping rear. He pumped his hips, letting her milk him of all his cum.

He rocked inside her until his tremors ceased and his legs nearly gave out. Lifting himself, he pulled her with him until they were sitting on his office chair. He removed the gag as he held her, pressing his lips to her forehead.

"Well, I must say that was the best lunch I've had in ages," he murmured. At her giggle, he smiled. He was truly lost where she was concerned. She could shave her head and paint herself purple and he would want her still.

Then she started to wriggle off his lap.

"Where do you think you're going? We still haven't had the lunch you packed yet."

"Can't. Since we got distracted, I will have to eat in a bit. It's nearly time for Liam's afternoon feeding. And he's just as demanding as his father," she murmured, sliding off his lap with a wince.

"I didn't hurt you, did I?" Fear clawed up his chest. Had he been too quick to push the envelope with her recovery?

"No. I'm sore but I think what we are doing is actually helping me heal a bit faster, so those muscles aren't just lying dormant and are getting a workout. If that makes any sense."

"It does. We'll do some more physical therapy on those muscles tonight," he promised with a wink and a wicked grin.

She blushed and nodded. "Okay, but I really do need to go."

He watched as she donned her bra, panties, tank top and shorts. She'd worn sandals—of all things—to the stables?

"We really need to get you some proper boots. Those might look sexy as hell but they are far from practical for ranch life. What if you had to outrun a rattler? You want that extra protection from their bite. Trust me on this."

"Rattlesnakes? Really?"

He nodded and replied, "You're in the country. While I do try to keep my ranch from being infested with them, there's a ton of open wilderness to contend with. I can't guarantee you won't run into the occasional wild animal out here. In fact, we need to have a conversation about the different predators in the area you need to be careful of coming across, along with some of the other wild animals you will want to steer clear of should you run into them."

"I'll look into getting some boots this week. You really think I will have to contend with a bear or mountain lion?"

"Good. Get really good ones, real leather, none of that suede crap. Don't go for fancy but comfort and practicality. And out here, there's no telling what you might come across. Thanks for lunch," he said, giving her a deep but quick kiss as he fastened his jeans. Then he ushered her out of his office.

He watched her glide out of the barn. Yeah, he was sunk where she was concerned.

CHAPTER 15

*L*ater that night, Jenna sat on the floor in her room with Liam. She'd eaten dinner early, since she'd skipped lunch. Or, rather, she'd had incredible pulse pounding sex with Carter instead of eating. She'd forgotten how hot it could be to have a Dom go all alpha on her. Her belly clenched at the memory.

She'd enjoyed every minute, even if she was a teeny bit sorer than she'd let on. All the sexual activity was helping her muscles regenerate, but it hadn't negated the twinges of pain entirely yet. And she could use a hot Epsom salt bath to help her muscles.

Liam reclined in his brand new bouncy seat. Her little man was fascinated by the movements and vibrations. They'd received delivery of the order for Liam this afternoon. She was assembling his new stroller when Carter walked into her room without knocking. Proof positive that they had crossed a threshold in his office today.

He was fresh from the shower, his dark hair damp, the ends curling on his neck, and she bit back a purr. Jenna didn't think she'd ever tire of looking at him, of the way he entered a room and every molecule in her being buzzed in response. The way his hazel eyes smoldered when he glanced at her. This afternoon, he'd been so fierce and dominant with her. She'd loved every minute of it.

But what did that mean for them? Jenna realized that she was the one who had changed their relationship this past week to include sex. Not that she was complaining about the bedroom activities, because at this point it would take being bound to his horse herd to drag her away. But it left her in a bit of a conundrum since they'd not discussed what their relationship was, precisely. Did he want more with her? Or was she just convenient?

Whenever she considered mentioning her concerns, her throat constricted and silenced her voice.

"Why didn't you wait for me to help you with that?" Carter asked, nodding at the myriad pieces spread out over the rug and joining her on the floor.

She shrugged and said, "It's not like I have other pressing things on my agenda. Liam's fed, and happy as a clam in his new bouncy seat. Aren't you, my love?"

Liam gave her a wide grin and oohhed.

"Still, let me do this for you," Carter said, picking up the assembly instructions and flipping through the directions.

Giving the Philips head screwdriver another crank on the piece she was attaching, she replied, "Or I could just finish. I'm almost done, and pretty handy when it's warranted."

Carter's glance slid her way, a dark slash of his brow raised. "I'm not saying you're not capable, you are more than that when you put your mind to something. But I want to help you."

"Fine. Have it. I'm just going a little stir crazy here," Jenna admitted and handed over the screwdriver, relinquishing control.

"Why?" he asked, taking over, his hands moving confidently as he added the last few parts to the stroller.

"Because I'm used to doing things, working non-stop. If you remember at all, on the island, I worked quite a bit. And yes, Liam takes up a fair portion of my day, but I don't really have anything else to do. Dottie will only allow me to help her out so much before she shoos me away. I'm a doer, Carter. Always have been, so the inactivity is driving me out of my ever-loving mind."

"Okay. Clearly you have something in mind," he said, standing the stroller up on its wheels and testing it.

"I need to go back to work. Nothing full time yet, but Lucy's Grocery Store is willing to work with me, since I have a newborn. Perhaps a day or two a week," she said, realizing that she would have to figure out babysitting for Liam.

"But you don't have to work. I've got you and Liam covered," Carter said with a shake of his head.

"I don't want you to support me, Carter. All my life I've worked and earned my keep. I won't stop now just because I have a child and we're sleeping with each other."

When Carter opened his mouth to reply, she continued, "I appreciate the fact that you want Liam taken care of financially and are willing to do so much for him—and for me. But it's a pride thing; I can't live off you and I won't. I need to be able to pull my own weight around here and contribute. I don't think that's a bad thing. Not to mention, it will keep me from going stir crazy out here in the boonies."

Carter did a final adjustment on the stroller and then turned his gaze back to her. "Fair enough. But what if I could offer you something better?"

"What do you mean?" she asked.

"The ranch hasn't had a bookkeeper in going on two years now. I just assumed the responsibility but with the weather we've been having lately, I've barely been able to tackle the books, let alone take care of more than making sure things are paid. It's why I didn't come to the house for lunch today." Carter gave her a wicked half grin.

"You would trust me with the bookkeeping for the ranch?" she asked, stunned.

"Why wouldn't I? You're smart. I can vouch for your work ethic because I've witnessed it firsthand. It's what you're in school for and there's no better teacher than real life experience. This way, when you do graduate with your degree, if you decide to start your own firm in Jackson, you'll already have one solid account," Carter said.

"And you would pay me?"

He shook his head. "The ranch would. You'd be an employee of the Double J and paid from those accounts. Just the same as Herb's, Kyle's, and Dottie's salaries. It's something you could start part-time while Liam's young and work around his schedule. We could give it a trial run for a month. If it doesn't work out, no harm, no foul."

"Let me think about it and get back to you," Jenna said, chewing her bottom lip. While it sounded good, she was worried about becoming more entangled within Carter's world. He was weaving her and Liam into the fabric of daily life here. And she worried about what that meant for her —for them.

"Where's the rest of the delivery, by the way? Did they only bring part of it?" Carter asked, surveying the stash.

"This is the stuff I ordered."

"But doesn't Liam need more than this? Jenna, I told you to get whatever he needed," Carter replied, exasperation seeping into his voice.

Rolling her eyes at him, she stated, "And I did. He doesn't need much. He's a baby, and one who will grow quickly. He's already not fitting into his newborn clothes anymore. It's wasteful, in my book. He has enough. Besides, aren't your friends throwing a shower for us tomorrow? He'll likely get some more clothing there and will be fine."

"Dammit, Jenna. On Sunday, we're going into town and I'm taking you shopping." Carter glowered in her direction.

She glared back and dug her heels in. "No. I'm not going to have you pay for everything. If I start working, I can manage, and pay for some of his things too."

Carter scowled, his arms crossed over his chest. "This is non-negotiable. Stop being so damn stubborn on this point. We have to pick out furniture for his nursery, anyhow. And we will get what he needs. You say he's growing quickly, well, then we need to plan ahead for the winter months and start to stock pile."

"I'm not the only one being mule-headed on this, Carter. Why do we have to plan ahead? Winter is months away yet," she said, not understanding why he was being so persistent— other than the fact that he was a Dom and wanted to get his way.

"Because when it snows here, the roads can become impassable. Oftentimes for days if we have blizzard conditions. What that means is you have to adopt a wholly different approach. It's one of the reasons we have a storage room in the basement with two industrial sized deep freezes. Dottie helps make sure we are stocked on meat, frozen fruits and vegetables. We overstock on pantry items and things like paper towels and toilet paper. I'm not being overbearing but trying to help you prepare. Life in Wyoming is a far different beast from what you are familiar with."

"Days? Stuck for days at a time?"

Carter shrugged as if it were no big deal. "That's life here in Wyoming, Jenna. I realize you're from Florida and this will be your first winter here, so think of it this way: imagine having to be prepared for a hurricane that lasted months, that could strand you without access to the outside world for a solid week, and make sure you are equipped for the worst case scenario. Especially with Liam, you will want stores of extra diapers and wipes for him. By then he might be on baby food and we would want to have the pantry stocked."

"I see your point," Jenna commented, the wheels turning in her mind. She did better with lists. If they really would be stranded, Carter was right. She'd have to consider what she would need for Liam during the winter months and have the foresight to ensure that he had what he needed.

Except it also meant that living here, with Carter, was becoming permanent. Skitters of fear raced along her spine. It was a level of commitment she wasn't entirely comfortable with.

She grimaced. It was a whole new way of being, of existing. But that's what she and Meghan had wanted when they'd moved here last month. A fresh start, and a new life away from pain, loss, and the reminders of their father's crippling disease. She wanted Liam to know Carter and had accomplished that feat, at least.

"Are you not happy here?" Carter asked, his expression unreadable as he studied her.

"I'm not unhappy," she replied.

"But?"

"Everything's just so new. I don't feel like I've found my footing yet. And it doesn't help that Liam's not sleeping through the night. So, it could simply be exhaustion on my part. Not to mention, my hormones are still all over the place and haven't returned to pre-pregnancy levels. It's perfectly normal, but it does make me question my reaction to things. Sorry, I know that's not really an answer. Do I think Liam and I could be happy here? Yes. I just need more time."

"We have all the time in the world. There's no rush, on anything," Carter murmured and turned away, but not before she caught the flash of disappointment in his eyes.

Was she screwing things up between them? Probably. Not that she knew what their relationship actually was to begin with. It was like she had a knack for destroying anything good that came into her life. Maybe she shouldn't have been honest with him but she knew that would be short-changing both of them. It was ingrained in her to be honest to her Dom. And regardless of whether they were permanent or temporary, she owed him her honesty and wouldn't start lying to him now to spare his feelings.

That didn't mean she wouldn't try to be kinder and less abrupt. She said, "I'm sorry. I know that wasn't what you wanted to hear."

Carter looked at her. "Jenna, why are you still acting like you're going to pick up and move at any moment? You're not. This is where you belong. You and Liam are staying here and that's final."

"So you just automatically get to decide my life for me? What if I don't want to stay here? You don't get to decide what's best for my life. You have no right."

He yanked her close and snarled, his visage stern as he scowled. "I have the only right. You're my sub, dammit. You have been since I set foot on the island last year, and nothing has changed that fact."

"Don't pull that Dom bullshit with me," she retorted, standing her ground while her body all but purred at his domi-nant claiming.

"Or you'll what? You seem to forget who's in charge," he snarled, his voice low and fierce.

"Let's get one thing straight: I don't belong to you. If I want to move to Timbuktu, I can and I will. And there's nothing you can do about it. Stop being an asshole and trying to control the universe," she said defiantly, her fists clenched against his chest, trying to push him away. It was a bit like a butterfly trying to move a mountain with the force of wind its wings generated, but Jenna was incensed at his attitude.

"That does it," he snapped. Carter shifted her body and drew her across his lap. Too late she realized his intentions when he gripped the waistband of her yoga pants and panties and yanked them down to her knees. Then he positioned his forearm across her lower back.

"Carter, what the hell do you think you're doing?" She tried to buck him off, but the man was more solid than granite.

"Doing something that I should have done the day the island was evacuated when you refused to come with me, and then again when I found you in Jackson," Carter snarled. His large palm connected forcefully with her rear and she yelped.

"You are my sub, Jenna. You know this deep down, yet you are refusing to admit it for some reason that escapes me." His hand cracked against her behind and moisture entered her vision at the brutal slice of pain.

"Your place is at my side, in my bed, and caring for our son." His hand whacked her bum with three forceful swats. Jenna bit her lip as pain radiated from her bottom. The sasquatch had crossed her last nerve.

"And what if I don't want that? Don't want you?" she cried through big, fat, angry tears.

"You're lying through your teeth. You want me. Why you're fighting it is what we are going to get to the bottom of," he stated, his hand cracked repeatedly against her butt. The sting caused fireballs of need to explode in her body. Instead of calming her, it had the opposite effect.

She snapped. "I don't want you, Sasquatch. Stop manhandling me or I'll—"

"Sasquatch? Appropriate, but you can cut the attitude. And as for not wanting me?" He dragged two of his fingers through her crease. Jenna moaned as he grazed her clit. Then he held his fingers in front of her face. They were coated with moisture.

"See this, darlin? That's your body telling me it loves my touch. Stop lying or you won't sit pretty for a week," he threatened, and peppered her behind. Her rear burned. Her cheeks were flaming. "Why are you denying it? Just tell me, Jenna, and your punishment will be over," he promised.

She dropped her face into her hands, wanting to hide as her tears began in earnest.

"You don't understand." She sobbed brokenly, feeling like delicate glass that would shatter into a billion pieces at the slightest touch.

Carter stilled his hand, massaging the fiery globes of her rear. "What don't I understand?" he asked quietly.

"What happens to me when it all goes away?" she said.

He shifted her in his arms until she was facing him. "I'm not going anywhere. When I say I'm all in, I mean it."

Her vision infused with her tears, she said, "You mean it now. People always mean it at the moment, but then forget that they said it."

Carter cupped her face in his hand, his gaze probing. "Where is this coming from? I've never once not come through for you. You can trust me, Jenna. I'm here, and I'm in this for the long haul. Question is, why do you think I'll desert you?"

"All my life I've had people I trusted tell me they would be there, that I could count on them, and that's never been the case. My mom said she'd always be there and committed suicide a week later. I was eight. Meghan was only two at the time. And my dad, he just fell apart. By the time I was thirteen, I ran our household. My dad taught history at the local high school, but the income wasn't nearly enough to raise two girls on his own. So I found odd jobs, babysat, mowed lawns and the like, until I was sixteen. Then I worked part time after school, raised Meghan, cooked, cleaned, and did pretty much everything. When Dad got sick, I left college in my sophomore year to care for him. I don't know how to be anything other than what I am. I've never been able to count on anyone. Not really."

"Jenna, Rome wasn't built in a day. I have never been anything but here for you. But you'll have to take a leap of faith and decide that you either trust me or you don't."

"I do trust you, but—"

"No buts, darlin'. I regret not hauling your ass onto the plane during the hurricane evac last year. But I can't change that fact. It's done. All I can do is show you that this is where you belong; with me, in my home and in my bed."

"I want you. I always have, and I'm trying. Please believe me," she said.

Carter swiped at her tears with his thumbs, his eyes boring into hers before he lowered his mouth and slanted his lips over hers. She moaned as he held her prisoner in his arms and ravished her mouth with his carnal, dominant kiss. It wasn't gentle. The kiss was hard and brutal. The kiss laid siege to the very fabric of her being.

Passion blasted between them. They'd always been volatile together. Carter swept his tongue inside her mouth, thrusting into the recesses and dragging her further into the quagmire of their explosive desire. Jenna placed her palms against his chest to try and put distance between them, to give herself a chance to think about everything he'd said. Except the moment she touched him, her hands went up in flames and curled into him. She dug her fingers in, gripped his shirt, and pulled him closer.

She mewled into his hungry mouth, lost in him. In the desire she felt for him. It didn't matter that they were sitting on the floor. They could have been standing on the ledge of an active volcano for all she knew or cared. Carter kissed her, and became her world. Everything else ceased to exist.

One of his hands snaked between her thighs to her heated center. At his touch against her sensitive core, she whimpered into his mouth. Carter's fingers slid inside her sheath, his thumb circled and flicked across her nub. Pleasure pulsed and throbbed. He controlled her body, commanded a response from her flesh. She writhed, rolling her hips as his fingers pumped inside her pussy. Her tissues clenched at him, wanting to draw him deeper.

But he set the pace, he controlled the force. Jenna surrendered in his arms, his caress. His kiss caused pleasure to coalesce in her form as she strained to reach the pinnacle of ecstasy. In the back of her mind, she realized that this entreaty was a lesson Carter was imparting. That he was backing his words with physical proof that she wanted him beyond the scope of her fears.

She should be furious. She should be fighting him. She should pack her things and go. Except she knew that if she did, she'd regret it forever.

The next graze of her clit with his calloused thumb made Jenna shatter around his thrusting fingers. She wailed into his fervent, hungry mouth. Her hips rocked into his hand as her tissues spasmed around his digits.

When Carter finally lifted his mouth from hers, his breathing was heavy. The magnitude of possessiveness clouding his visage made her tremble. He withdrew his fingers from her sheath, lifted them up to his mouth, and sucked them inside. His gaze never left hers as he cleaned her dew off his fingers. The man was erotic and sexy, and wanted her every bit as much as she desired him.

Was she that damaged that she was willing to ruin everything? His erection pressed against her bottom through his sweats. But it was the emotion she spied in his gaze…

"Carter, I—"

Liam interrupted with a howl of frustration. She closed her eyes.

Love you.

163

Then she tried to scramble off Carter's lap, aghast that she'd nearly told him.

"We're not done talking about this," he said.

"Fine, but Liam needs me right now," she said, squirming in his lap. He let her go. She yanked her pants back into position before kneeling before their son. Lifting him out of his new seat, she glanced at Carter over his head.

He was correct. They weren't done with each other. Not by any means. What Jenna truly wanted from him, more than anything, was his love.

But maybe love wasn't in the cards, and the best she could hope for was being his submissive, being owned, and being cared for. Yet as hot as the fires of ecstasy burned between them, she worried that it wasn't enough for the long haul.

She didn't just want his dominance and protection, or the stability he offered. She wanted Carter's heart.

CHAPTER 16

*J*enna fidgeted in her seat as Carter parked his truck near the club. Jackson Hole was crowded with tourists today, even in the oppressive heat.

"Relax, Jenna. You're not going before a firing squad," Carter murmured, casting her a glance.

"I know. I'm just a little nervous," she admitted. Today was another line of demarcation in their relationship, even if he didn't see it.

"But you've already met the guys, and they loved you. In fact, they've all been texting me, trying to finagle a dinner invitation so they can eat more of your cooking. You have nothing to be afraid of and I will be with you the whole time."

It wasn't the Doms she was worried about. "I know. It's silly of me. It's a new club, and we have Liam. This is one of his first outings, and I'm not sure how he will handle it."

"We'll stay as long as we can, but they understand we have an infant," Carter said, helping her out of his truck before getting the stroller and transferring Liam into it. She grabbed the diaper bag and her purse. Carter pushed the stroller with one hand and put the other on her lower back, leading her toward a club on the corner. The harmless contact caused shivers to flare along her spine.

The exterior was constructed with a slate gray stone façade that resembled the color of the nearby mountains. There was a mahogany wooden trim porch and front overhang. At the street corner was a double door entry of wood and glass. The club's symbol, a cowboy on a bucking bronco, was etched into the glass. She read the name.

"Am I missing something? I thought the name was Cuffs & Spurs."

"It is, for the lower level. But for this to be a valid business, we named it The Teton Cowboy. The main level is open to the public most days and does brisk business. Although, from the looks of it, it seems like Spencer closed the place down for us this afternoon." He tapped the sign that apologized for the inconvenience but stated that The Teton Cowboy was closed until six that evening for a private party.

Jenna didn't think that Spencer liked her. Not after over-hearing him the other night. It touched her that he would do this—for her, and more likely for Carter.

They entered into what she could only describe as John Wayne's favorite hangout. Her dad had loved old Western films and this place called to mind every one of them. There was a wall bar that had to be a good fifty feet in length. The barstools were the most unique feature. Competing with the glossy gold wooden and brass bar were brown leather saddles for patrons to sit upon. Saddles that acted as seats. What a weird and kind of cool idea.

In the seating area, packed with tables, there was a group already in attendance. She recognized most of the Doms from poker night at the ranch, although there were two men she didn't recognize. Meghan was here, making her sigh with relief that she knew one person there well. She was over near the bar, chatting with Garrett while Spencer's gaze shot daggers in her direction. Jenna could only imagine what her sister had said to him. Those two were like nitroglycerin and matches. They didn't belong anywhere near each other.

It was the group of women present that interested Jenna. At their entrance, everyone turned toward them. She let Carter lead her around the room and make introductions. She'd never keep all their names straight, today at least, but they all seemed nice enough.

They were curious about her and they fawned over Liam. Karolina and Tibby both held him. Anne, Billie, and Paige were gracious, if a little shy. Jenna hit it off with Faith and Natalie. But Sasha and Rachel seemed a bit sullen, making her wonder if they'd had their sights set on becoming Carter's submissive. Or, worse, they'd already been with him.

He was entitled to have a past but that didn't stop the jealousy from clawing at her, which was new for Jenna. Then again, there'd never been any Dom like Carter in her life. Most of her relationships with other Doms had been open and short-lived.

Carter introduced her to Joshua Barrett, the local vet who oversaw much of the care of the horses on the ranch. The six-foot veterinarian with a wide, kind smile was the only man in the room not wearing a cowboy hat. And then she met Derrick Wimbly, Joshua's business partner and a horse breeding specialist, who helped Carter oversee breeding season. The man was almost as tall as his partner, and tufts of his midnight hair peeped out from beneath his hat. He had the bluest eyes.

Spencer, bless the man, had thought of everything. There was fall off the bone barbeque ribs, along with a selection of delicious sides. They ate until they were all full amidst the laughter and friendly banter. Some of the club's wait staff was there, collecting plates, offering refills on drinks.

Liam started to fuss in his stroller.

"Problem?" Carter asked as she moved to pick their son up.

"No. I suspect he's hungry. And likely needs a diaper change while I'm at it," she replied.

"If you want some privacy, near the back corner over there by the stage there are a few comfortable booths that would do the trick nicely." Carter indicated.

"That should work. We'll be back in a few," she said, slinging the diaper bag over her shoulder. She soothed Liam, rubbing his back as they ventured into the corner.

She liked The Teton Cowboy and would love to see the place when it wasn't closed for a private party. She also wondered where the entrance to Cuffs & Spurs was located. They settled into a back corner. Liam calmed as soon as he was nursing and Jenna was able to watch the interactions of the Doms and subs at the shower.

Jenna had lied to Carter. She did like it here. That was part of the problem. She could envision herself being folded seamlessly into the group. So why was she holding herself back? Why was she hesitating when she was so in love with him?

Meghan joined her as she was burping Liam.

"What's up, sis?" Meghan asked, sliding into the booth, looking fresh and beautiful in an aquamarine sundress.

Jenna glanced down at Liam, avoiding eye contact, and replied, "I don't know. Why do you ask?"

"You just look unhappy. You've been smiling since you walked through the door and you forget, I know you. It's not genuine. This is a party. So what gives? Did you and Carter fight?" Meghan asked, needling her.

"A little. I don't know if I can give him what he wants."

Meghan snorted. "Please, you already are. That man is boots over Stetson for you. And for Liam. I'll admit, I had my reservations about him at first, but he's a decent guy. And he doesn't look half bad in Levi's."

"You should see him out of them," Jenna commented and then blushed. She couldn't believe she'd said that.

Meghan chuckled. "I'm sure he makes quite a yummy picture. Whatever it is, you'll get through it. You always have. I'm not saying any of this has been easy. I know I was a burden on you for so many years."

"No, you weren't. I was happy to—"

Meghan interjected. "Just let me finish. You've been both stand-in mom and big sister for me. You carried the burdens of our family, of raising me on your shoulders. It's your time now, Jenna. Don't waste it. Take your happiness where you can find it and grab hold of it. And I think that man over there will make you ridiculously happy if you allow him to. The only one who is stopping that is you."

"I know. I'm a complete head-case. I keep waiting for the other shoe to drop. Like: surprise, you were happy for two seconds, and now we're going to pull the rug out from underneath you," she replied with a sigh.

"Jenna, do you really think that man over there would allow something to happen to you? I'm sure if you asked him to bring back dinosaurs, he would figure out a way to genetically engineer them and bring them back from extinction for you. Stop dipping your toes in the happiness pool and jump in."

Jenna blinked back moisture from her eyes. Was that what she was doing? Probably. "I'll try. How's that?"

"In the words of a really smart dude: do or do not, there is no try. Just do it for me, because I can't stand to see you miserable and want you to take your happiness where you find it. And I know you well enough to know that you love him and are scared to death of your feelings for him. I can't help you with those, but I can give you a shove in his direction."

"You and your pop culture references." Jenna shook her head, side-stepping a bit. She did love him, but she wasn't certain he loved her. Cared for her, wanted her as his sub? Yes. But love?

169

"Hey, I just want you to live long and prosper." Meghan gave her a saucy grin and winked.

Jenna caught Carter staring at them and he waved them back over. "Thanks. I think we need to rejoin the party. Looks like it's present time."

"Just promise me you will think about it," Meghan said as they walked the short distance back to the group.

"I will," she said.

Putting Liam back in his stroller, she and Carter opened gifts. The club members had outdone themselves. There were bottles and blankets. A chest full of clothing, tiny shoes, even a pair that looked like little cowboy boots, a rocking horse, toys, books. And then the piece de resistance from the Masters of Cuffs & Spurs: a gorgeous mahogany wooden crib with all the essentials.

"Thank you all so much," Jenna said after opening the last of the gifts. She was overwhelmed by the generosity and fought back tears. Once the presents were open and the cake had been eaten, attendees started to disperse. Jenna offered to host a sub meeting at the ranch. She made plans with Faith and Natalie to come visit.

She felt good. Remarkably so.

Her sister sparred with Spencer before she left to head to work that evening. When it came to those two, Jenna didn't know whether she should put them in a room and let them duke it out or attempt to keep them separate from one another. Especially since Meghan seemed inclined to bait Spencer whenever they occupied the same space.

After saying goodbye to her sister and the rest of the subs, the Doms started packing up Carter's truck. While they were occupied, Jenna wandered through the club and found the entrance to Cuffs & Spurs. Holding Liam close, she descended the stairs.

Down here, the cowboy theme persisted, but that was

where any similarity to the bar upstairs ended. There was another wall bar that was half the size of the one upstairs. The barstools were saddles, too, but there were obvious silver loops at the front and rear to restrain a sub's hands. And then again, the loops were present on the lower rung to restrain a sub's feet. Scene areas were cordoned off with black velvet rope along the walls. There weren't any private rooms that she could see.

There was a seating area with brown leather couches, and a smattering of dungeon furniture. The one that was a bit of a surprise was the mechanical bull in the center of the club. It wasn't so much the bull as what was on it. Dead center on the thing's back was what looked like a saddle for a submissive to sit on, and in the center of that was a vac-u-lock attachment for dildos. And there were also silver loops to attach a sub's wrists and ankles.

The sight stirred her. She could imagine being strapped to it, the dildo plunging into her pussy as the bull bucked, while the entire room watched. She hadn't been to a club since Pleasure Island but she wanted to come here, with Carter. It shocked her how much she wanted it, and how hot it made her to think of Carter watching her ride the bull.

A hand slid around her waist. "See something you like?" Carter murmured and nipped her earlobe.

"Yes," she admitted.

"You can tell me all about it on the car ride home. When Liam's a little bit bigger and you can leave him for an evening, we'll come to the club," Carter said.

Deep down, Jenna knew they'd turned another invisible corner. Yes, she'd already met his friends, but this was different. They'd gone out in public as a couple. Carter had shown her off in front of other submissives and Doms, like he already considered her his.

Maybe her sister was right, and she was an idiot.

CHAPTER 17

*L*ast night Jenna had begged off and slept alone.

It had felt foreign. Strange, really, that she and Carter had only been back in each other's lives a little over a week and she already had separation anxiety. But she'd needed the night to get her head on straight, or at least attempt it. It had given her time to make some decisions.

Jenna was unsure that being with Carter was a good idea, but wild horses couldn't drag her away from him. She'd fought it, fought her feelings for him, hadn't wanted to surrender to them. But it was like trying to swim upstream: a lot of work and pointless in the end because it wasn't giving her any peace or satisfaction.

She loved Carter.

She just didn't know what to do with that love. But today, after a full inventory of all the gifts from his friends, Carter had dragged her and Liam into town to shop. Not necessarily her most favorite thing in the world to do. Mainly because, over the years, she'd had to stick to a fairly frugal budget. Today's little excursion had been like something out of a fantasy, and one she wasn't entirely comfortable with.

They were now the proud owners of the baby aisles from the local superstore center. Carter had been true to his word. But that was him, honorable to a fault. He made a promise, he kept it. In fact, he'd purchased so much for Liam, he had to hire one of the workers just getting off their shift to follow behind them in their truck with the rest of their loot.

When they returned, she'd been exhausted, and so had Liam. They had ended up taking a nap while Carter had unloaded the two truckloads of baby goods.

Jenna was in the rocker, nursing Liam, when Carter strode in. The man took her breath away. Striking and sinfully handsome—a mere glance at him and her body purred.

"Did you two have a good nap?" he asked as his gaze roamed over her, causing tendrils of need to slide through her veins.

"Yes, we did. I can't believe how worn out I was when we returned," she said, shifting Liam to her shoulder to burp him.

"Well, when you finish burping him, we should go across the hall and you can check out the nursery," Carter murmured.

"You finished it? Already?" They had bought a mountain of items. He couldn't have put it all together while they'd slept.

"Most of the furniture, yes. You will have to tell me where you want everything in his room. But the bulk has been put together. I will leave it to you to organize it how you see fit," he said, sitting down in the leather chair beside her.

The man amazed her. Which was why she had made at least one decision that she believed would work well for both of them. She said, "I did want to let you know that I have thought about your offer about being the ranch's bookkeeper."

"And?"

"I accept the position. Maybe we should install the temporary basis deal so we can make sure it's the right fit."

"Good. You can start tomorrow," Carter said with a devastating smile.

"I'll have to bring Liam with me to the stables, but we can manage and adjust as needed."

"Yes, you can, and we'll figure it out as we proceed. I have every confidence in you. If you're ready, let's go across the hall," he said and stood.

Carter picked Liam up. He always seemed to do that—hold Liam whenever he got the chance. It was one of the many things she loved about him. He really was already such a wonderful, attentive father.

The door to Liam's nursery was directly across the hallway from Carter's bedroom. They walked the short distance. Carter, his gaze steady on her, held the door open. She walked in and stood rooted to the spot. It was amazing.

"Carter. It's wonderful," she said.

He'd erected the crib and furniture. Put the mattress and bedding together in the crib. He'd added the mobile. She loved the little forest critters; the foxes, deer, and rabbits. So did Liam. She turned on the mobile and Liam grinned, a line of drool running down his chin.

"You like your room, my love? Your daddy did a wonderful job, didn't he?" Jenna said. Carter had also brought in all the presents they'd received yesterday and had stacked things in the corner for her to wade through.

"You really like it?" Carter asked.

"I can't believe you did all this while we took a nap," she said, walking around the room, touching the dresser and changing table. He'd hung up the pictures and designs, and added shelving for Liam's books. The chest they'd been given was open, with the pile of toys inside. Carter had thought of everything.

Yes, he'd done this for Liam, but it wasn't lost on her that he'd partially done it for her as well.

"I might have had a little help. Spencer," he admitted with a sly grin.

"He was here? I didn't hear a word." Which meant she'd been beyond exhausted.

Carter rolled his shoulders with a shrug like it was no big deal. Going on instinct, she went to him, leading with her heart and not her head for once. She slid a hand around his neck, leaned up on tiptoes, and kissed him with everything she was. He held Liam in one arm but his other slid around her waist, holding her close, and kissed her back with enough heat to singe the soles of her feet.

Then Liam squirmed, and she knew they needed to stop, but she adored kissing this man. Carter lifted his mouth, his gaze dark with hunger, his grip tight on her waist.

"I have one more thing I wanted to show you," he said.

"Okay, lead the way," she said, wondering what the man had up his sleeve. He led them back across the hall, but this time to his room. Other than during the tour of the house, she'd not ventured into his room. Strange, really, that she hadn't crossed this threshold. Deep down, she knew it was her way of erecting a barrier between them.

His room was richly appointed, just as most of the rooms were, but utterly masculine in appearance. It reminded her of Carter. All the furniture in here was extra-large, from his custom made oak four-poster bed, to the leather bench and seating area with two leather recliners in a deep espresso color. She spied the open door to his bathroom and caught a glimpse inside.

Yet it was what he'd erected at the foot of his massive wooden bed that stalled her forward progression into his domain. It was another bassinette, with a reflux pillow inside.

"I'd like you and Liam to start joining me in here at night. Sleep in here with me," Carter said, observing her reaction to his room.

"I don't know. Do I have to decide tonight?" Her heart

wanted him so much. It was her head that was the problem. She wished she wasn't so conflicted.

"That wasn't a request. As my sub, Jenna, this is where you belong, and you know it. Frankly, if I have to tie you to the bed to see it done, then I will," he chewed out, his hazel eyes flashing with fury. The man would do it, too.

It was just a room. She knew that. But once she was in here, there would be a permanence there. Right now, she at least had a retreat. Except, then she saw it: a brief glimmer of pain in Carter's gaze. It was gone in a blink, replaced by an uncompromising, furious Dom.

"Can we compromise?" she said, regretting the hurt she was causing. He didn't deserve that.

Frustrated, he ran a hand through his hair and asked, "What did you have in mind?"

"We rotate nights between your room and mine. I'm not trying to be difficult, but babies don't like change. Something as simple as moving Liam over one room could make him cranky. I'm just asking that we ease into it," Jenna said.

"Fine. But tonight, I want you in here. I've wanted you in my bed for nearly a year, and I'll not wait any longer," Carter said. His visage brooked no room for argument. How could she deny him that when he'd been so wonderful to her? And she was just the most wretched woman alive. She couldn't deny him.

To soften and smooth the tension between them, she demurred and said, "Yes, Sir. Liam and I will sleep in here with you."

CHAPTER 18

*T*he next day, Carter showed Jenna the office she would be using at the stables. The interior room wasn't large, only about ten feet by ten feet, with a desk, few shelves and computer, but she somehow looked right there.

Her office was part of a series of five. Carter's was two doors away. He didn't mind the separation. In fact, it was probably good that she wasn't right next door. If they were going to be working together, distance would be crucial. He'd carted in file folders of receipts, invoices and payments that needed to be added into the system. He showed her the computer program the ranch used and then left her to sort through it. She'd brought Liam down with her. He could see that he would need to get some duplicates of things for Liam here at the stables so Jenna could work.

Eventually, she'd need a playpen and other supplies down here to make her life easier. That was part of his mission, to make her life better.

Dottie had delivered boxed lunches for everyone. He grabbed two, along with a couple of waters, and headed to

Jenna's office. He wasn't certain what he would find. He knew his accounting was a mess so he was amazed to see Jenna sitting at the desk, a stack of files, neat and orderly, beside her.

"Do you realize you've been overpaying for extra feed for months?" she asked, not looking up from the computer. Her fingers were typing with speed.

"No, I didn't." He shook his head and had to hide his grin.

"Well, you have, by quite a bit in my estimate. I already contacted the feed store. They've agreed to take the amount off the next few billing statements."

He'd always known she was whip smart intelligent. This just proved he'd been right to offer her the position.

"You figured that out in, what, two hours?" he said, a bit taken aback. He himself had stared at the pile of receipts with dawning horror and avoidance.

"Yeah. Numbers have always been my thing," she said and shrugged one delicate shoulder. It made her tits jiggle and he nearly sawed off his tongue.

"Here, I have lunch. Why don't you join me at the table and take a break?" He indicated the small table in the corner with two chairs.

"Well, if the boss says I must, I must," she replied.

"Where's Liam?" he asked, not seeing him anywhere.

"Dottie. She stopped by and said she'd watch him until three for me. I'd just fed him, so he should be fine with her for the time being," she explained.

He gave her a sly grin and flipped the lock on her office door. Plans for their lunch had just changed.

"Carter? What are you doing?" Jenna asked, a blush spreading over her cheeks. The woman knew exactly what he was doing.

"Strip, and prop that pretty ass of yours over on the table," he commanded.

She sat back in her chair and said, "Carter, we're working. This is what I was worried about: that we would mix business with other things."

"You're officially off the clock for the next hour. So right now, you're just my sub and I plan to fuck you. Clothes off, now. Don't make me tell you again."

He noticed her nipples had beaded beneath her top and felt his cock swell.

Jenna set down the file she'd been working on and hit a few buttons on the computer, likely saving her work. Then she stood and walked over to the table. He set their lunches on her desk. They'd get to the food eventually. Right now, he hungered for her.

He watched as she removed her bright yellow top. And then her cotton bra. Who knew that cotton could be sexy? He knew she wore it because it was easier for her to nurse their son, but he'd never look at cotton deridingly again. The heavy globes of her boobs made his mouth water. He'd always loved her tits, but now she was nursing their son they were exceptional.

Then she slid her jeans down her lithe, toned legs. Her black lace panties followed the same path.

Carter closed the distance between them. Lifting her up by the waist, he deposited her on the table. Gripping the back of her head, tilting her face up to his, he claimed her lips in a demanding, torrid exchange. She'd caved and slept in his room last night. Liam had done perfectly fine with the change of scenery. It was Jenna who'd had a hard time.

He wanted to prove to her that they were meant to be. Imprint himself so deeply on her heart and soul that she wouldn't ever think of leaving. He wasn't a man who was fanciful or who believed in fairy tales, but he knew deep in his gut that if soulmates were real, Jenna was his. Then his free hand trailed between her thighs and he found her drenched.

"Christ, Jenna. I can't wait. I need to be inside you now," he said, freeing his turgid shaft as he pressed her upper torso down to lie back against the table. At his words, she mewled in the back of her throat.

He rubbed his cock through her folds and hissed at the silky smooth feel of her flesh. He pressed forward, furrowing his dick inside her quivering heat until he sank inside and was balls deep.

"Cup your tits for me, darlin'," he commanded.

She did as he asked, gripping the large, pillowy glands. He positioned her legs so that her calves rested on each of his shoulders. He gripped her thighs as he moved, pumping his cock in short brutal digs. He pumped hard. The table vibrated beneath her with his movements. He watched the play of emotions cross her face as he fucked her, loving the way her tits jiggled.

Christ, she was beautiful. Open and erotic, and her pussy fit him like a fucking glove. He loved the little mewls she made. The way her sheath clenched around his cock and tried to pull him deeper as he penetrated her.

Her blue eyes were half-closed in her passion, her face a mask of pure, unadulterated desire. He changed the angle and leaned forward, penetrating her more deeply.

"Carter?"

"Come, Jenna. Come for me now."

Her eyes went wide as she came. Her body trembled and quaked in his arms. He growled as he unleashed his passion, fucking her with a frenzy and a mind for reaching his own blistering climax. Her pussy spasmed around him a second time and took him over the edge.

"Jenna," he bellowed as he came, thrusting wildly into her sweet cunt.

He rocked inside her until every drop of semen and every

shudder had stopped. Carter kissed her, telling her with more than words that he loved her. He knew he needed to tell her his feelings, but he worried that they wouldn't be returned.

Yet the way she kissed him back and clung to him gave him hope.

CHAPTER 19

*J*enna settled into a rhythm that week with her new schedule. On Mondays, Wednesdays, and Fridays, she would spend a few hours in what was now her office to work on the accounts for the ranch. On Tuesday and Thursday afternoons, she did her online coursework. Meghan came out to the ranch to watch Liam on those days.

Carter was taking full advantage of having her work in such close proximity.

It was Friday, and it had been a full week. She was tired, not from Liam keeping her up, but from working. Jenna felt good, really, startlingly good for the first time in ages. Liam had slept an entire five hour stretch last night, which meant she'd gotten one heck of a lot more sleep than she had gotten in months. She was working again. And it felt so good to be useful, to know that she was drawing a salary and income. That she wasn't dependent on anyone.

It was late Friday afternoon and she had a question about one of the accounts before she could head home. She went searching for Carter. Every day she watched him work in the stables with the horses, she was amazed by him. The man worked incredibly hard. She'd known cerebrally that running a ranch, especially one as big as his, would take a lot of time and energy. But until she'd started doing the books, she'd had no idea how intricate his work was, nor how much he was in the thick of it, day in and day out.

Jenna had a newfound respect for the man. And she had to admit, the more time she spent with him, the deeper in love she fell. He hadn't pushed her on consolidating their bedrooms, but she knew she was the holdout.

It was fear. Plain and simple.

But when you'd lived the entire past twenty years of your existence with the other shoe dropping, it was difficult not to expect the same thing in this situation. And perhaps if she wasn't so in love with Carter she could hardly see straight, it wouldn't matter. But it felt like there was this huge, enormous elephant in the room. That eventually bad luck would catch up with her and take away all the joy and happiness Carter brought to her life.

She felt complete with him.

He wasn't in his office, which meant he could be anywhere. Both Kyle and Herb were at lunch. This week they'd hired two new hands, Joe MacIntosh and Dave Boyd, to work with the horses. They were both presently out in the fields checking on the mares since they'd caught a teensy break in the oppressive heat.

Carter emerged from one of the stalls.

"Hey there, darlin', aren't you a sight?" His enigmatic gaze raked over her.

She blushed. She couldn't help it when he went all soft and countrified. Clearing her throat, she said, "I have a question about one of the accounts when you get a minute."

"I have a minute. But I don't want to talk business. Not after finally seeing you in a proper pair of boots. Come with me." He gripped her hand and tugged her along behind him.

"Where are we going?" She asked.

Carter pulled her into a nearby stall that was currently unoccupied, then pressed her back up against the wall and kissed her. This wasn't a tepid peck either, but a full on kiss that made her brainless in less than five seconds. Whatever she was going to ask him about the accounts fled with every thrust of his tongue inside her mouth.

Carter's fingers undid her jeans and then his hand slid under her panties to stroke her folds. She moaned into his mouth.

"Hush," he ordered against her lips.

Then he plunged two fingers inside her channel and she was lost. She rocked into his hand as he plunged his fingers. He wasn't shy but finger-fucked her brutally. The force, the hard thrusts, rocketed her body to a startling, intense orgasm that left her whimpering into his mouth.

Then he removed his hand and pulled her to the ground. He positioned her on all fours, then drew her jeans and panties down to her knees. It trapped her, she couldn't spread her legs wide at all. But Carter seemed unconcerned.

At the sound of his zipper lowering she almost purred. She couldn't believe how hot this man made her. Every time, her desire for him increased. And then his thick cock was pushing inside her pussy. The way her legs were positioned made her channel tighter. With his girth, it felt amazing, and her eyes slid closed as they rolled back in her head. He gripped her hips, his fingers bruising as they dug in and he established a punishing fast, hard pace.

Carter pounded his cock inside her. When she couldn't contain her moans, he slid a palm over her mouth and silenced her. This wasn't a gentle meandering tempo but a race to the damn finish line. He was fucking her senseless and she loved it. Loved him. Couldn't say no to him.

She came, wailing into his palm. Tremors wracked her

frame at the explosive force of her orgasm. Carter hissed, stiffening as he plunged. Then hot streams of semen filled her pussy, sending another ripple of spasms through her body.

He lay against her back as he held her for a few minutes while their heart rates returned to normal. Jenna wanted to slide into a heap on the floor of the stall and not move.

But Carter withdrew his softening shaft and moved away. Then he helped her back onto her feet, and they both readjusted their clothing before he said, "You had something you needed with the accounts?"

"Yeah, if you will follow me to my office. There's an account that I don't know what it's for," she said.

Carter nodded as they left the stall and walked toward the bank of offices.

"Probably the new one I set up for Liam," he commented near her door.

Already in her office, she turned and said, "What? Carter—"

"If you're going to reprimand me, just realize I will pay you back in kind when we are alone and redden that ass of yours," he warned her with a stern glance.

Had she been that horrible a shrew when he was just being kind and considerate, wanting to take care of Liam? Probably. Proof positive that sleep deprivation and inactivity were bad bedfellows for her. Instead of berating him, she walked over to him, slid her arms around his waist and hugged him.

"Thank you, Carter. Liam is lucky to have you as his father," she murmured into his chest.

For a moment, he stood stock still before he enfolded her in his arms. He kissed her forehead and said, "Thank you for that."

CHAPTER 20

*C*arter startled awake. He'd gone to bed alone tonight. After finding Jenna and Liam asleep already, he'd given her a reprieve, not wanting to wake her. He could see the weariness in her gaze every day. Taking care of their son, the midnight hours she was up caring for him, were draining her. So he'd chosen not to disturb her, to give her the night to herself.

Yet now she was here. In his room, his bed. A vision in seductive white. Carter was instantly hard. Fuck, he wanted to claim her. Make his mark on her to warn other Doms away. She set a walkie-talkie style baby monitor remote on his nightstand.

"Need something, Jenna?" he asked, his voice rough from sleep and the lust pounding through his body.

She straddled him and drew her nightgown up over her head, revealing her gorgeous body. Her tits swayed, heavy and enticing. Motherhood looked good on her.

"Yes, Sir. You, please. I need you," she begged and leaned forward, nipped his chin, and rocked her hips against his cock. At the feel of her breasts pressed against his chest, he growled, then rolled over, pinning her body beneath his. Her admission made him feel like he could take on the world. It was progress in his quest to claim her, not just for the night or temporarily, but forever. He wanted her, like this, in his bed and his life, for as long as he drew breath into his lungs.

Carter lowered his mouth, possessing hers with a guttural moan. He wanted her surrender, her submission, but more importantly, he wanted her heart. He explored her mouth. Instead of giving her the flash bang fireworks that always seemed to be present whenever they touched, he meandered. Kissing her deeply, thrusting his tongue inside in long, languid strokes.

Her body softened beneath his, from the livewire of need she'd been into a slow burn of aching desire. Her hands clutched at his shoulders. She returned his kiss, her tongue sliding along his, and liquid tugs of need pooled in his core. As hard as he was, he wanted to draw it out. Dominate the very fabric of her being until he was the only one she wanted.

He kissed her until she was clawing at his shoulders and rocking her hips against his. He lifted his head and nearly lost his nerve as she looked at him with such passion and desire. She made him lose control. It took everything in him not to plunge ahead and forget his seductive campaign.

He circled her wrists, removing them from his neck. He drew her arms above her head with one hand. Reaching over to his nightstand with the other, he grabbed a pair of leather cuffs. The same ones she'd worn on the island.

"You kept them?" she murmured the moment she spied them.

"Of course I did. They look good on you. And I've been waiting for the right moment to put them back on you," he said, fastening them around her delicate wrists. Then he connected them to a loop on his headboard.

"Carter," Jenna purred.

He caressed her cheek. "Just enjoy, darlin'. Come as many times as you need to."

She moaned, and he felt it in his chest. By the time he was done with her tonight, her body would crave none other but his, forever. After a brief, hungry kiss, he moved to her boobs. Cupping the heavy globes in his hands, he took his time exploring them, laving her engorged nipples. They were nearly always swollen and puckered. He fucking loved it, enjoying the taste of her as he sucked on the buds.

Then he moved, traveling south until his face was nestled between her thighs. Christ, she made a picture, restrained and naked in his bed. Her thighs spread before him. Her gaze was at half mast, passion blazing in the blue depths of her eyes. It was the most beautiful sight he'd ever seen. Love for her swamped him and drove him onward. Spreading her pussy folds, he swiped his tongue across her clit. At her garbled groan, satisfaction speared through him

And then he ate her pussy, letting her flavor linger on his tongue. Her musky scent filled his nostrils and spurred him on. Her cries pierced the stillness as he teased her nub until it swelled.

"Sir," she cried. Her dew flooded his mouth and he growled, wanting more from her, wanting all of her.

He feasted on her cunt, penetrating her sheath, holding her hips steady, watching the rise and fall of her breasts as desire overrode her. He loved the way she trembled in his arms. How she strained in his cuffs—the only cuffs she would ever wear again if he had anything to do with it. Her sharp mewls, as she came again and again against his mouth.

Soon she was mindless and begging, her pleas adding embers to the inferno of desire raging through his bloodstream. Yet he didn't stop. Sweat slicked his form. His dick strained to feel the hot clasp of her pussy, and still he drove her body up another peak.

And then he felt it. The moment she let go and surrendered herself fully into his hands. He bit down on her clit and she screamed. Her body quaked as she climaxed.

Carter lifted his head, his chin coated with her juices, and crawled his way up her body until they were chest to chest. Her breasts pressed against him, tiny trails of milk leaking from them.

Grasping his dick, he fit the crest between her swollen folds, poised to penetrate, and growled, "Look at me."

Her eyelids fluttered open. Only then did he slide home, thrusting until he was buried so deep, his crown grazed the lip of her womb. Her eyes began to slide shut once more. He gripped her throat with one hand and said, "Keep your eyes on me, darlin', or I will stop and make you watch me masturbate."

Her gaze snapped back open and she moaned, "Yes, Sir."

His other hand palmed her ass, holding her steady as he ground his hips, his cock plunging deep. He fucking loved how her cunt squeezed him. She was so damn tight. Her Kegel muscles fluttered around his girth, trying to draw him deeper.

He controlled his strokes and measured his thrusts, watching her expression as he delved deep with each penetration. She writhed beneath him. His fingers dug into her ass.

Sweat slicked his back. Yet still he pressed on, drawing her legs up around his waist. Changing the angle, pounding deeper. He reveled in her moans. In the way her arms strained their bonds.

Carter increased his tempo. His own needs battered at his control. It was all Jenna. She'd been the only sub to ever upend his control, make him crave her flesh, her body, like he needed air to breathe.

"Please, Sir!" she cried raggedly.

His control snapped. Carter let loose and hammered his cock inside her quaking heat. Over and over, he plunged. Lightning arced along his spine. Jenna's moans spurred him

ANYA SUMMERS

onward. He gathered her close and buried his face against her shoulder. He slammed his cock in short, brutal digs.

His dick swelled.

"Oh god, Sir," Jenna wailed. Her pussy clamped around his thrusting member.

Her climax set off a chain reaction. Carter thrust, his body strained. His cock surged as semen poured into her quaking pussy. He glided in and out, rocking his hips until the last drop.

"I can't wait to put you on a St. Andrew's Cross again and flog your sweet ass," he murmured against her throat. Her pussy clenched around his cock and he chuckled. "I think someone else wants that too."

He reached up above their heads and undid her restraints, unlatching the cuffs from the headboard. But he left them on her wrists. They were where they belonged. He gave her a brief, tender kiss before he withdrew his softening shaft from her channel. Then he shifted, rolling onto his back. He drew her body with his so that she lay against his side, her head pillowed on his chest.

"What are we doing here, Carter? Because if it's just scratching an itch, I think it would be best if we stop. That tonight should be it. For Liam's sake, I don't want things to end badly, and if we're just screwing each other because we're convenient, then—"

Carter tensed beside her. He cupped her chin and drew her gaze up to his, then said, "You're not convenient, Jenna. I haven't been with another sub, another woman, since our time together on the island. There's been no one but you. Do you understand?"

"Wait, what? You haven't? Why not?" she asked.

"I have feelings for you, Jenna. And I think, if you admit it, you have feelings for me too. From the very beginning, this has always been more than scratching an itch."

"I do," she admitted, then shifted her gaze away.

"But?" He hated that he had to press her. But they had reached a tipping point in their relationship. He felt it, and knew she did too.

"I'm terrified, Carter," she admitted, and he spied the sheen of moisture lining her lashes.

Christ, why hadn't he seen that? Maybe because she was always so fierce, so independent, so determined to forge ahead on her own that he'd never for one second believed she was afraid. Every protective instinct he had barreled to the forefront. He wanted to shield her, have her lean against him and let him battle her monsters. He asked, tracing his thumb over her cheek, "Why? You know that you're safe with me."

"Because what happens to me when you get bored and don't want me anymore? I learned at a really young age not to depend upon anyone. I don't know if I have it in me to trust someone fully, to submit completely. And eventually that lack of ability in me will wear thin and you won't want me anymore," she admitted, a few stray tears escaping.

Why hadn't he seen just how traumatized she was by the last year? Hell, by a lifetime of having to be so incredibly strong in the face of such a daunting task as caring for everyone else. It struck him then. And yes, he was a bit slow on the uptake. She'd not had anyone take care of her since she was a little girl. For all that she was submissive—and she was—she'd spent such a long time holding things together, she didn't know how to let another care for her.

He made the vow here and now, that he would prove it to her. Teach her how to let him care for her. That was his job as her Dom. And he was hers in every sense of the word.

Cradling her face, he murmured, "Baby, listen. Life's not certain. You know that. But I know I want you more than anything in my life. Trust me to care for you. Give me your cares and worries. I won't leave you alone to face them. You have to know that by now."

"Because of Liam?" she asked, and her lower lip trembled.

"No. Even without him, I would want you. I'm turning the tables. Am I just convenient for you? Was there another Dom after me? I'm okay if there was, we made no commitment to each other on the island. But am I keeping you from someone you would rather be with?"

She shook her head and replied, "No, there's been no one since. And I'm not sure, Carter. What we had on the island seems so long ago… after everything that's happened since then, I don't know if it's smart of me—or us—to go down this path again. That doesn't mean I don't want you, because I do, with every fiber of my being. I'm just not sure it's wise, though, for either of us."

"I see," he replied. His heart squeezed painfully. Carter couldn't do half measures with her anymore. He couldn't love her and not have her in his bed permanently. It was clear that she wasn't on the same page as him.

He slid from his bed, unmindful of his nudity—or hers. Then he scooped her up in his arms. He carried her back into her room as she sputtered and clutched at his shoulders.

In her room, with the nightlight ablaze, he saw that Liam was sleeping peacefully in his bassinette. He deposited Jenna on her bed and withdrew from her. His heart felt like it was being wrenched from his chest.

"You let me know when you get that figured out. Until then, I ask that you stay out of my room," Carter murmured and turned away. He had to, feeling his heart break. He was playing for keeps and he wasn't certain she was all in. As much as he loved her, he wouldn't force her to love him back. Either she loved him or she didn't, but until she made up her mind, he was done playing house with her. He didn't want it to be play, he wanted it in truth, wanted it to be real. Wanted her to be the one who, forty years from now, he looked across the table at and smiled, knowing they'd made it together.

"Carter?" Jenna said when he reached the door, her voice ragged.

He turned and looked at her in the bed, the sheets clutched to her chest. Her golden hair tumbled around her shoulders and her lips were swollen from his kisses. "Yes?"

"I'm sorry."

The finality of it struck him. He felt like King Tut had just kicked him in the gut. All the oxygen expelled from his lungs and he needed to escape before she witnessed the devastation her words had wrought. With a brief nod, he fled, closing the door quietly behind him so he didn't disturb Liam.

He retrieved a pair of sweats from his room, then strode down to his stocked bar in the game room and proceeded to do something he hadn't done in years. He drank until he passed out, until he no longer felt like he was hemorrhaging internally.

CHAPTER 21

*J*enna was at a crossroads and uncertain about the direction she should take. She'd messed up with Carter. Big time. The man was barely speaking to her. And well, why would he? She'd all but told him she didn't trust him—when that wasn't the case. She didn't trust herself; trust herself to love him and not lose herself in him.

Jenna noticed the drastic change in Carter since that fateful night. And it was not for the better. He'd withdrawn. Erected barriers between them. They conversed about work as she tallied and waded through the ranch accounts. They made small talk over dinner. He spent every evening with Liam. Those two were bonding like mad. She could tell they would be thick as thieves as Liam grew. Carter didn't hold back his enthusiasm or his warmth from their son. He took him to the stables. Read to him. She'd started pumping breast-milk for bottles and Carter would feed him. Carter held nothing back when it came to Liam. It was her he distanced himself from.

There were no more kisses or midnight lovemaking sessions. No teasing. No holding her while she fed Liam. He rarely ventured past her bedroom door. A week passed, then another, and the distance between them was killing her.

She discovered his dungeon one day while Liam was napping, comically enough, in the basement behind the locked door. She'd located the key easily behind the bar in the game room. The dungeon was filled with every piece of naughty furniture imaginable. A ghost of an idea surfaced, which she quickly smothered that night when Carter barely even glanced in her direction over dinner.

Today, Meghan was watching Liam while she completed her online class, microeconomics. She was in the sunroom and submitting her work when Meghan strolled in with Liam. She was outfitted in her resort uniform already; skin-tight tan cargo pants and a fitted black polo, her blonde hair pulled back in a thick braid.

"What have you two been up to?" Jenna asked as they approached her. She closed her laptop, her attention diverted to her son.

"We did some tummy time and some bouncy seat, then we read some stories and played," Meghan said, handing him over.

"Say, you love hanging out with your Aunt Meghan, don't you, my love?" Liam grinned and kicked his feet.

Meghan joined her on the lounger, sitting near the end, and asked, "What's going on, Jenna?"

"I don't know what you mean."

Meghan rolled her eyes and said, "Between you and Carter. I've noticed the strain between the two of you the last few times I've been here. What happened? I thought things were going so well."

Deflated, Jenna confessed, "I messed things up. It's my fault and I don't know how to fix it."

"Do you want to?"

"Yeah, I do, but I think I pushed him too far. Serves me right. I should never have let things get so complicated between us, should have kept my distance and made it all about Liam."

"Jenna, I don't buy that. You've got to stop living in the past. I know you had it rough taking care of all of us, but you have to know that Carter's not Dad. He's not going to fall apart when something bad happens and make you pick up the pieces."

"Meghan!" Jenna exclaimed.

"What? I loved Dad with everything I am but that doesn't mean I didn't see his faults or love him any less because of them. He placed a heavy burden on your shoulders at a young age because he couldn't deal. That's on Dad, a reflection of him, not you. And then again when he got sick, begging promises out of you that you never should have had to live up to. Including taking care of me and helping me with college. I'm sorry I let you handle that burden for me. I didn't really understand the toll it was taking on you. I'm going to pay you back every cent. I know I don't have to, but I want to. You can put it into a college fund for this little guy if you don't want it. But I'm going to give you a piece of advice. A man like Carter doesn't come along very often. He's a rare find. I know you love him."

Jenna admitted, "I do, but how do you know that?"

"Because I know you. And you don't get bent out of shape for nothing, only for those you care about. Jenna, you would donate body parts to the people you love if they needed them. It's time you started giving yourself the same care. I've never seen you so happy as you've been with Carter—when you allowed yourself to be. So fix it. I think you know how, you're just too afraid to take the leap."

"But what if he doesn't want me anymore? What if I killed whatever was there because I'm an idiot?" Jenna whispered her deepest fear.

"Jenna, any other man would have tossed you out. While I might not have been his cheerleader from the start, I've watched him with you and the man adores you. He's not going to let you down and make you carry his burdens like Dad did. In fact, I think if you let him, he'd shoulder yours."

"What would you do, if you were in my shoes?" Jenna asked.

"For the right guy, the real question is what wouldn't I do," Meghan replied, her gaze steady and filled with warmth.

There was a knock on the door. Jenna and Meghan glanced over. Spencer filled the doorway, a gift box in his hands. He wore a black tee that stretched across his chest with the name of a band on it. His jeans were fitted, stressed at the knees. His aviator sunglasses were hooked into the neckline of his shirt.

At the sight of him, Meghan stood and said, "I've got to get to work. Think about what I said."

Her sister marched toward the doorway that Spencer currently occupied.

"Do you mind?" Meghan gestured in her attempt to pass by him.

"Actually, I do. You don't have to rush off on my account," Spencer replied, glancing at Meghan, his black gaze unreadable as he stared at her.

"Please. Like you bother me. I have to get to work at the resort, not that it's any of your business. But I will send you a bill if my pay is docked because you wouldn't let me pass."

"What you deserve, little brat, is a red ass," Spencer quipped.

"You think that's going to scare me or make me cower and tremble before you? Please. I've known better and had better. Put your hands on me and I will break your thing off," Meghan threatened sweetly with a gamine grin.

"Meghan!" Jenna said, aghast that she'd threatened a Dom that way.

Meghan shrugged. "He deserves it for being a dick. Catch you later, sis."

Spencer stepped back, and she thought she heard him say to Meghan, "One day, little brat, I will make you eat those words."

Meghan glared up at him and then smiled. "In your wet dreams, dickwad." Then she flounced out of the room, her footsteps retreating down the hall. Spencer watched her leave with a shuttered expression.

"Sorry about my sister, she can be a little testy at times," Jenna said. She was going to have to work overtime to keep those two apart. They were the epitome of oil and water—chemical components that couldn't be anywhere near the other without dire consequences.

"She's her own person. There's nothing for you to apologize for. I had a little something for Liam that I had ordered and didn't arrive in time for the shower," Spencer said, approaching with the box in hand.

"You didn't have to drive all the way out here just to deliver this. It's very sweet of you," Jenna replied, putting Liam in his carrier seat and taking the box from his hands.

"Carter and I have a meeting about club business tonight. He couldn't come into town so I drove out here. It's not an extra trip."

"You really didn't have to do this," she said, lifting the top of the box. Inside was a tiny cowboy hat. "Oh my gosh, where did you find this? It's adorable. I can't believe you found a hat this small."

Spencer shrugged. "Carter's the first member of our little club to have offspring. It's appropriate. When you're ready and fully healed, you should come to the club with him one night. I know you hit it off with a few of the subs, and it would do you good to forge friendships with them. It can be pretty lonely at times living out here, and it would be good for you to have some other women to talk to besides that one." He indicated to the space her sister had recently occupied.

"Thank you. I appreciate the invitation, but I don't know that Carter will take me. He's... never mind, we're not what you think or assume we are," Jenna said, the reality of their situation feeling like a dagger to the heart.

Spencer slid his hands into his jeans pockets and pierced her with an inquisitive gaze. "Look, Jenna, I realize you don't know me well but I'm going to give you a word of advice."

"Okay," she replied.

"Cut the bullshit. It's obvious to me and anyone else that you care for him. All you're doing is denying you both a chance and for what? I might add. Get your head out of your ass. Carter's one of my best friends. I watched him search heaven and earth for you for months. He never stopped looking for you, never even set foot in Cuffs & Spurs. He wants you more than I've ever seen him want anyone. And if you honestly can't care for him, make the break now and save him the heartache," Spencer said with a ruthless undertone in his voice.

She sat back in her seat, a little stunned by his diatribe. Perhaps she shouldn't be. It was just that everyone else seemed to see things clearly when all she saw was murky water.

"Just think about it and do it fast, because while Carter's the best man I know, even he has his limits. So don't yank his chain if you have no intention of following through. Decide whether you're all in or not, and do it soon," Spencer warned.

She finally found her voice and replied, "I'm trying, but it's complicated."

He shrugged. "So uncomplicate it. Ask yourself this: do you want him, and are you willing to risk your heart?"

Jenna said, "Yes, but I'm terrified. What if—"

"Sweetheart, living your life safe that way, playing the 'what if' game, isn't really living and you know it. Seems to me, you're not just afraid of Carter but of truly living. Take it from someone who knows life is far too fucking short to dither back and forth over something this important. And here's another thing to consider: Carter would walk through hellfire for you. That's not a man who's going anywhere, he's as solid as the mountains surrounding Jackson and twice as steady. Give him your trust, he deserves it."

Liam chose that moment to stir in his seat and begin to fuss. Jenna dropped her gaze to her son, who looked more and more like Carter every day. She lifted him out of his carrier to calm him.

Spencer tipped his Stetson and said, "You two take care now, you hear?"

"You too. Thank you, Spencer. For everything. I will think over what you said," Jenna said.

He gave her a warm glance and Jenna realized he was also giving her his friendship, in a roundabout way. He said, "Anytime."

He left her in the sunroom, leaving her a good deal to consider. Both Spencer and Meghan had. Glancing down at Liam as he latched his mouth to her breast and fed, Jenna knew deep down they were both right. She'd held herself back from loving Carter for so many reasons, they were too numerous to count. She'd also been unfairly holding a measuring stick up to Carter that shouldn't exist.

She knew who and what she wanted. She just had to figure out how to get him back.

CHAPTER 22

*L*ate Saturday evening, Carter ambled into the kitchen for a beer after a long day in the stables and an evening spent entertaining. He'd been putting in extra time at the stables, picking up whatever slack he could to avoid the truth: he and Jenna were, at best, uneasy roommates. Roommates who shared a common interest, their son.

Jenna's sister was staying the night. She'd joined them for dinner and had interrupted some of his time with Liam. He liked Meghan, enjoyed her company, and she clearly doted on her nephew. But she was another barrier erected between him and Jenna. The separation, the distance seemed damn near insurmountable. Spencer had urged Carter to 'go all Dom on her cute ass'. His words.

He took a long draught of his beer. The thing was, he'd tried that. And it had failed. The kind of 'didn't see the iceberg until it was too late and struck the hull' fail. Clearly, she didn't have the same feelings for him that he did for her. He should let her go. Stop holding on to something that wasn't ever going to happen.

As if his thinking about her had conjured her appearance,

Jenna padded into the kitchen in a powder blue silk robe that made his mouth water and his cock stand at attention. It would be a lot easier to let her go if he didn't want her to distraction.

There was hesitation and uncertainty in her gaze as she approached. And why was that? Because he'd pushed her. He was a fool. Her scent was everywhere he went—the kitchen, his bedroom, the stables, even the game room—and he was living in hell. Looking at her now, her golden tresses spilling in enticing waves over her shoulders, the image of his every fantasy brought to life, craving her touch, yearning to feel her again, but being unable to touch her was a special slice of hell.

Tension riddled his frame. He needed to escape and lock himself in his room. Otherwise he was bound to do something he'd regret. He grunted, "What can I do for you Jenna?"

"Could you come with me, please?" she asked, and held a delicate hand out for him to take. Her eyes were bright blue pools and he felt he could drown within them. It would be so easy to back her up against the kitchen island and kiss her brainless. Erase the wall between them.

He asked, "Is it Liam? What's going on?"

"Just follow me, please," she pleaded and then he noticed the slight tremor in her hand. If she was brave enough to approach him, he would go with her.

Curious at her entreaty, he did as she asked and slid his hand around hers. He had to bite back the moan that wanted to escape at the pleasure coursing through him at feeling her touch again. Jenna turned on her heel and tugged him along behind her. She could be leading him to the gates of hell and he would follow her. He expected her to lead him upstairs, to his room or hers. It didn't matter. He was all in.

But she didn't take him up the stairs. Instead she went down, into his basement and the hallway to his personal dungeon. The door was slightly ajar, and the lights inside were ablaze. Dumbfounded, Carter let Jenna tow him inside before shutting the door behind him. She released his hand and then sashayed over to padded leather horse. He followed her, like a dog with a scent. Then she turned toward him. She untied her robe, letting it fall to the floor and pool at her feet. Beneath it, she was gloriously nude except for his cuffs. The sleeves of her robe had hidden that she was wearing them.

Christ, he never thought he'd see them on her wrists again.

She grabbed something off the horse and then knelt at his feet. She held up his black leather flogger and her eyes beseeched him. "Please, Sir."

He held still, his heart slowed. The electric current that was always present anytime they were near each other sparked and crackled. "Are you sure, darlin'? I don't want to hurt you."

"I need you to hurt me. I think that's what we've both needed. And I want you to, Carter. I need you, Sir. I know I ruined things between us." She bowed her head and he spied tears in her eyes.

He cupped her chin and drew her face up until their gazes met. "You didn't ruin things. We both did."

"You don't understand, Carter. I was punishing myself, I believed that I didn't deserve you. And I hurt you. I'm so sorry. Please forgive me. I never meant to cause you so much trouble."

Jenna kneeling before him, submitting to him, was the most beautiful, erotic sight in the world, and a gift he would cherish. He wanted her like this every night for the rest of their lives.

He hauled her up into his arms and kissed her. "Darlin', I don't want you to ever change. Not your fire or your spirit or the way you challenge me, because you give me what I need. Now, let's get you up on the bench, shall we?"

He lifted her up, setting her back down on the horse. How he had craved to bring her down here, to have her like this. He locked her in, attaching the cuffs at her wrists to the bench. Then he added leather restraints around her ankles and a strap across her lower back, and another across her upper torso, just beneath her cleavage.

He accepted the flogger from her hand. Cupping her chin, he gave her a wicked kiss that was all tongue and teeth.

"Use your safeword if you need it," he said, kneeling down to speak to her.

"Sir?" she asked before he stood.

"Yes?"

"Don't be gentle. I need the pain and so do you," she said.

"Baby," he murmured. If he didn't already love her to distraction, he would have fallen right then and there. "Just trust me to take care of you, all right?"

She nodded, her gaze infused with emotion that rocked him. He stood and divested himself of his tank top and sweats. He left his boxer briefs on for the time being. Because he wanted this to be as pleasurable as possible for her, he went to his dresser stocked with goodies and withdrew a small bullet vibrator with remote.

He returned and went to her rear. Her pussy was on display for him, the pretty pink lips spread. He inserted the bullet into her pussy and then turned it onto a medium setting. At her pleasured gasp, he smiled. This was only the beginning.

With her ass on display, Carter gripped the flogger in his hand, wound back, and cracked the leather across her butt cheeks. At her moan, pleasure flooded him. He set a rhythm, tuning in to every nuance, every cry and gasp. He watched the lines of her back, her body. Her hands, previously fisted against the leather, began to relax as he struck.

Her moans of pain turned to cries of ecstasy. Carter's need for her increased. She relaxed into his dominance. Let go of her control with every whack of leather across her bum. She was stunning in her surrender, in the gift she was giving him as she ceded control of her body into his hands.

He struck again and again, doing as she'd asked, not holding back but unleashing his nature upon her. He was so hard, his cock strained to feel the silken clasp of her cunt. And still, he didn't relent or stop. All the pain and suffering they had endured these last few weeks withered away with each sharp strike to her flesh. He loved the way her ass cheeks reddened and burned for him. Loved the mewls of pleasure she emitted with each blow. Loved seeing the dew coating her pussy and dripping onto the bench in her arousal.

With the next blow he landed, Jenna wailed and came, her body shuddering and trembling in her restraints. Tears poured from her closed lids. Her mouth was open, her sighs and moans music to his ears.

He would never forget tonight, nor the way she'd given him her surrender, freely and without question.

～

JENNA WAS in a haze as Carter knelt before her. The pride and care in his gaze warmed the recesses of her heart. She'd been right to trust him. But she wasn't done with him yet. She wanted everything from him.

When he moved to undo her restraints, his hands at her wrists, she murmured, "Please, Sir. Don't remove them yet."

Carter stilled. His glance connected with hers. He asked, "Are you sure you're up for it? I don't want to hurt you."

This was the reason why she loved him. He was steady and sure, honorable to a fault, and he would always put her well-being first. Deny himself and ensure she didn't hurt. He was everything, and she'd been a fool for holding herself back from him. She removed all her hesitations, letting her love for him show on her features and in her words. "Carter, fuck me. Like you did when we were at lookout point. Don't hold back. Give me all of you. I need you."

He cupped her face, his gaze searching. His thumbs brushed

her cheeks, the whispered caress zinging through her into the soles of her feet. With a guttural groan, he slanted his lips over hers. His torrid kiss stole the very air from her lungs. His tongue dueled with hers, drinking down her cries.

It was hard to believe she'd just climaxed, because his drugging, soul-stirring kiss made her ascend right back up into a pleasure-filled haze. She'd known deep down from the moment he'd first kissed her that there was no one else for her. He was it for her, he was everything. She poured her heart into her kiss. Holding nothing back. Giving him all of her, and more.

Carter released her lips. His gaze was clouded with lust and so much more, it humbled her. This big, dominant alpha, her Sasquatch, looked at her with such heart-rending emotion blazing within his hazel depths, she felt it keenly in her entire being.

Carter stood before her on the horse, his massive form blocking out the rest of his dungeon, wearing only a pair of black boxer briefs. She spied his erection. The thick shaft stretched the material and made her mouth water. She licked her lips when he shucked his pants, his cock bobbing into her line of sight.

He gripped his member with one hand and cupped her face with the other.

"Open up," he ordered, his voice low and infused with lust.

She did as he commanded. He fed the head of his cock into her mouth. She swished her tongue over the crown and lapped at the pearlescent bead of pre-cum before sucking his length inside her mouth. Carter's hands clasped the back of her head, holding her steady while he pumped his shaft in short digs.

He was so large, she had a difficult time taking him all the way down. The bullet still vibrated in her pussy while Carter fucked her mouth. Her fingers dug into the bench as pleasure bombarded her senses. She moaned around his cock, her mewls of ecstasy muffled.

Then Carter withdrew his shaft from her mouth and waltzed around the horse until he stood behind her. He shut off the bullet and removed it from her pussy. She whimpered at the loss. But then the head of his cock penetrated her sheath. Her mouth dropped open on a moan as he slid all the way home. That was what it felt like when he loved her—that she was finally home.

He held still, giving her body a second to adjust to his girth.

"Sir." She whimpered, craving the friction, the way it felt when he moved inside her.

His hands dug into her hips as he slid out until only the tip remained before slamming his cock inside until he hit the lip of her womb. He did it again. And again. His thrusts walking that razor-sharp line between pleasure and pain.

Jenna was overjoyed, her mouth open as she keened and dug her fingers into the horse. Carter pumped his hips, his cock pounded her sheath, sending delicious torrents of desire radiating through her body. Her nipples throbbed. Her pussy pulsed. She clenched her Kegels and elicited a groan from Carter.

She did it a second time. It was all the urging he needed. He unleashed his carnal desires upon her body and fucked her. He wasn't gentle or controlled as he jackhammered inside her pussy. Carter went wild. His hips rocked. The slap of flesh filled the dungeon, along with their combined moans.

Jenna could feel the etchings of her climax. She held on as long as she could, but Carter going dominant caveman on her was the hottest thing ever and she simply handed her release, her body, over to him.

He bent over her back, his hands gripped her shoulders, and he penetrated her deeper from this angle. His strokes pummeled her composure.

"Oh god, Sir!" She wailed as her pussy spasmed around his plunging cock. Her body exploded like a cataclysmic volcano. Quakes wracked her frame.

Carter strained, his cock jerking. "Jenna," he bellowed. Hot liquid streamed into her quivering folds, causing another series of explosions in her, with twin responses in her breasts. Milk leaked from her boobs onto the horse. Her pussy wept with dew and Carter's semen. Her body was slick with sweat.

And she'd never been so happy.

Carter turned her head and captured her mouth in a tender brush of lips. It always stunned her that a man so big and fierce could be so gentle and loving. She whimpered as he withdrew from her body. He left her for a minute and returned with warm washcloths, cleaning between her thighs. And then he removed her restraints and helped clean the seepage from her breasts and the bench. He kept kissing her, caressing her as he did, running a cloth over her breasts and down her torso. Then he helped her off the horse.

When her knees wobbled, he scooped her up in his arms. Unmindful of their nudity, he carried her from his dungeon.

"But someone might see us," she murmured against his chest.

"The only one here—besides our son—is your sister. And I doubt she's awake," he said. He bypassed the door to her room and went directly to his.

He laid her down upon his bed. "This is where you belong from here on out. I won't take no for an answer, not even if I have to tie you to my bed."

"There's no place I would rather be," she said sleepily. At Carter's breathtaking smile, she murmured, "Come to bed, Sir."

"I will. As soon as I collect our son." He kissed her on the nose, then retrieved Liam from his room and laid him in the bassinette at the foot of the bed.

Tonight had been a return to who they had been on the

island. A reclaiming. Jenna opened her arms to Carter as he joined her. He enveloped her in his embrace, their bodies entwined with the other, even as they fell asleep. She was right where she had belonged all along. And now that she was here, she didn't plan to waste another minute.

CHAPTER 23

The following morning, after Meghan left the ranch, Carter took Jenna and Liam on a picnic lunch. His arm was around Jenna's waist while they walked, her head against his shoulder as he pushed Liam in his stroller. He took them to a small abutment of land with a copse of trees that would provide ample shade for Liam and what he had planned.

Last night had changed their relationship for the better, and it was time to seize on their progress. When they reached the abutment, they worked together, setting up their picnic. He parked Liam's stroller next to one of the trees. They spread a large blanket over the ground. And then Carter lifted the detachable carrier and set it on the blanket with the picnic basket Dottie had put together for them. He'd snuck a few more items inside.

They sat overlooking his land underneath the copse of trees. There was a gentle breeze carrying a hint of pine and grass. They still hadn't gotten any rain, although it had cooled some. But that was a worry for another day. Today, he had plans to see through to completion.

"It's so beautiful up here, Carter. Thank you for bringing us.

And Liam loves the leaves, don't you, my love?" Jenna said, as Liam yawned and shut his eyes in his seat.

"I can see he's real impressed with them. You like it here, Jenna? Living with me?" Carter asked.

"Yes. I know I was hesitant at first, but I love it here. Why? Is something wrong? Do you not want us here anymore?" she asked and bit her lower lip, but not before he noticed it was trembling.

He tugged her onto his lap. Framing her face with his hands, he stared into her bright blue eyes. "I love you, Jenna. I want you and Liam to stay with me, not just for now, but always."

Her gaze widened, moisture lined her lashes and she said, "You love me?"

He stroked a hand down her back. "More than life itself, darlin'. I've loved you since that very first moment when you dunked me in the ocean."

"Carter, I love you. So much. I'm sorry for everything I've put you through, that I didn't come with you when you asked me to on the island. I've been so afraid of trusting you and counting on you because of my past," she murmured, tears flowing over her cheeks.

"But you love me?" he asked, feeling lighter than he had in ages. A grin spread over his face and his heart expanded as euphoria took hold.

"Yeah, I do, with all my heart. You're the best man I know."

Never taking his eyes off her, he reached into his pocket and withdrew the small gold band. He said, "That should do it. Marry me, Jenna. Be my family, my wife, my partner, my submissive. I want all of you, forever."

"Yes," she replied, openly weeping now—but they were tears of joy. Her eyes no longer held shadows, but sparkled at him with love and devotion, more than any Dom, any man could hope for. He slid the ring over her finger and smiled when it fit perfectly. Some things were just meant to be.

"It's beautiful, Carter."

"It was my mother's engagement ring," he said, as the tiny diamond glittered in the sunlight. "She gave it to me when I was a boy and said to only give it to the one woman I couldn't live without. Since you barreled into me on the docks of Pleasure Island, you've been it for me. My life doesn't work without you in it."

"Carter," she murmured, tears still pouring over her gorgeous face.

His heart bursting with joy, Carter kissed her, knowing there was a whole lifetime that awaited them. One filled with love, laughter and, if the fates saw fit to bless them, more children. And then Liam decided to let them know they were not alone. Carter released Jenna as she scrambled off his lap and retrieved their son, who was squalling in fury.

"I know, my love. You didn't get your lunch. Mama's got you," Jenna said, settling with her back against Carter's front. He would never grow tired of watching their son at her breast.

"And then his father would very much like to eat his lunch too," he murmured suggestively in her ear.

She chuckled and replied breathily, "Yes, Sir. His mother would like that very much."

She leaned against him, and he knew he had never loved anyone as much as he loved the two beings in his arms. For a man who'd always thought he'd end up being a lifelong bachelor, Jenna had upended his world from the moment he set eyes on her, and he didn't regret a single minute.

"Carter?" Jenna asked.

"Hmm?"

"You don't want a big wedding, do you?" she asked.

"It doesn't really matter to me. As long as you're mine. Why, don't you?" he asked.

"Not really. Maybe a reception to celebrate it. But if we could just go before a justice of the peace, maybe on Tuesday, I think that would work well, don't you?"

"You want to get married in two days?" he asked.

"Well, I think it would be fitting, considering it's the anniversary of the day we met, don't you?" Jenna asked and glanced up at him. In her eyes, he saw his present and his future. He saw a lifetime of a love greater than he could have ever hoped to find. It was enough to make a man like him believe in things like fate, destiny and soulmates. Because Jenna was his fate.

"I'm in. Let me see what I can do to put something together. And then you're mine, forever," he murmured. It wouldn't be easy to pull off, but in order to have her there, bound to him in every way that counted, he would move the mountains surrounding his ranch if need be.

"Me too. I'm sorry it took me a while to get here, but I'm on board with forever." Her love for him shone through the smile she gave him, and peace settled over him.

"It doesn't matter how long, love, just that you got here. I'd do it all over again in a heartbeat. And now that our boy is asleep with his belly full, I think it's time I ate, don't you?" He heard her sharp intake of breath and adored the way her pupils dilated as she nodded.

"Good, put him in his seat and then lie on your back with your thighs spread for me."

As Jenna did as he asked and he sank between her thighs, Carter understood that the journey to win her love had been the only one worthwhile.

213

EPILOGUE

TWO DAYS LATER

*J*enna was back in her room, standing before the full-length mirror and gazing at her appearance. She'd found an ivory empire-waist gown in town yesterday. Her shoes were silver sparkly ones that she'd borrowed from Meghan. Dottie had proven to be not just a whiz in the kitchen but also great at fancy women's hairstyles. She had styled Jenna's hair in elegant waves and curls, then twisted those into an elegant up-do.

Her sister was in her room, in a mauve, ankle-length gown, standing in as her maid of honor. Meghan walked over and said, "Here's a finishing touch." She handed Jenna a jewelry case.

"You didn't have to do this," she said, incredibly touched, and opened the box. She gasped at the contents. "Meghan, are these what I think they are?" she asked, glancing at her sister.

"Yep. Mom's pearls. When you were liquidating everything, I thought it would be nice to keep one thing that was hers and snagged the set. I figured they could be the something old that each of us wears on our wedding day. I think it's only fitting, don't you?" Meghan said with grin.

"I can't believe you did that!" Jenna exclaimed.

"Don't be mad. I will pay you for them. I know it cost—"

She enveloped Meghan in her arms and said, "Thank you. I never thought I would want something of hers, need something to remember her by, but getting to wear these today, of all days. It's the best present I could ever have asked for. Help me put them on."

"Oh, I'm so glad you're not mad," Meghan replied with relief.

"When it's your turn, I will give them back to you," Jenna promised.

"Well, that will be a while, so enjoy them."

Blinking back moisture in her eyes, Jenna affixed the teardrop pearl earrings. Then Meghan fastened the string of pearls around her neck. Jenna caressed the pearls as she stared in the mirror.

"See, they are perfect. I'm just so happy for you," Meghan said, giving her a small hug from behind.

At the knock on the door, Jenna said, "Come in."

Herb Henderson opened the door to her room, holding his hat in his hands. The old cowboy was duded up in a suit and tie. He said, "Don't you make a pretty picture? The both of you. They're ready for you downstairs."

"Thanks, Herb," Jenna said and strode over to him. Liam was already downstairs with Dottie and enjoying the attention, she was certain. Herb had come to her last night and offered to walk her down the aisle since her dad wasn't there. Between him and Dottie, the two of them were acting more and more like surrogate parents toward her and beaming grandparents toward Liam. Life had taken on a sweetness Jenna had never experienced before. But she was grabbing hold of it, no longer afraid of what her future might hold, because she knew it would be full of love.

"Be nice to Spencer, Meghan," she murmured.

"I will be if he is, but I promise not to ruin anything for you today," Meghan said, handing her the small bouquet of orchids before going ahead of her out of the room.

Jenna looped her arm through Herb's and let him lead her down the front stairs. Claude DeBussy's *Claire de Lune* filled the air as they descended the staircase into the great room. Carter had called in a million favors and had transformed the great room into a stunning hall filled with chairs, and lined with tables laden with food. Candles glowed. Flowered garlands hung from the ceiling. Jenna had no idea how he'd pulled it off.

In the room were all his friends, both Doms and subs from the club. Dottie stood in the front row of chairs, holding their son. But it was the man standing before the hearth that drew all her attention. Carter was dressed in a tailored black suit and tie, his cowboy hat suspiciously absent. His eyes glowed with love when he spied her. Meghan made her trek down the aisle with Spencer, looking decidedly dapper in his midnight suit, serving as the best man, and Jenna was amazed that they both were on their best behavior with not one snipe toward the other.

Mason stood front and center as the officiant in a dark gray suit and tie.

But she couldn't take her eyes off Carter; her steady, gorgeous cowboy was perfect. He was perfect for her. And she would love him forever. Herb guided Jenna down the aisle toward him, her Sasquatch, who had shown her the true meaning of love. When Herb transferred her hand into Carter's, warmth flooded through her and tears of joy pricked the corners of her eyes. And an emotion she had almost forgotten suffused her chest as they said their vows.

Joy.

She would never take him or their life together for granted. Jenna knew how swiftly that all could change. But she would celebrate the joy with him for however many moments they had together.

When Mason declared them husband and wife, Carter kissed her, and she knew that not a day would pass when she wouldn't show him how much she loved him.

Afterward, their gathering of friends and family indulged in the feast Dottie had whipped up for the occasion. Jenna took a break from the festivities to feed Liam. When she returned, she stood near the window, swaying with Liam as he dozed with his belly full. Their small wedding celebration was still going strong, laughter and happiness infused their home. Carter joined her near the window. Her husband slid his arms around them and swayed with the music.

"I can't believe you put this all together so quickly. Tonight was perfect. Thank you," she said and brushed her lips over his.

"Anything for you, and it's only the start." Then a strange look crossed Carter's face. It was then that she heard it, above the sound of the music playing.

"What's that noise?" she asked, glancing around as it increased in volume and tempo.

Carter's handsome face broke into a grin and he said, "Rain. The drought is over." Then he raised a dark brow and asked, "So, Mrs. Jones, could I convince you to leave the reception for our own private celebration?"

"I'm all yours," she replied. In every way that mattered.

Hand in hand, they left the great room, with a thumbs up from Spencer, who would see to everyone else. They took Liam and set their sleeping son in his crib before they hastened across the hall to their bedroom. When the door closed behind them and it was just the two of them, Carter swept her up into his arms, carrying her to their bed.

"No regrets?" he asked as he laid her down.

"None as long as you love me," she replied.

"Always," he promised.

And then she surrendered herself into his arms, knowing she'd finally found her way home.

~The End~

HIS WICKED LOVE

CUFFS & SPURS BOOK TWO

Read on for an exclusive sneak peek of His Wicked Love, Cuffs & Spurs Book 2, available May 2018…

LATE SEPTEMBER

*W*ell, if those numbers didn't just chafe his ass.

Mason checked and re-checked the account ledgers. He'd been over them more times than any sane person would, but he wanted—needed—to be certain they were correct. The loss they'd sustained three months ago had been substantial. With what was left, they'd be lucky if the Black Elkhorn Lodge and Resort didn't shut its doors by Christmas.

"Are you sure about the numbers?" Cole asked.

Mason glanced across the expanse of his mahogany wooden desk at his brother. There were lines of tension in his shoulders and tanned features that were so much like their dad's, including the dark chocolate shade of his hair that he wore past his shoulders and his brown eyes nearly the color of soot.

Whereas Mason took more after their mom, with his lighter shade of brown hair and eye color—in a manly way, of course.

His gut twisted. Despair and dread seized him.

Mason detested himself for their current plight: the lodge nearly bankrupt. And it was all his fault.

Before all this, Mason had prided himself on reading other people. He'd been cocky about it. As a Dom, he'd considered his ability to size up a person to be top notch. But their last chef had proven him wrong. His arrogance had cost them. Mason hadn't seen the fraud and deceit behind the chef's apron before the no-good piece of trash had embezzled nearly every penny the lodge had.

He could still remember when he'd discovered the theft. The disbelief, the anger. His normal fun-loving personality had vanished overnight. The lodge, the dream their parents had conceptualized and that he and Cole had actualized, had tail-spun out of control. They had gone from having excess capital with savings to spare, to barely limping along and teetering on the brink of collapse.

In the last three months, they'd had to liquidate their invest-ment portfolio just to keep their noses above water. But the costs of running the lodge were considerable. It took capital to make this place run.

"I'm sure. We are well and truly fucked. If we make it until Christmas and are able to pack guests in, maybe we can string things along enough to begin rebuilding," Mason replied. But word had spread about their legal woes no matter how much damage control they'd tried to do. Without a functioning restaurant on the property, the Black Elkhorn Lodge and Resort had received cancellations in droves. The once pros-perous getaway hemorrhaged funds daily.

"Well, with the restaurant currently closed, we're losing a stream of revenue right there," Cole said, telling Mason something he already knew. Still, he was glad they were both on the same page.

Frustrated, he slammed the account ledgers shut and irritably ran a hand over his face. The irritation was all self-directed. Mason couldn't remember the last time he'd genuinely smiled. In the three months since the bottom had been yanked out of their business and a person he'd trusted had robbed them blind, there hadn't been much reason to smile. When he observed himself in the mirror every morning, he no longer recognized the person in it. The haggard expression and grim line of his mouth. The permanent scowl and self-loathing.

Life, for Mason, had once been a bountiful banquet, and he'd never given it deeper thought than the fun to be had. Now, it was a steaming pile of horse manure. He replied, "I realize that. While you were leading the fishing expedition trip this past week, I contacted Le Cordon Bleu on the west coast for a recommendation. We need a chef running the restaurant if we have any hope of staving off further losses. I figured we need all the help we can get at this point. Not to mention, it could be a potential draw in our advertising to have a fully trained chef from such a reputable institution. As much as we adore her, Tibby can't handle the load or full responsibility. Not that she's not capable, but she balances her time here with her daughter's needs. I can't make a single mom give me more time than she's able. Our new chef should arrive today."

Mason could only hope that re-opening the restaurant would staunch the flow of cancellations. They'd attempted to keep it open with Tibby and Faith pulling extra shifts here and there. He'd had them pare down the menu to just the basics. And those two had nearly staged a coup—not that he blamed them one iota. The onus was on him, not his employees, to improve the situation at the lodge. They already gave the lodge one hundred and ten percent. The rest had to come from him.

Mason had made the executive decision to close the restaurant temporarily a month ago. He'd directed Tibby and Faith to prepare boxed lunches for sale, limiting their hours, with the promise that it was temporary so he didn't lose them. Mason had made sure their paychecks didn't reflect the loss of hours. Since then, guests had cancelled their reservations in droves.

Mason didn't blame his guests one bit. The Black Elkhorn Lodge and Resort wasn't close to the downtown hub. Their lodge was about bringing people back to nature. That was one of the premier selling points. And normally, with a fully functioning restaurant on the property, the place tended to thrive. Except most people didn't want to have to drive forty minutes just to grab a bite to eat.

Each of the lodges had a small kitchen with a stovetop, as well as gas grills. But people on vacation liked to eat out. Many wanted to kick back and relax. Re-opening the restaurant would, he hoped, get customers to rebook their stays with them.

"Just like that?" Cole asked, his face filled with concern. Mason was just thankful that when the shit hit the fan, Cole never once pointed the finger at him. He would have deserved it. They both knew who was at fault for their dire situation, but instead of hanging Mason out to dry, his older brother had stood by him.

Mason sighed and said, "Her background check came back clean and, to be honest, we're in a pickle. Tibby and Faith have at least been able to supply boxed lunches for the hikers, but with closing the restaurant, they've been picking up more catering jobs. If we want the slightest chance of keeping the lodge from hemorrhaging even more money, we need the restaurant back open for guests this week. Billie informed me this morning that there were two more cancellations today due to the fact that the restaurant is closed."

"Shit. All right. If you're sure about this new chef..." Cole replied with a grimace. Mason knew Cole would rather be out at his private cabin, avoiding people and surrounded by nature than dealing with the running of the lodge. It's why their partnership had always worked—if not seamlessly, at least without too many blips. He ran the business side and catered to guests, while Cole was in charge of leading hiking, fishing, hunting, and sight-seeing expeditions, away from the bulk of civilization.

"I'm not," Mason admitted with a shrug in an attempt to ease the anxiety building up. "But the problem is we don't have much of a choice."

The only thing that would ease his mind, take him out of his current default state of tension, would be playing with a sub at Cuffs & Spurs. Being balls-deep inside a willing woman was the only cure, even if it was a temporary reprieve. Or, at least it, used to be. Problem was, he'd not had a chance to make it into town and the club since the top blew on his world.

"Any word on the legal proceedings against the culprit?" Cole asked, leaning back in his leather chair, avoiding use of the chef's name. They both had stopped using the thief's name. It was easier to use separation, make it feel a little less personal than it had been.

Mason wished that the legal matters had been concluded. Then he would have a definitive answer on when they would get paid for all their accounts. Some weren't willing to work with them at all and were demanding payment. With a shake of his head, he said, "No. Not yet. Other than they haven't found what they actually *did* with the stolen funds and that the money was all gone. The prosecutor has assured me that part of the sentencing will include restitution but that the court would most likely allow the defendant to make payments, which doesn't help us one bit."

Cole cursed under his breath, his face stern and lines of

worry present in his normally calm demeanor. He asked, "When does the new chef arrive?"

"Today at some point, out of Los Angeles," Mason replied. He could only hope his instincts were better than the last with this one and that they were worth the recommendation. The lodge couldn't afford another fiasco or for his judgment to be off in the slightest. One wrong move at this point and everything he and Cole had built with their dad would go up in smoke.

Cole snorted. "You mean part of our plan to keep this place open rests on the shoulders of someone from the land of Hollywood? Brother, I hate to tell you, but the chances of someone from the west coast willingly trading in for life here is slim."

Mason understood that all too well. This new chef, an Emily Fox, just needed to stay long enough to get them back into the black. If she didn't work out after that, well, they'd cross that bridge when they came to it. "We just need someone for now. It doesn't have to be permanent. In fact, I mentioned in passing during my conversation with her that it was a temporary arrangement, with a trial run included."

And the rest of their exchanges had occurred via email. In what little communication they'd had, Miss Fox had been blunt and to the point. For the time being, that was what they needed.

Cole shrugged. "At least that gives us an out. I have a few expeditions to lead this week. Day trips, so I will be around at night to help out."

"Focus on the trips. I've got the lodge covered. And Alex's trail rides are busy this time of year. So that will help," Mason added. Their buddy, Alex, used the Black Elkhorn Lodge stables to run his trail riding company. It was profitable for both parties. While Alex had his own employees taking guests on trail rides, if there was any spillover, Cole or himself picked up the ride. Likewise, on the lodge, if Cole and Mason needed an extra hand, Alex filled in when he could.

Thankfully their previous chef's sticky fingers hadn't extended to the stables. It didn't hurt that Hunt Trail Rides was a separate company, either.

Didn't mean there wasn't a good chance that they weren't royally fucked.

"Are you sure this new chef can cook?" Cole asked, a pensive expression creasing his brow.

Fuck if I know. "She comes highly recommended. Has a been a sous chef for two years."

"Actually, it's four years, but who's counting, right?" said a sultry female voice from his office doorway.

Mason glanced up and was glad he was seated. Emily Fox's resume and background checks had provided him with a boatload of facts about his new hire. But they hadn't prepared him for the red-haired siren currently standing in the wooden door frame. The long waves of her hair reminded him of the sunset, the myriad hues of burnt orange and sienna hung over delicate shoulders and more than ample cleavage before ending above her trim waist. Her skin was smooth and the color of iridescent pearls, which only seemed to magnify the natural pale pink hue of her lips that were not overly plump but perfectly formed.

Yet it was her eyes that were the real killer. On top of a voluptuous form that made the Dom in Mason want to weep in thanks, her hazel eyes were large pools that sparkled with lively zest and were surrounded by a wealth of inky lashes. Intelligence flashed in her gaze. The electricity of it zapped through him.

"You must be Emily Fox," Mason said, finding his voice after nearly swallowing his tongue. Standing, now that he'd found his legs, he shoved away the unwanted and rather inconvenient lust she evoked in him.

"You'd be right about that," she said, with a hint of sarcasm that she softened with a grin as she placed her free hand on her denim clad hip. The other clutched the handle of a small leather satchel about the size of his goody bag. He must have been in a mood when they'd briefly talked on the phone because the sound hadn't affected him as it did now. The dulcet tones curled along his spine, into his gut, and made his dick twitch.

"I'm Mason Stewart. This is my brother and business partner, Cole," Mason informed her. His gaze roved over her form. While she was dressed casually, in a pair of well-worn blue jeans and fitted mint green Henley top that accentuated her curves, with a black jacket tied around her waist, Miss Fox was anything but casual. She was stunning—exotic, even. He couldn't help but wonder what she looked like naked.

Yet her demeanor didn't scream *Rodeo Drive*. That was good. It made her appear accessible and down to earth. As though, perhaps, if he and Cole played their cards right, she wouldn't mind trading in city life for country life in Wyoming.

"Pleasure." Emily smiled and nodded towards Cole, who tipped his hat in her direction in greeting. From the expression on Cole's face, Mason surmised he wasn't the only one a bit taken aback by her looks. It should make him feel better that he wasn't the only who'd been momentarily struck dumb, but it didn't. He couldn't afford to be attracted to the newest chef. The paradox of it, given their current situation, was not lost on him.

"I'm glad you made it early. Hopefully the drive wasn't too hard on you. If you like, I can have the front desk get your belongings to your cabin. Then I can show you the restaurant and where you will be working," Mason said as he emerged from behind his desk and walked toward her. He gestured with his hand outstretched to take the case from her and help her out. Miss Fox really was a small thing. While he was six one, he had to look down to meet her gaze. He hadn't known what to expect—certainly not the vision before him.

Yet instead of handing it over, she shifted the case behind her back and held her other palm up, stalling his forward progression.

"Hold up, cowboy, no one touches my knives without losing body parts. I know I agreed to accept the position over the phone, but I need to see the kitchen first before we go any further," Emily said, her sultry voice making him think of sex. Long, languorous, Tantric style sex before a roaring fire. Sex that left a body boneless and too sated to move. Her voice was sex, plain and simple. And it made his dick hard in his jeans. Mason tempered the unexpected and rather unwanted desire she stirred within him. Or tried to.

Instead he settled on annoyance with a simmering underbelly of lust, which only served to piss him off. It had been way too long since he'd availed himself of the subs at Cuffs & Spurs. And his knee-jerk reaction to his new chef proved that. If Miss Fox was going to prove to be a mistake, he'd rather know now. And if her bossy attitude didn't end, he would toss her out on her ass. Contract or no.

"If you want to lug a heavy suitcase, be my guest, sweetheart. I think we need a demonstration, a sample of your skills, before we go any further. Don't you?" Mason challenged, letting his annoyance creep into his voice. She'd accepted the position without the clause of needing to see the kitchen first. So she thought she could toss in an extra demand, put a wrench in his plans to bring the lodge back from the brink, test who was in charge? It wasn't her. Miss Fox could try but she would fail. This was his place and he would fight like a rabid dog to save it, to protect it further from outside harm. He wouldn't ever allow the lodge or himself to be overrun by a pretty face.

She smiled. The air was charged between them, electrified,

as she stared him down, then said, "Cowboy, once you've had my cooking, you will be my slave and beg me to stay."

An image of Emily, collared, naked, and on her knees begging him to take her flashed through his mind. The unbidden thought unleashed a windfall of lust and it roared through his bloodstream. Mason tensed, beating back the unsolicited desire. Compartmentalizing the unwanted, erotic images, he narrowed his gaze. "Doubtful. I could take my pick from twenty line cooks today from one of the restaurants in town."

She rolled her eyes in an exasperated fashion and asked, "Then why did you call me?"

"That's what I'm beginning to wonder," Mason retorted, not admitting that he wanted a chef at the top of their game. That he believed if they offered culinary delights not found at other resorts or restaurants, they would attract customers, and maintaining the current menu that was a crowd favorite was paramount.

She was their Hail Mary Pass, even though she didn't know it. Nor would he tell her that. She already had an overabundance of confidence.

Cole intervened, severing the electric livewire connection as he stepped between them. Mason finally inhaled a deep breath while Cole gave him a brief glance with his brows raised high enough they nearly disappeared beneath his Stetson, and a 'what the hell?' expression. Then Cole shifted fully toward Miss Fox, his face calm with the pleasant smile he typically used to win over a sub, and said, "Emily, why don't I take you over to the restaurant and you can see if it's to your liking? We updated the kitchen two years ago and have all the latest equipment. Not that I have any idea what all those gadgets do."

It was the gamine grin, the spread of her pale pink lips exposing her straight, white teeth, and transforming her face into breathtaking. And it was directed at his brother. It shoved

Mason toward caveman status. He wanted to snarl at Cole to back off, not to touch her, that she was his. Which was fucking asinine, and only fueled his internal engines to near record levels.

"That would be fabulous. Thank you. Is he always like this?" she asked Cole, indicating Mason with a jaunty tilt of her head. Her hair shifted, making it shimmer.

A half grin spread over Cole's face and he replied, "No. Sometimes he's worse."

Emily's full-bodied, sexy laugh sucker-punched Mason in the sternum. The sound skittered along his spine and pooled in his groin. The throaty, jazz singer sound made him wonder what she sounded like when she came. It made him yearn to discover whether she was a screamer or issued almost silent, throaty moans. There was a part of him that wanted to bend her over his desk and fuck her until his legs buckled.

"Good to know," Emily responded with another shake of her head which made the waterfall of red tresses shift and move like flames. The color was so vibrant, Mason ached to feel the strands in his hands. Would they be as soft as he imagined, or would they singe his flesh?

"It is; better to be armed and prepared. If you'll follow me," Cole murmured, diffusing the situation and ignoring Mason.

"Honey, I'd follow you anywhere," Emily flirted. With his brother. Jealousy gripped Mason, which was idiotic at best. He couldn't want Emily. Wouldn't allow himself to desire her. One, she was his employee and there were some roads that were better left untraveled. Two, he wasn't sure he liked her. She was brash and mouthy, and most likely as vanilla as they came.

But that didn't seem to matter to his dick, who liked the thought of playing boss and naughty secretary with her a little too much.

Except then Cole picked up the ball Emily had lobbed his

way and responded, "Likewise, sweetheart. Mason, you coming?"

Almost.

And from a damn fantasy. He shook his head, attempting to distill the lust raging through his veins. He bit out, "I'll be right behind you two."

Mason watched Cole lead Emily from his office. His gaze, trained on her perfectly formed, heart-shaped ass, did nothing to detract from the fantasy. He adjusted himself and winced at the discomfort.

Breathing deeply, he called on his training, on the stalwart control that made him a Master, to corral his needs to a more manageable state. Using that control, he remembered the last time he'd allowed lust to guide his actions. It was akin to dousing himself with a bucket of ice water.

The absolute last thing Mason would do would be to allow his hormones to do his thinking for him. He'd done that once, and look where that had gotten them.

His Wicked Love, Book 2 (Available May 2018)

ANYA SUMMERS

Born in St. Louis, Missouri, Anya grew up listening to Cardinals baseball and reading anything she could get her hands on. She remembers her mother saying if only she would read the right type of books instead binging her way through the romance aisles at the bookstore, she'd have been a doctor. While Anya never did get that doctorate, she graduated cum laude from the University of Missouri-St. Louis with an M.A. in History.

Anya is a bestselling and award-winning author published in multiple fiction genres. She also writes urban fantasy and paranormal romance under the name Maggie Mae Gallagher. A total geek at her core, when she is not writing, she adores attending the latest comic con or spending time with her family. She currently lives in the Midwest with her two furry felines.

Don't miss these exciting titles by Anya Summers and Blushing Books!

Love Me, Master Me, Book 6
Submit To Me, Book 7
Her Wired Dom, Book 8

Pleasure Island Series
Her Master and Commander, Book 1
Her Music Masters, Book 2
Their Shy Submissive, (Novella) Book 3
Her Lawful Master, Book 4
Her Rockstar Dom, Book 5
Duets and Dominance, Book 6
Her Undercover Doms (Novella) Book 7
Ménage in Paradise, Book 8
Her Rodeo Masters, Book 9

Cuffs and Spurs Series
His Scandalous Love, Book 1
His Wicked Love, Book 2 (Available May 2018)

Visit her on social media here:
http//www.facebook.com/AnyaSummersAuthor
Twitter: @AnyaBSummers
Goodreads:
https://www.goodreads.com/author/show/15183606.Anya_S
ummers
Sign-up for Anya Summers Newsletter

Connect with Anya Summers:
www.anyasummers.com

Made in the USA
Coppell, TX
15 December 2019

13003887R00139